Omen of the Hawks

Omen of the Hawks

A Story of Washakie's Shoshones
in Pre-reservation Days

by
Virginia Cole Trenholm

Tŭvo Waipŭ, Writing Woman

P.O. Box 7802 The Woodlands, Texas 77387

Other Books by
Virginia Cole Trenholm

Author of
The Arapahoes, Our People
(The Civilization of the American Indian Series, Volume 105)
Footprints on the Frontier
Amanda Mary and the Dog Soldiers
West of Plymouth

Co-author with Maurine Carley of
The Shoshonis: Sentinels of the Rockies
Wyoming Pageant (a textbook)

Editor of
Wyoming Blue Book
(a political history in three volumes)

ISBN 0-943255-26-0

Library of Congress Catalogue Number 89-63585

Printed in The United States of America
First Edition

Cover Illustration by Shoshone Artist Floyd Osborne of Fort Washakie, Wyoming. *Courtesy of Marion Huseas, Cheyenne, Wyoming.*

To the first families of Wyoming,
the Shoshones,
who were here when the white man arrived.

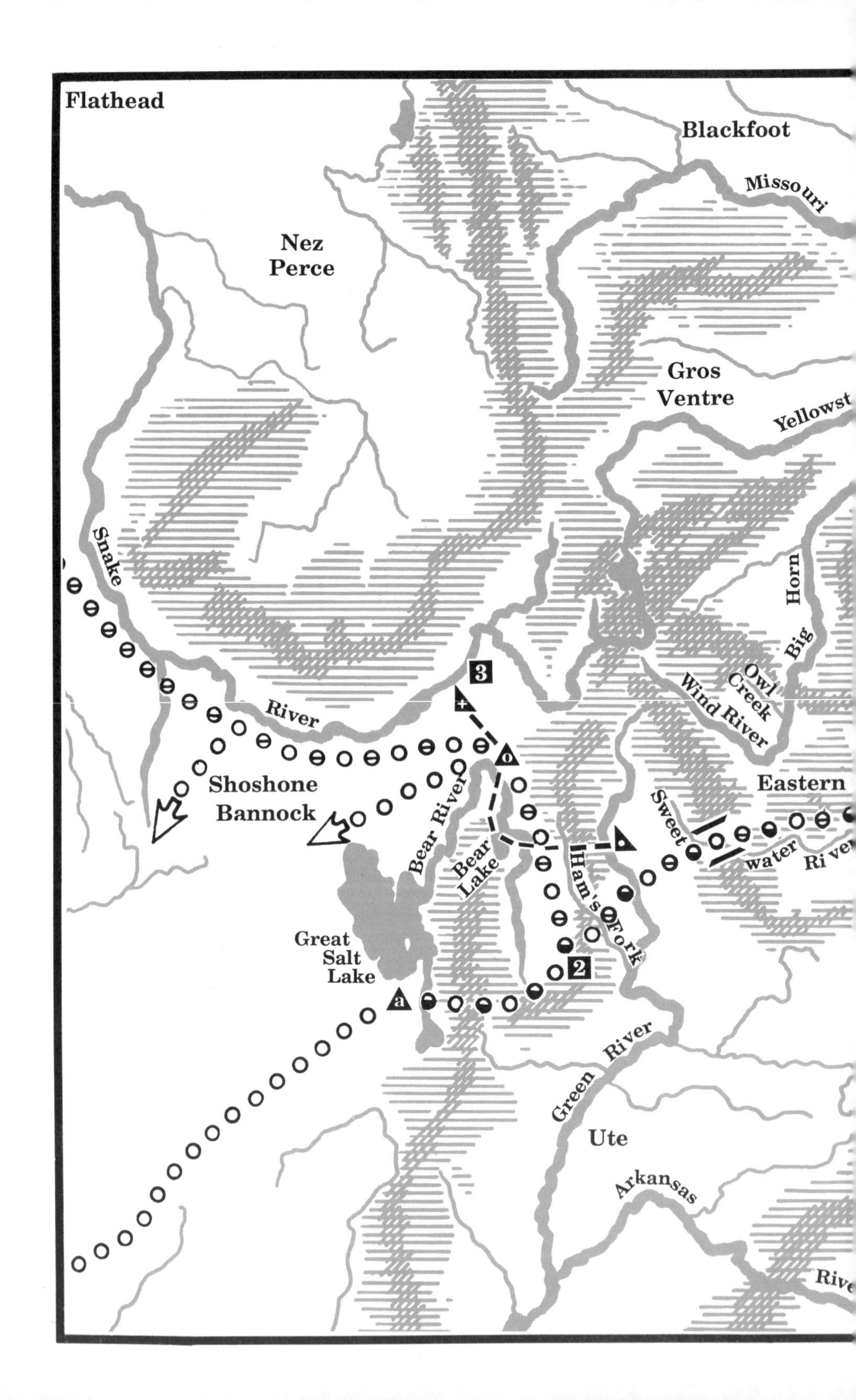

Flathead
Blackfoot
Missouri
Nez
Perce
Gros
Ventre
Yellowst
Snake
River
Big
Horn
Owl
Creek
Wind River
Shoshone
Bannock
Eastern
Bear River
Bear
Lake
Ham's Fork
Sweet
water
River
Great
Salt
Lake
Green
River
Ute
Arkansas
Rive

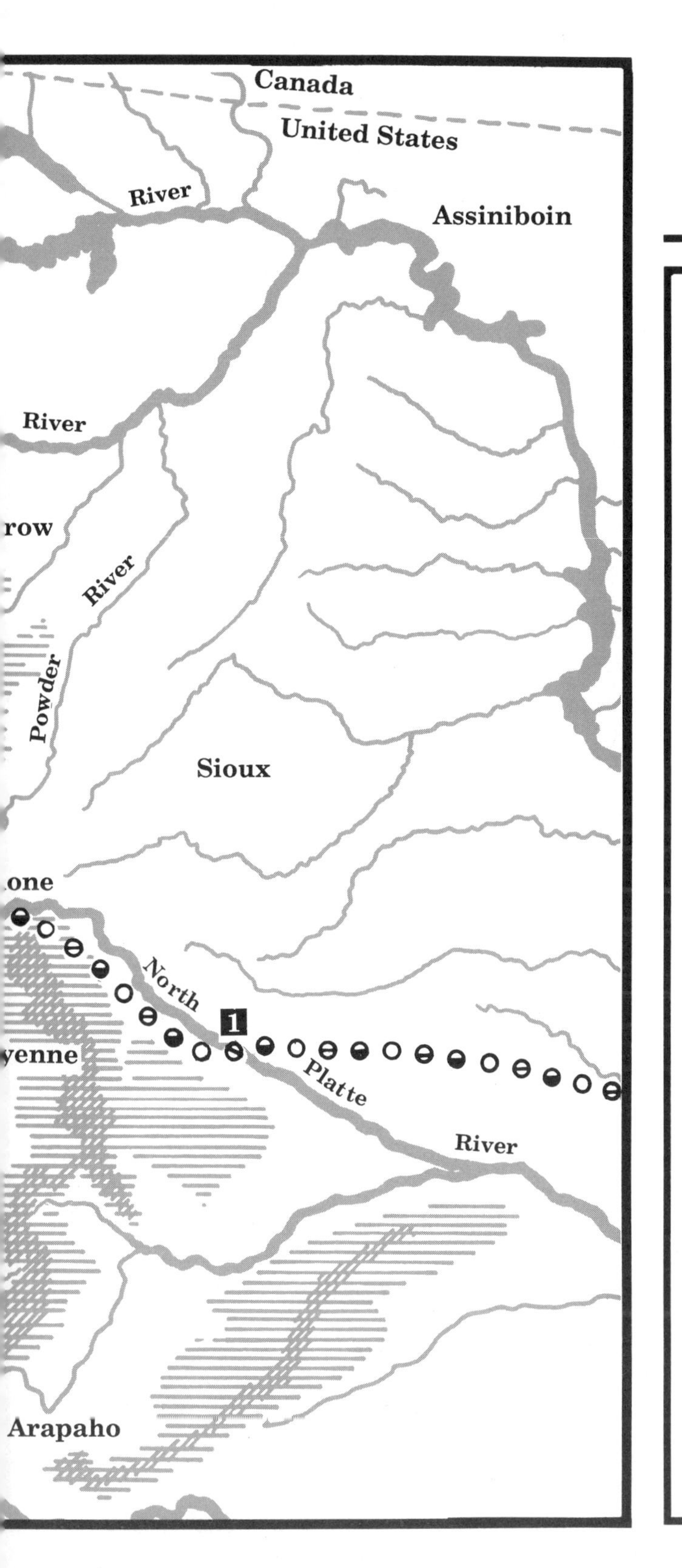

Canada
United States
River
Assiniboin
River
rrow
River
Powder
Sioux
one
North
Platte
River
yenne
Arapaho

Tribes and Trails in the Rockies 1851
—Legend—
Mountains
1 Fort Laramie
2 Fort Bridger
3 Fort Hall
South Pass
Oregon Trail
Morman Trail
California Trail
Washakie's Camp
Naroyan's Camp
Kamŭ Kaupa's Trail to Washakie's Camp
Salt Lake City
Soda Springs

Prologue

Emigrants, streaming westward on the "White-top Wagon Road" in the mid 1800s, pulverized the soil and left permanent scars on solid rock along trails and cut-offs through Shoshone country west of the Rockies. Horses and oxen devoured the grass, and hunters killed all wildlife within range of their guns. While the ribbon of destruction widened, resentment mounted, for the survival of the natives was threatened.

Particularly hard pressed were the followers of Naroyan, or "Snag" as the white man called him. As chief of a mixed band of Northern Shoshones and Bannocks in Southeastern Idaho, he had the difficult task of maintaining order between the two factions. The Shoshones were inclined to be more friendly than their fractious allies, but there were those among them who shared their animosity toward the white invaders.

Naroyan had the disposition of his uncle, Chief Cameahwait, who, a generation earlier, befriended Lewis and Clark in the high country of Montana, and his aunt, Cameahwait's sister, Sacajawea who accompanied the expedition to the West Coast. His determination to conform to the white man's demands ultimately led to tragedy. On his way to Bannock City, Montana, to forfeit an Indian child, reportedly a white captive, he was shot by a drunken miner who later bragged that he wanted to add another notch to his gun.

As the respected chief lay dying, he expressed his wish that his mild-mannered nephew Tendoy, rather than his son Peggi, be named his successor. Peggi, a mystic, had proven himself an able warrior, but his father feared that peace could not be maintained because of his violent nature.

Naroyan urged that Tendoy be friendly because he would someday have to travel the white man's road. Though aroused by his murder, the tribal leaders respected his wishes and elected Tendoy their chief the day following his death.

"Omen of the Hawks," an authentic historical novel about the early West, begins in Naroyan's camp. The action soon shifts to Green River, where Washakie has strict control over the Eastern Shoshones. The scattered bands recognize him as head chief of their nation, but they are less apt to comply with his peaceful attitude. Order is needed for defense against the hostile Blackfeet and Crows, the unpredictable Utes, as well as the formidable Platte River Indians, the Sioux, Cheyennes and Arapahoes.

The Eastern Shoshones, or Green River Snakes as they are called at the time of our story, have assumed a synthetic Plains culture while remaining true to their origin. First known as "Grass House People," they are generally friendly, unlike the Plains Indians who accept warfare as a way of life. The Snakes fight creditably when forced, but their battles are intertribal.

The story is unique because of the role Washakie's Shoshones played in the opening of the West. The chief vowed that he would never harm a white man, and he remained true to his word though his patience was sometimes strained to the breaking point. Those for and against his policy helped establish the mood for the story. In order to understand his behavior, one must consider his nature as well as his culture, his country and his time. He could not have prevented westward expansion, but had he been inclined he could have made it costly; for he occupied a strategic position at South Pass, the only practical access to the Western Slope known to the emigrants. Instead of collecting toll from the throngs who followed the trails, he flung wide the gates so that all might enter.

When migration to the coast began to taper off, the weary, land-hungry emigrants found the country inviting. The most significant settlement in the Shoshone domain was at Salt Lake, the Mecca of Mormonism. Beginning with Brigham Young, a second period of migration was underway. Countless immigrants entered Salt Lake Valley, which they considered their Promised Land.

Diaries and reminiscences of early arrivals tell about Indian-White relations. The Saints, following Brigham Young's policy of "feed 'em, don't fight 'em," had little trouble with the natives. James Brown, who led the first missionaries to Washakie's camp, gives a graphic account in his memoirs. (*see* James S. Brown, *Life of a Pioneer*, George Q. Cannon & Sons, Salt Lake

City, UT, 1900.) He recounts his experiences and records some of Washakie's dramatic orations which, slightly edited, appear in this volume. Percival D. Lowe's *Five Years a Dragoon* (Franklin Hudson Publishing Company, Kansas City, MO, 1906) is the primary source of information regarding the historic Horse Creek Council; the *Deseret News*, for the Ute-Shoshone councils in Salt Lake City.

The first scholar to study systematically the Eastern Shoshone dialect was E. Ballou, who was stationed at Wind River from 1880-1881. Other studies followed, the most recent being Melinda Tidzump's *Shoshone Thesaurus*, University of North Dakota, 1970. She is a direct descendant of Washakie and Ahwaipŭtsi. David Shaul, a linguist at Purdue, screened vocabularies and word lists at the Smithsonian Institution and helped the author select the Shoshone words used in this story. At Fort Washakie, Rupert Weeks (now deceased) and Irene Pingree checked the Glossary which follows the Epilogue.

1

"The old blood creeps with the snail;
the young blood leaps with the torrent."
—Washakie

Gold! . . . White man! . . . Crazy!

Kamŭ Kaupa, the Bannock boy, reeled forward for a better view of the scene below although he knew it by heart. When the wind blew from the direction of the setting sun, he would cautiously find his way to his hideout, under a low-branched pine tree on a promontory overlooking Warm Springs, the emigrants' favorite campsite. He was ever watchful for a shifting breeze. If the white man's dog should pick up his scent, the chase would begin, and he would be hunted down like a timber wolf.

Bitterness welled in his heart as he watched the incessant action taking place below. Men, women and children always moving about. Why did the white men not rest on this stop along the White-top Wagon Road? Tall men, short men, old men, young men driving stakes, repairing wagons, shoeing horses . . . . When they found nothing better to do, they would chop wood like old women.

"Pth!" The Bannock boy spat contemptuously at the thought of such unmanly conduct.

Occasionally, a snowy-bearded old man would settle down for a while to play a musical instrument unlike anything he had ever heard. At other times the old grandfathers would just whittle to pass the time away.

Anything to be doing something! . . . Tiresome.

Kamŭ Kaupa could hear bits of conversation, unintelligible except for the profanity which had crept into the vocabulary of his father, Pia Isha (Big Wolf) and his cronies who were troublemakers in Naroyan's mixed band of Shoshones and Bannocks to which they belonged. The renegades spent much of their time lolling around Fort Hall. Even though Kamŭ Kaupa had wanted to, he had never set foot inside the fort; but he had seen many trinkets brought back to camp—mirrors, beads, ribbons, all kinds of finery. His mother, Mŭatsi or Little Moon, had none of these. Since Isha, as the boy chose to call his father, traded only for whiskey, she did not have gay flowered calico to wrap around herself. She still had to tan the hides for her clothing.

The boy looked disdainfully upon the women below. They, too, were busy. He could see them suckling their young, airing bedding, washing at the springs, and cooking. Always cooking! The tantalizing smell of frying bacon, hot bread and steaming coffee tormented him as he had eaten nothing all day.

His attention was attracted by two lovers, hand in hand, slipping from curious eyes but not too far away for safety. Screened from their companions by a covered wagon, they clung to each other while their lips met in an ardent kiss. The young Indian was puzzled by their behavior because they had no blanket to seclude them from the outside world. Their love making was brought abruptly to an end by a shrill-voiced old woman who came railing toward them.

"Ugh!" exclaimed Kamŭ Kaupa in disgust.

He then watched four little girls lightheartedly skipping around. Could one of them be Daidŭtsi, the little one, about whom he had dreamed the night before? In his dream she had screamed in terror; why he did not know. Before he could reach her side, she had disappeared. In her place there stood a yellow-throated, wax-white sego lily, all alone on the prairie. No, the golden-haired *daidŭtsi* was not there. Just why he thought of her by the Shoshone term rather than the Bannock *tsŭa'a,* little girl, he was not sure. The Shoshone word seemed somehow to fit her.

His interest shifted to two half-grown boys, perhaps his age. No one had ever told him how old he was. They were wrestling and pommelling each other with their fists. He was not sure whether they were fighting or playing a war game. A lanky youth looked on for a while. Then he took a bite of the food he carried in his hand and gave the remainder to the dog, begging at his feet.

Food! Why did the young braves fight among themselves when they had all they needed to eat? Clothing to keep them warm when snow comes? And horses?

Kamŭ Kaupa had always wanted a horse. Before long, he would slip to the white man's camp and take the finest one he could find so that he would no longer be a Walker. After that, he would return to his tepee and kill Isha. He had always known that he must. That was the only way he could stop his beating Little Moon. Long ago he had decided that he would someday split his head open and take out his poisonous tongue. He was a bad Indian, always full of whiskey and wanting to fight someone who could not match his strength.

Overhead, a buzzard glided gracefully through the cloudless sky as its shadow, cast on the busy scene below, raced to keep pace with it. Something dead! Kamŭ Kaupa wished vehemently that it might be Isha together with all the emigrants below. Next to him he hated them because of the hardships they had brought to his people.

Dried pine needles pressed intricate designs on his bronze belly. His bony but sinewy arms and legs bore briar scratches, and his back was scarred from beatings at the hands of his brutal father. Life had been hard; the hurt of it showed in his eyes. With a grimy hand, he pushed aside a tangled lock while he viewed the strange behavior of the emigrants. He had risked his life in order to observe the scene, and he did not intend to miss any of the action.

He was so engrossed in thought that he failed to notice that the wind had shifted until the white man's dog had picked up his scent. Persistently barking, it came running in his direction. If only he could get his hands on the little traitor! Taking its stance a short distance away, it continued to bark until the entire camp was alerted.

With a quick aim, Kamŭ Kaupa let fly an arrow, but it failed to hit a vital spot. The dog turned and, with tail between its legs, went yelping back to camp. The emigrants, apparently fearing that they were surrounded by Indians, screamed at each other like a flock of frightened blackbirds. Immediately, the young Bannock was up and away.

Shadows were lengthening and the sun, a fiery ball, was beginning its descent in the western sky. Soon it would nestle behind the slate blue foothills, and the land would be flooded with darkness. Evil spirits would stalk from one Indian camp to another in search of their enemies, and one of the treacherous Little People, a Ninimbu or dwarf, might lurk around to bring misfortune to anyone who crossed his path. Few had seen the Little People besides Bull Elk, Pariha Ungu, who had described them as chubby, elfin creatures whose invisible arrows caused endless misfortune.

Kamŭ Kaupa realized that he must hurry in order to reach camp by nightfall. Adjusting the strap of his quiver over his bare shoulder, he started homeward. He would kill a rabbit or a prairie dog along the way for his mother, and she would cook it in the pot Isha brought to camp following an attack on the emigrant road. She would say nothing, just look proud because her son never came home from the hunt empty-handed.

He kept well to the timber at the base of the foothills where there was little chance of being observed. The ground was carpeted with a variety of wild flowers. In places, patches of blue lupine seemed to vie for attention with large splashes of red, Indian paintbrush. Ordinarily, the boy would have been impressed by their beauty. When there was no one around to observe his weakness, he would even pluck some of the blossoms and marvel at their texture. He had been tempted at times to take them to his mother, but he feared that she might laugh at him or beat him. The Bannocks needed food not flowers. He must hurry because it was getting late.

Progress was slow and hunting poor a mile or so to the side of the wagon road, but beyond that the white hunters dared not go. Several recent attacks had been made on the emigrants. He knew because Isha had returned to his tepee with miscellaneous prizes, including a bloody scalp which he had displayed triumphantly.

"*Taibo'o*!" he had boasted. His explanation was unnecessary, because the loose locks hanging at his belt indicated that they had belonged to a white man.

On the way toward an old travois trail, Kamŭ Kaupa crossed a buffalo wallow where the bony remains of two bulls told of a fight to the death. Reconstructing the battle in his imagination, he could almost see the angry bulls as they bellowed and pawed the earth until they had made a wide basin, now a stagnant waterhole on the low side. The bleached bones of the victor protruded above the low waterline where he had apparently died of injury or overexertion as he wallowed in the cool earth following the conflict. The bones of the vanquished lay scattered where the hungry wolves had cleaned them.

When the boy reached what he thought to be a point of safety, he flattened himself at the edge of a spring for a refreshing drink. His view was obscured by a clump of chokecherry bushes, intertwined with wild grapevines where the water flowed to the right to join a larger stream.

Suddenly there was a sloshing sound. Puzzled as to what it might be, he peered through the bushes to see a sight that took his breath. And yet it so thrilled him that for a moment he was unaware of his danger. There sat a female black bear, working in the mud. Using her left paw, the boy always heard that bears were left-handed, she slapped and patted the oozy substance until it was the consistency that she wanted. Then picking up as much as she could carry, she made her way to the water's edge where she looked briefly at her reflection. Apparently dissatisfied with what she saw, she began applying the mud mixture to the left side of her face.

In the midst of her beauty treatment, she lifted her head and sniffed in all directions. Fortunately, the wind favored the boy, for it blew his scent away from her. Even so, his heart stood still when he realized that he was viewing a mother bear on the fight. She growled as she crashed through the thicket and began wading across the stream. Creeping forward to find the cause of her displeasure, he saw two cubs on the opposite bank. They must have done something to annoy her. When she reached them, she cuffed them both soundly and sent them reeling.

Kamŭ Kaupa's sympathy was with the cubs, cowering before her savage might. They were probably as unaware of the cause of their punishment as he had often been when suffering like treatment at the hands of Isha. The injustice of her action caused him to disregard caution, to spring into the open and take aim before she could deal a second blow. When the singing arrow plowed a furrow in the hide on her shoulder, she roared furiously and whirled toward her attacker, who stood horror-stricken on the opposite bank. Too late, he realized his mistake.

"Fool!" his spirit cried within him. It would now be a race for his life with the odds against him. Spurred on by the smarting injury in her shoulder, she began to cross the stream in swift strides. The cubs, in their attempt to keep up with her, came splashing at her heels.

Kamŭ Kaupa realized that there was not a bush that she could not crush nor a tree that she could not climb. His only hope lay in outdistancing her. He sped along a trail that ran out at a natural crossing. Rather than follow a path leading farther from camp, he was forced to run over a stretch of open country, littered with stones and cacti. But he was so frightened that he paid little attention to the pain they caused. On and on he raced, with the bear in pursuit. He imagined he could feel her hot breath, she came so near to him.

Glancing over his shoulder, he saw her stop and wait for her fretful cubs. When they caught up with her, she struck them down and resumed the chase. A second time it looked as if she might catch him, but again she paused until they reached her side. Picking up one, she boxed it ahead of her and carried the other to the spot where it landed. After picking it up, she gave it a fling. Then she picked up the other.

The game, which was rough and time consuming, was obviously to the boy's advantage. He wondered how long it would continue, but when one of the cubs landed it must have injured a paw because it began to whimper for sympathy. Its mother looked toward the boy, then at her offspring. Apparently overcome by mother love, she turned her attention to her young and abandoned the chase.

When Kamŭ Kaupa felt that it was safe to pause for breath, he watched her settle herself in a sitting position. The cubs, pressing against her, began to nurse. The boy would always be grateful to them for saving his life and to their mother for the lesson she had taught him. She had impressed upon him the wisdom of the old Indian rule—never arouse a wŭda to anger. He well knew this rule, for Pariha Ungu had told him many times. How crazy he had been to shoot wildly across the stream! He would know better next time.

The lesson she taught him also applied to Isha. He must bide his time until he could grow strong enough to handle him.

A cottontail jumped from behind a sagebrush near the path ahead. Instead of shooting it or running it down for the mere pleasure of the sport, he appeared not to notice. Zigzagging back and forth, it teased him into action, but still he did not respond. He trudged along until he had regained his composure sufficiently to upbraid himself for not killing it. He was a fool for arousing the bear and an old woman for letting the rabbit get away. The thought of facing his mother empty-handed distressed him.

When he came in sight of her tepee, he noticed that his father had returned. The presence of the renegade indicated trouble. There Isha lay, outstretched, indolently watching Little Moon stir up the fire to cook their supper. His contemptible manner reminded the boy of the story Pariha Ungu had told about Isŭf, as the Shoshones called Wolf, father of the Bannocks. According to the old Shoshone prophet, Isŭf was the one who shut up all wild life, preventing the Indians from hunting. Kamŭ Kaupa knew it happened because Pariha Ungu said so. The Indians who were born to hunt did not like the plan, so Izapŭ, Coyote, father of the Shoshones, set the animals free. Pariha Ungu maintained that this was the story back of the Wolf Dance.

The water in the cast iron kettle bubbled expectantly, but the young Indian realized there would be no supper. Too exhausted to run away, he walked dejectedly toward his mother. He was prepared to accept his punishment.

She took a sharp look at him. "Kamŭ Kaupa sick?" she asked.

"*Kai*—no." There was no excuse, at least none that she would understand.

Isha got to his feet and took an unsteady step in his direction. The boy trembled; his father seemed bigger and meaner than usual. The flinty glare in his eyes indicated a heart without feeling, and his long upper lip pointed downward over a cruel mouth. His short forelock was tied to stand erect, the distinguishing sign of the Bannock, while the braids on his shoulders were wrapped in otter fur and bright red, tradecloth. His two-piece buckskin suit, glazed with grease, was decorated with scalp locks and fringe down the arms of his shirt and on the outer seams of his leggings. His moccasins, painted red at the instep, indicated that he had stepped in the blood of an enemy.

"Plenty hungry," he growled, his tongue thick. "Whatcha bring?"

"Nothing." Kamŭ Kaupa hung his head.

"Nothing! Sonabitch!" Isha staggered toward the campfire. When he leaned over to pick up a stick, he lost his balance and came near pitching headlong into the flames. Righting himself, he turned on the boy and brandished his weapon.

Kamŭ Kaupa, his black eyes blazing with rage, stood his ground as if hypnotized. His brothers and sisters, cowering by the tepee, dared not come to his aid. Even Little Moon knew better than to interfere.

When his assailant began beating him, Kamŭ Kaupa made no effort to break away. Although the pain was almost unbearable, he would not give him the satisfaction of hearing his cry if it killed him. The animosity he felt at that moment was so like a fire that it almost consumed him, but he gave no outward sign. Had the bear not taught him a lesson in self-restraint? This was no time to antagonize his father.

Unable to draw a whimper from the boy, Isha dropped the stick in disgust and reeled toward the half-starved horse, hobbled nearby. The hobbles were unnecessary because the animal was too listless to move. When Isha reached its side, he backed up against it and looked menacingly toward his family. The scene was one of utter misery. The children, deep-eyed from fear and hunger, looked little better off than the poverty stricken Digger Indians.

Little Moon, after inspecting the broken skin on her son's shoulder, hastened into the tepee. When she returned, she carried a small rawhide container of bear grease, which she began to apply to his abrasions.

"Stop!" Isha rushed at her, knocked the ointment from her hand and gave her a vicious blow. "Go to your blanket!" he ordered.

The children were still speechless after he had followed her into the tepee. Kamŭ Kaupa was not sorry that his father had to go to bed hungry, but he wished that he had brought something for Little Moon and the children. He looked disconsolately into the pot. His mother had shown her faith in him, and he had failed her.

2

The flap entrance of the shabby skin lodge was open, but the interior was stuffy and Isha's snoring unbearable. Kamŭ Kaupa, unable to stand it any longer, crept from his blanket and stealthily made his way outside. The crisp mountain air on his smarting wounds would be more soothing than his mother's ointment.

The pleasant smudge smell of many campfires greeted him when he stepped into the night, and the cool moonlight gave purpose to his plan. He would go to Pariha Ungu's campfire, where he would find comfort and personal guidance. No one had ever tried to understand him but the Shoshone holy man. He had once been tall and as straight as a pine tree, but meditation over the trials of his people had brought deep lines of care to his face and had caused his back to curve like a moon in its last quarter.

The old prophet knew all there was to know about everything. Besides teaching Kamŭ Kaupa how to hunt and fish, he had also coached him in the ways of a warrior. Whenever the time should come to lift his first scalp, that time would not be far away, he would be able to do it with the greatest speed. The old Indian had shown him how.

More than that, Pariha Ungu had instilled in him his philosophy and his hatred for the white man. Not content with robbing the streams of the beaver, the intruders had turned to the destruction of the Indian's source of livelihood, the buffalo. White men were sometimes known to take nothing but the hide or the tongue. Pariha Ungu considered this sacrilege because buffalo were put on earth for the Indians' use, not to be left lying on the prairie for wild animals to devour. As a consequence of the white man's reckless slaughter, the buffalo would one day be gone.

Kamŭ Kaupa found the old Indian, as he knew he would, sitting by the dying embers of his campfire. He was deep in study, his scarred face grotesque and his cadaverous body protected from the night chill by a soiled, badly faded blanket. Motionless, he was hunched forward in the moonlight. During the snowy moons the holy man would tell of his valor in days gone by. He had cause to boast because he had been a great warrior until a Blackfoot arrow pierced his left eye.

The young Bannock, sitting down beside him, said not a word to disturb him. He would speak when ready. He was a man of meditation, not of words. After deliberately puffing on his long-stemmed, redstone pipe four times, the old Indian spoke; but he did not say, "*Ha,*" the usual greeting and questioning "yes" of the Shoshones. Nor did he say, "*Yawa,*" the Bannock form of greeting. Obviously he was expecting him.

"Pariha Ungu wonder why you not come sooner." His lack of surprise was not unusual, but his statement was perplexing. "Pariha Ungu only holy man in Naroyan's band. Only Indian who can talk with Our Father, Dam Apŭ. You know?"

The boy, warming himself before the fire, nodded.

"In Bear Dream, Dam Apŭ through Wŭda, tell Pariha Ungu many things." Kamŭ Kaupa could not help shuddering at a mention of the animal. He had already had more than he could endure for one day.

"You cold?" The old man threw a pitch-pine log on the fire. That meant that he had much to say; otherwise he would have chosen a stick. "Wŭda says Pariha Ungu's spirit will leave before another moon. First, he should give Kamŭ Kaupa his Medicine Arrow to take to Washakie, great Shoshone chief. It will bring good medicine to him and to his people."

The boy found it difficult to follow what he was saying, he was so weary. He wished that the old Indian would be quiet and give him a chance to relate his troubles. . . . When he realized that he was talking about him, he began to listen.

"Wŭda says you very brave. Sometime be great warrior." Then interrupting himself, he cautioned, "Remember, never bother Wŭda. He's strong and wise." How well Kamŭ Kaupa knew the truth of this! But how did his old friend find out what had happened? Could the bear have told him?

From the folds of his blanket, Pariha Ungu produced the butt end of his pemmican as if it had been saved for the occasion. It was greasy and dirty, but it was food. "Here, eat so you be strong. When sun come again, you go on long journey."

The boy, gnawing greedily, had no idea where he might be going nor did it matter. In the willows, a dog barked; and the night air was filled with the musk odor of a skunk.

When the old prophet laid a fatherly hand on the boy's shoulder, he felt the welts. "Pia Isha?" he asked, touching them gently.

In need of human sympathy Kamŭ Kaupa sidled closer. "*Aha,*" he confided.

"*Kesandŭ*—no good! Pia Isha not your father."

Kamŭ Kaupa looked at him in astonishment. What was he saying?

"Your father, father before him, both Shoshone, Snake Indian." He made their tribal sign, a serpentine motion. "Pia Isha take Mŭatsi after your father is killed by Sioux."

Wide-eyed in amazement, Kamŭ Kaupa tried to understand. So that was why his grandmother, Mua Pavan, and his mother, Mŭatsi, had Shoshone rather than Bannock names! He stared at a dying ember, out of reach of the flaming log. One thought alone was clear. Isha was not his father! This knowledge was enough to fire his imagination and cause his heart to sing—*Isha was not his father*!

Reaching into his buckskin quiver, Pariha Ungu drew out an arrow. He inspected it carefully while the black obsidian head glistened in the firelight. The shaft, darkened by age, was branded with the crudely drawn miniature of an elk. Holding the arrowhead in his hand, the old Indian tested its sharp edge with a gnarled thumb. Then he explained its significance.

"This come from upper Yellowstone country. There evil spirits fight underground. Send up big smoke. Big Noise. Bad medicine for many tribes, not Shoshone and Bannock. They guard Medicine Mountain. Scare other Indians away."

He told of an experience near Yellowstone Lake to prove it. According to his story all of the enemy tribes knew about Medicine Mountain, and they wanted the obsidian for their arrows. Once when a band of Cheyennes came, the Bannocks led them on so that they got to "Big Smoke" when it blew up. He gestured to show the way Old Faithful, as the white man called it, spouted into the air.

"Enemy plenty scared. Never come back." He claimed that the Shoshones and Bannocks often fought the Blackfeet over possession of the mountain. It was in one such battle that Pariha Ungu lost an eye. "Look." He showed Kamŭ Kaupa the arrow with its shiny black head. "This hit Pariha Ungu here." He placed his cupped hand over the empty socket and badly scarred side of his face. "I always keep it. It is perfect arrowhead." He handled it lovingly as if it were an exquisite work of art. "Use wisely. Do not waste."

After the old Indian had mused awhile, he asked, "You shoot straight?"

The boy nodded.

"Pariha Ungu teach Washakie to shoot straight. He stayed many moons in Naroyan's camp after his father was killed by Blackfoot. He become chief of Shoshone after Mowumha die."

He was quiet a moment. Then he continued, "Washakie very brave. Blackfoot arrow hit him. Make double scar here." He placed a finger on his left cheek just below the empty socket. "He get revenge when they steal Shoshone horses. He follow four days. When he return, he bring back many many horses covered with scalps." The old Indian's voice rang with pride as he recalled one of the acts of bravery that led to Washakie's chieftainship. "Blackfoot still fear 'im."

The boy sat looking at the arrow in silence.

Pariha Ungu picked up his tobacco pouch, the bladder of a Blackfoot about which he had boasted many times in council. This he considered just exchange for an eye. He slowly filled his pipe. After lighting it, he offered it to Dam Apŭ, then toward the rising sun, the earth and the four cardinal points. Following the ceremony, he handed it to his companion, a rare honor accorded one so young. Kamŭ Kaupa took a puff and choked on the smoke. He tried again. This time his stomach seemed to bounce up into his throat.

The old Indian's bony frame looked as if it might come apart at the joints when he threw aside his blanket and stood erect, his face lifted toward the star-lit sky. Then chanting in his sonorous voice, he shuffled his feet and slowly lifted the arrow with both hands toward the heavens four times. After that, he breathed upon it lustily as he transmitted the blessing of Dam Apŭ into the arrow. He lowered it in homage to Mother Earth. Finally, he thrust it in all of the four directions from which his imaginary enemies might come. Then he handed the arrow to the boy. "Keep, my son. Take it to Washakie. Give him Medicine Arrow. He will know it is one Pariha Ungu always carry. He will take you in his tepee. Tell him, in Bear Dream Dam Apŭ says Kamŭ Kaupa must learn Medicine Arrow Dance. Always do it before going on warpath. It will please Dam Apŭ."

When Kamŭ Kaupa rehearsed the dance, Pariha Ungu called it more than good. It was *tivizant,* very good! The Indians, who were accustomed to hearing the Shoshone holy man burst forth in song any time of the day or night, were undisturbed.

The boy, who had a natural fear of the dark, did not like the thought of starting on his mission. What if he were to encounter one of the Little People? "Ninimbu?" he asked.

"While you carry Medicine Arrow, Ninimbu not hurt you. Wait till sun come again. You have full day before Pia Isha miss you. . . . Remember grass will stand again, but soft ground not. Leave no tracks."

Suddenly, the picture of the hungry children flashed upon the boy's memory. "*Kai*!" he protested. "Kamŭ Kaupa cannot go. My family will starve."

The old Indian looked at him a long time. What he saw must have pleased him because he said, "You would make good chief. Have people in your heart.

Family will not starve. They will learn to take care of themselves the way you do."

The boy was still reluctant. "Washakie, where—"

With his pipe stem, Pariha Ungu pointed the way southeast in the direction of Soda Springs. Kamŭ Kaupa would have to cross the Oregon Trail as well as Bear River after leaving Naroyan's camp on the east bank of the Snake. In this way he would avoid traveling the emigrant road. At the same time, he would have access to water at least part of the way.

The old Indian admonished him to stay well away from the Medicine Road of the emigrants, except in crossing. Then he was to observe the utmost caution. In sight of Bear Lake, he would cross the river and the trail a second time, then follow travois tracks leading eastward to Ham's Fork. This would be the beginning of the most difficult part of his journey because there were no streams to follow, and there was little water to be found along the way. He would have to depend entirely on his sense of direction.

After leaving Ham's Fork, he would go across country on an old Indian trail until he reached Green River, the last stream he would be forced to cross. On the far side, he would turn right, and follow fresh tracks that would take him to Washakie's camp. Just how Pariha Ungu knew where his friend was to be found, he did not say. Wŭda must have told him.

Kamŭ Kaupa considered the journey with solemn wonder. He had always experienced a thrill of pleasure when camp was to be moved even though his job of replacing lodgepoles was difficult. He also had to find the heavy stones to hold down the edge of the tepee so that the wind would not get under it and blow it over. Even so, the anticipation of new scenery and the prospect of more plentiful game stirred him. He would flex his puny muscles and glory in his imaginative strength. Was he not the provider for his family? His mother and the children would fold and pack the weather-beaten lodgeskin on the travois poles, hitched to the slat-sided horse. Somehow there had been comfort in going down the trail together though their lot was hard.

His heart was suddenly gripped with fear over the prospect of setting out upon a journey into the unknown. There was no way of telling what lay ahead. But when Pariha Ungu gently urged, "Go, my son," he despised himself for his timidity. He resolved that he would carry out his wishes no matter what happened. His determination dispelled his momentary weakness.

"Kamŭ Kaupa will take Medicine Arrow to Washakie, then come back," he promised.

"*Kai,* stay with Shoshones. Pariha Ungu will not be here—Dam Apŭ has spoken. Washakie will make you fine warrior. Maybe Shoshone want you for chief when he joins me in spirit world. Remember, do good for your people. Be honest. Listen to wise counsel."

The boy's heart was heavy, for he realized that these were the last words of advice he would have from his wise, old friend. He stood by the fire a moment, unable to find words to tell him how he would be missed, how his teachings would stay with him all the days of his life. Then he turned so that the holy man could not see the tears in his eyes. With his head swimming as much from the conversation as from the tobacco, he ran home.

Little Moon, her back toward Isha, lay sleeping while her mate, in a drunken stupor, sprawled half out of the blanket. Moonlight pouring through the flap opening seemed to center him out in the dark interior. The boy stared down at the scoundrel whom he had always thought to be his father. In spite of his hatred, he could not help admiring his sinewy build, so characteristic of the true Bannock.

Perhaps there would be no need after all for a tomahawk. With the sharp edge of the Medicine Arrow he could someday remove Isha's scalp in one piece. As a Bannock, he could not display it on the end of a lance or a lodgepole. That would not be proper. But if he were no longer a Bannock, that is, if he were a warrior of some other tribe perhaps he could claim his scalp, hang it over the entrance of his tepee and boast of his deed in council. The thought that Isha would not be able to enter the spirit world without it made him tingle with pleasure.

3

Dam Apŭ had given light to another day when Kamŭ Kaupa crept from his blanket. He tried not to awaken Isha, who lay fast asleep. Little Moon was nowhere to be seen because she had taken her digging stick and had gone in search of food for her hungry children. No one needed to tell Kamŭ Kaupa; he knew. Wistfully, he wished that he could find her, but if he tried, it would only delay him. He must get as far away as he could before Isha would be aroused by pangs of hunger.

He found the Medicine Arrow in the sagebrush where he had hidden it the night before. Looking at it in daylight when he could see it better, he wondered at its significance. Then he carefully put it in his quiver and started on his journey. He had nothing to guide him except his keen sense of direction and the knowledge of the heavenly bodies Pariha Ungu had instilled in him.

The fear that engulfed him the night before had fled. In its place was the comforting thought that Dam Apŭ had directed that he be sent to Washakie. Nothing could happen to him while he was the bearer of the sacred Medicine Arrow, Pariha Ungu had said.

When he was far enough from the camp that he

was comparatively safe, he took the arrow from the quiver once again and inspected it thoroughly. This was the first Medicine Arrow he had seen, and he was awed by it. Then he felt the urge to rehearse the dance the holy man had taught him. Standing on the top of a knoll where he seemed nearer the Spirit Above, he lifted his face and earnestly prayed.

"Dam Apŭ, guide me. Help me find Shoshone chief. Make me big, strong warrior, wise like Pariha Ungu." He lifted the arrow four times. Then with gusto he breathed upon it and lowered it slowly to the ground. Finally, he went through the motion of thrusting it at his imaginary enemies.

Before resuming his journey, he surveyed the area he knew and loved so well. He was sad to think of leaving the vibrant, rugged land of the wapiti. In places deep valleys snuggled between towering snow-capped peaks that constantly pointed upward toward a nobler life. Clear water from melting snows and hidden springs rippled down the forest-covered mountainsides only to gain tempo and rush recklessly onward as it neared the confluence of a larger stream below. There were shimmering lakes abounding with fish and mountain meadows teeming with elk and deer. Sure-footed mountain sheep watched from crags above, and there were bears, black, left-handed bears, that went out of their way to avoid trouble.

The high plains beyond the Tetons had once been thick with herds of buffalo. Pariha Ungu had been there. That was before the white man came to plot the destruction of the Indian. How could he survive without food, lodgeskins and clothing, all of which the buffalo must provide? Nibbling every edible leaf that he could find or root he could pry from the ground, Kamŭ Kaupa determined that the white man must go. He would one day be a great warrior, a Shoshone warrior maybe, and drive him out. Moreover, he would settle his score with Isha.

Although there was no time limit to his excursion, the boy did not tarry along the way. He moved forward mile after mile at a consistently slow pace, for he had a long journey ahead and there was no need of tiring himself at the start. His single item of clothing was a buckskin clout, and his other possessions a ragged blanket, a willow bow and a quiver containing the Medicine Arrow with his own assortment. Though footsore, he remained strong in his resolve. If only he had a horse to carry him!

The country in which he traveled the first several days was familiar; he saw a number of former campsites used by Naroyan's band. Beyond that, all was a never-ending land, holding out the exciting promise of a new and better life. It was like the white man's quest for gold Pariha Ungu had told him about. Only his search was for something more precious, for he envisioned the Shoshone camp as a land of plenty, where warriors brought more than scalps to their families. Children laughed and played, and women had colored beads to decorate their clothing. There would be quantities of food, even some to throw to the dogs like in the white man's camp. His anticipation became keener each day.

He had little difficulty finding the two crossings of Bear River as the Indian trails were easy to follow. Without loss of his blanket or his quiver, he was able to swim and at the same time tow a makeshift raft to the opposite bank. He saw various kinds of small game which he did not shoot because he was afraid that if he tried to roast the meat he might attract unfriendly Indians. He feared nothing more than a hostile. The night sounds that once terrified him, the howl of a wolf or the bark of a coyote, did not even awaken him as he lay clutching the Medicine Arrow, safe in the arms of Mother Earth.

He lived as the buffalo, entirely on vegetation; but he, too, needed water. After leaving Bear River, he chewed licorice stalks to stimulate the flow of saliva. Even so, he was craving a drink when he spied Ham's Fork in the distance. His throat was so dry and parched that he could scarcely swallow, and his feet were numb with pain. So far, he had managed to stay away from the trails after each hazardous crossing, and he had not encountered a single soul. Because of the scarcity of water in the country, there would most certainly be a well-used trail at the willow-fringed stream in the distance. Even so, he picked up speed just as an animal does at the smell of water.

Once on the river bank, he restrained himself from diving into the snow-fed stream; for he knew that if he were to gulp too much water when he was hot from exertion he would sicken. Carefully, he began splattering a little water on himself and rinsing out his mouth. His spirits soared, and he was wild with joy when, splashing and sputtering, he finally submerged himself. He bobbed up and down until he was completely refreshed; then he hid in a sheltered nook and went to sleep.

Judging by the position of the sun, he had not slept long when he was aroused by his instinct of self-preservation. There was the sound of hooves in the distance. Ninimbu was his first thought! But it could not be one of the mischievous dwarfs because they did not ride horses. Anyway, Pariha Ungu had assured him that he would not be bothered while he carried the Medicine Arrow. Could a white hunter have strayed so far in search of game? While the boy hid behind a chokecherry bush, the sound came nearer. Listening anxiously, he was sure that the horse had a rider, so he parted the bushes to see.

The picture before him was one he would not forget. The horse, a sleek sorrel stallion with white flowing mane and tail, was as resplendent as his rider in his ceremonial array. Both horse and rider were bedecked with feathers and wolves' tails and ornamented with beads, pieces of metal, and the teeth and claws of wild animals. Big Chief must be Shoshone the boy reflected; no Bannock ever appeared in such splendor!

When the chieftain neared the thicket at the water's edge, his horse, startled by something in the grass, shied sharply to one side. The rider was caught off guard. In a flash, the great chief and all of his riggings crashed to the ground ingloriously.

Kamŭ Kaupa caught his breath. Then unmindful of his own danger, he stepped from his hiding place to see what had happened. The chief, a heap of buckskin and feathers, did not move. His head had struck a stone, and his warbonnet was already becoming soaked with blood. The horse, startled by a rattlesnake, galloped on a few paces, then turned to look back at its master. As if unable to be of assistance, it slowly began nibbling the buffalo grass at its feet. Still the chief did not move.

The snake, emitting a strong reptile odor, coiled in striking distance of the unconscious man. Venomously eyeing its prey, it rattled continuously. Kamŭ Kaupa, in a flash, drew the Medicine Arrow from his quiver and, taking careful aim, severed its head. The snake then writhed convulsively.

The boy, rushing to the stream, filled his quiver and ran back with all possible speed before the water leaked out at the bottom. He tore the kerchief from Big Chief's neck and began bathing the dirt and blood from the wound on his scalp. It was not deep, but the bleeding had to be stopped before the chief regained consciousness because it was hard to tell what might happen then.

When Kamŭ Kaupa was wiping the blood from his face, he observed a double scar. What was it that Pariha Ungu had said about the Blackfeet making a scar on Washakie's face! The boy's hands trembled until he could scarcely tie the kerchief around his head, for he realized that this was Washakie, the great chief of the Shoshones. He looked with reverential fear upon the classic features, the prominent nose, the high cheekbones, the generous mouth and the somewhat narrow forehead of the handsome Indian. Kamŭ Kaupa was terrified when he opened his eyes.

"*Ha*!" Big Chief spoke.

"You bad hurt?"

Washakie lifted his hand to his head, then closed his eyes. The boy feared that the spirit had left his body. When he bent over him anxiously, the chief's dark, penetrating eyes suddenly opened wide. He propped himself on his elbow so that he could see what had taken place, the headless rattler still writhing at his side, the horse calmly grazing nearby and the frightened young Indian caring for his wounds. The scene spoke for itself. As the chief sat up, he noticed the arrow and reached for it, but the boy snatched it from under his hand.

"Where'd you get it?" Big Chief snapped. "Speak! Tell me your name!"

Kamŭ Kaupa," the boy managed to answer, though Indian-like he was reluctant to admit it. Fearing to look up, he concentrated his attention on the arrow, which he held tightly with both hands. Although he had made the long journey for the purpose of delivering it to Washakie, he now clung to it as if it meant more than life itself.

"Kamŭ Kaupa, Rabbit Leg! Bannock boy. You have

no right to carry Pariha Ungu's Medicine Arrow!" Washakie, staggering to his feet, held out his hand. His voice was so gruff that the boy started to run.

"Stay!" the chief commanded. "How do I know you did not steal it? Maybe kill my friend, Pariha Ungu. Do not talk crooked talk. Tell me!" His voice was so frightening it was no wonder the Blackfeet quaked at a mere mentioned of his name.

Kamŭ Kaupa reluctantly handed over the arrow. Still Big Chief was not satisfied.

"Speak!" he demanded. He squeezed the boy's thin arm so hard that tears came to his eyes, but he would not utter a sound. He would some day be a warrior, and warriors do not cry. He must not be afraid, he told himself. True, he would always be a Bannock because he belonged to his mother's tribe, but he had come to live with his father's people, the Eastern Shoshones or Green River Snakes as Pariha Ungu called them. He hoped to be accepted as one of them just as Washakie, also of mixed blood, had been. Pariha Ungu had explained that it was the chief's mother who was Shoshone, not his father. Kamŭ Kaupa threw his head back and looked into Big Chief's eyes. Then he spoke fearlessly.

"Pariha Ungu is my friend. He gave his Medicine Arrow to me." Still Washakie was not convinced. He shook the boy, but he was no longer able to frighten him. "He told me to take it to Washakie. He said you would take me in your tepee."

Big Chief stared at him in disbelief.

"Pariha Ungu will not be here, but he will be glad, glad that Washakie take Kamŭ Kaupa. Pariha Ungu is still alive, but in Bear Dream, Dam Apŭ told him his spirit will go away before another moon. He is very old, but still very brave." The boy, with parted lips, was breathing hard, as if he had just completed a race. He looked into the chief's face for a sign of understanding. Not seeing one, he went on, "Pariha Ungu told about Washakie's bravery. When Blackfoot stole Shoshone horses, he followed and got many horses he brought back all covered with scalps. He—"

"Ho!" ejaculated the chief as he released his grip. He settled himself cross-legged. The boy's words were like salve to his vanity.

The hot sun had disappeared, and a rosy haze had settled over the landscape. Soon it would be dark, but Washakie was in no hurry. Indians never hurry unless going into battle or pursuing the enemy. Just white man. White man crazy to hurry.

Washakie sat motionless while he listened to Kamŭ Kaupa's account of his beatings at the hands of Isha and of his slipping to Pariha Ungu for comfort. Words began to tumble from the boy's lips after he had gained the chief's confidence. Mention of the name of the Shoshone prophet caused Big Chief to interrupt so that he could eulogize his old friend and give details of his encounter with the Blackfeet. . . . He stopped short, waiting for the boy to continue.

"Pariha Ungu says Kamŭ Kaupa is not all

Bannock, not Isha's son, but son and grandson of and Shoshone warriors. Mua Pavan, my grandmother, Mŭatsi, my mother—" He did not finish because Washakie was acting strange. His mouth worked, but no words came. His eyes bulged as if he were trying to see but could not. Maybe Big Chief hurt inside?

"Mua Pavan? Moon on the Water? Mua Pavan?" Washakie repeated as if unable to comprehend.

"*Aha,* Mua Pavan, my grandmother, died when my mother, Mŭatsi, was born."

The chief continued to stare at the boy. "Pariha Ungu did not name Shoshone warrior who claimed Mua Pavan?"

"Just Shoshone."

"Washakie will tell you. I paid two ponies for her because she was so beautiful. When I took her to my lodge, my other wives were jealous and they beat her when I was away. Soon she stopped smiling and talking and just cried. We then called her Waipŭ Yagakantŭ, Crying Woman. I did not want her in my blanket any more.

"One day when I come in, I found her people visiting her. She did not see me stand and watch her laugh and talk with them. I got mad and struck her. She started to cry, so I gave her a blanket and a horse and told her to go home with her people. I did not want to see her again. When she was leaving, she talked and laughed, she was so happy! . . . Washakie did not know about Mŭatsi." There was a note of sadness in his voice. After a moment's silence, he stated, "Pariha Ungu sent Kamŭ Kaupa because he is grandson of Washakie!"

Big Chief must be bad hurt! Maybe crazy in the head!

"The heart of Washakie is glad." His face broke into a happy smile. "You have another name?"

The boy shook his head.

"It is not good for Indian to have only one name. That is why Pia Isha has only one. He will always be *kesandŭ,* no good. There is no name worse than Wolf his people can call him."

Washakie was quiet a moment. Then he said, "Here. Take Medicine Arrow. " He handed it to the boy. "Your name will be Kamŭ Kaupa no more. You saved the life of Washakie so you will have new name and right to boast in council. I will call you—" He held out his hand as if reaching for something. The boy, too confused to know what he was doing, handed the arrow back to him.

"Black Arrow!" The chief thoughtfully studied the object in his hand. Then with a sudden inspiration he exclaimed, "*Tupaku,* Black Arrow! Washakie will call you Tupaku for Medicine Arrow. Tupaku will be your name!"

Well pleased with his proclamation, the chief reached for a skin of pemmican suspended in a buckskin pouch from the left side of his belt. He began slicing off pieces which he popped into his mouth.

Meanwhile, Tupaku watched, hungry eyed. After the chief had satisfied his appetite, he cut pieces for the boy, who devoured them with the zest of a half-starved animal. The food was unlike anything he had ever tasted. The meat was not the usual elk or deer, but tender, half-grown rabbit, finely chopped together with the spicy breast of sage hen. To this had been added dried currants and fawn fat. While Tupaku devoured his food, he listened to Big Chief's account of the way in which he earned his name and his right to boast in council.

It happened in the year of the great prairie fire, "When-Fire-Burn-Grass," Washakie told him. "I shoot my first buffalo. It is fine bull. I ride up beside him and whing, I sink my arrow to feathers behind his front leg. He drop." The chief paused as he appraised the boy. "I was young like you. It was fine bull. I never forget how big!"

He smoked for a moment in silence while he reflected upon the merits of his game. "No one had a gun, so each hunter claimed his kill by his arrow. I gave mine to old woman who had no one hunt for her. I just kept head. I had watched Pariha Ungu make rawhide shield from tough hide on bull's neck, so I made rattle from skin on its pate. I put little rocks in it, and tied it on the end of hollow stick. Then, Pooh!"

His bronze cheeks puffed in dramatic demonstration. "I blew it up, tied it and hung it on lodgepole. When it dried, it rattled like gourd."

The Bannock boy gazed spellbound at the narrator, who, thus encouraged, made the most of a good story. He told of a day when the Shoshone braves were hunting in the Big Horns, and a Sioux war party was spotted in the hills. Without warriors, the old men, women and children were defenseless in their camp in the peaceful Sweetwater Valley. War whoops rang out, and the Sioux descended upon the quiet camp.

"Quickly I paint red spots on my face and jump on my horse. With rattle shaking, I gallop toward enemy. I shout a warning, *enga-tasŭa*!" Smallpox, the dread disease of the Indian!

The warriors, with lances and spears clattering, whirled their ponies around so quickly that even Washakie was astounded. The feathers on their bonnets fluttered behind them as they disappeared through the dust. Laughing heartily over the joke he had played on the enemy he was sure that they did not stop until they had reached their camp somewhere along the Platte. This event proved to be his first act of valor and the one which earned for him his name Wŭ-(with a handle) saki-(shakes) pŭ-(object, rattle), or Washakie. He was no longer Pina Quanah, smell of sugar, the name given him at birth.

After he had finished his story, he told how he had lately been pursued by the Ninimbi, who had repeatedly shot him with invisible arrows. The little demons of misfortune had caused him to be thrown from his horse. "But Tupaku good medicine," he added confidently. "He shoot straight, kill *togoa* and fix head. Pariha Ungu is wise to send him to live with Washakie. It is well."

The boy stared at him. His mind had worked slowly. It had taken time for him to adjust to the fact that he was not a full-blooded Bannock. Mulling over the idea since his talk with Pariha Ungu, he had finally convinced himself that it was so. Now it was hard for him to believe that Washakie spoke true words because he had absorbed little of what he had said. Still confused, he got to his feet and turned away.

"Stop!" ordered the chief. "Tupaku must never leave Washakie! I have spoken."

4

With a hand on the young Bannock's shoulder, Washakie limped toward his horse, still grazing a few feet away. Flipping the reins over its head, he mounted Indian fashion from the right and instructed the boy to jump on behind. They made an odd looking pair as they rode through the dusk, Big Chief in his finery, but with a blood-stained turban, and the Bannock boy, as naked as any warrior.

Tupaku could tell that they were going in an easterly direction, but he could see little because of the broad back in front of him. He was glad that Big Chief did not talk, for he could hear familiar night sounds—the moan of pine trees fanned by an uncertain breeze, the cry of a nighthawk flying low and a coyote howl in the distance. A coyote howl when the moon was full meant good fortune, but Tupaku did not need to be told. This night, at least, he was not a Walker.

Never before had he been on a horse so grand! He reveled in the heady smell of horse flesh and in the fawn-like texture of its hair. He touched the animal gently, lovingly. It was not like the scrawny old nag he used to ride, One Eye, she was called, because in her livelier days Isha had blinded one of her eyes so that she would be easy to catch. The horse, like the one now used to move the family, had belonged solely to Isha. When One Eye died, he shared the carcass with his Digger friends, all of them sitting around the remains and feasting until the last morsel was consumed. The boy had not forgiven him.

Before crossing the third and last river, Washakie alighted, leaving Tupaku alone on the horse. There was a lump in his throat, he was so happy!

The chief lifted his arms in supplication. "Dam Apŭ, watch over my people," he prayed. "Make us strong to defend ourselves against those who black their hearts toward us. Do not let Crow destroy us!" Then he added as if to himself, "Tupaku is good medicine." Together, the two crossed the stream and turned toward the south, just as Pariha Ungu had signified.

When they arrived at the outskirts of the Shoshone village, Big Chief reached for his musical gourd, hanging with the accouterments of war from his belt. The gourd, covered with many rattles, formed his accompaniment as he burst into song. While the sound reverberated through the hills, he composed words to his own liking. Much in the manner of a town crier, he chanted his good fortune.

"Ah'hah-ne-ne, ah'hah-ne-ne!
Washakie bring good medicine,
Good medicine for my people.
Ah'hah-ne-ne, ah'hah-ne-ne!
Tupaku save life of Washakie.
Save life of all my people."

Indians, running from every direction, came yelling, all at once. Shouting words of welcome to their chief, they crowded around to see his medicine bundle. He had lately read two such bundles, one containing the bones of a *pohakantŭ* or medicine man. The other, among its assorted contents, held a fine petrified hairball, carried to attract the buffalo. To their surprise, their chief did not have a medicine bundle but a naked, rawboned Bannock, who in appearance was neither a man nor a child.

"Tupaku killed *togoa* before it strike Washakie when he was bad hurt from fall. He saved the life of your chief. Now he has come with Pariha Ungu's Medicine Arrow to help all Shoshone." He held the arrow high so that all might see. "The Bannock boy who will carry this Medicine Arrow to battle against Crow is son of Washakie!" With that, the adoption was complete.

"Ha'a! Ha'a!" The warriors shouted as they crowded around, trying to touch the chief's good medicine.

Wide-eyed and speechless Tupaku looked at his people, the bold Shoshone warriors. They were all he could see, the women and children having been pushed into the background. He was terrified when he was carried on the shoulders of the surging crowd toward an enormous campfire. For a moment he thought that he was to be roasted in the flames, but no, he was deposited gently on a rocky knoll where he could be seen plainly in the firelight.

From there, he watched Washakie and the other bonneted warriors assemble for the Afraid Dance, the prelude to the War Dance. Several singers, men and women, were beating their hand drums and chanting, while the chief and sub-chiefs responded to the rhythm with a marching step without changing position. Pariha Ungu had described this dance so well that Tupaku recognized it, and he knew that its purpose was to announce that the enemy was near. The dance, lasting but a short time, stopped as abruptly as it had started. Warriors, who a moment before had stood motionless, now sprang to action. They beat their blankets while their war chief shouted, "Shoshone will go on warpath when sun comes again!"

Washakie silenced the drums that had already begun to beat for the War Dance. "First we must have sacred Medicine Arrow Dance Pariha Ungu send by Tupaku. Come, my son," he called, "and dance it so my people will know Dam Apŭ is with us."

How the Bannock boy managed to reach his side he was not sure. Once there, he forgot the drums, the feathers, the sea of painted faces peering at him. He closed his eyes and began a repetitious chant while he raised the Medicine Arrow skyward. By the time he had lowered it to the ground, the entire congregation had joined him. When he was thrusting the arrow toward his unknown enemies, the sound was deafening.

Washakie, climbing on a boulder, silenced his Indians so that he might deliver one of the speeches for which he was famous. He had spent so many years mingling with his white trapper-trader friends that he could express himself more fluently than any other Indian in the tribe. As he frequently said, he had been a young man with Jim Bridger.

"My people." He stood with hands lifted to silence them. "My people, our runners say that Sioux take many scalps from Crow. We know what that means. They will come to fight Shoshone to recover their loss. They do not know about Tupaku, our Good Medicine. Our runners say they camp on Owl Creek. Their families, too. Crow will strike when sun is high. Shoshone are ready. Tupaku ready. Shoshone will win!" It was the kind of speech the tribesmen liked to hear. Inspired by his words, they zealously entered into the rhythm of the War Dance. All of the warriors beat their chests and flourished their weapons to the beat of the drum. Their ardent medicine making would not only please Dam Apŭ, but it would also frighten the enemy wherever he might be.

It was so frenzied that a Mormon camp nearby was alerted by the noise. Although Washakie had befriended the Saints, there were those who distrusted his motives. Their fears seemed justified by the realization that the Shoshones were on the warpath. Huddling the women and children in the center of the wagon corral for protection, the men armed themselves and took up posts around the outside. They dared not sleep as they feared an attack might take place at any time.

Finally, Washakie led Tupaku to his tepee where he insisted that he rest. There amidst the shadowy blanketed forms of sleeping women and children, the chief found his faithful wife, Hanŭbi, Corn Woman. At the sound of his voice, she came forward, her moccasined feet treading lightly on the hard dirt floor. In the firelight, she appeared young enough to be his daughter. Her genial face beamed and her teeth flashed white in a broad smile of welcome, for busy tongues had already informed her of the presence of the Bannock boy.

"My son," was all the explanation Washakie gave or Hanŭbi expected. "Blanket him with Nanagi." Tupaku did not realize at the time that an honor was being bestowed upon him, that the child Nanagi, Echo, had been favored since birth. To Hanŭbi, the gesture meant that the chief's two sons would share equally in their father's esteem. Before leaving, Washakie strode to one side of the lodge, opened a rawhide chest and transferred several miscellaneous articles to another nearby. Then he pulled the empty one forward and presented it to Tupaku, who was delighted by the magnificent, white buffalo robe covering it.

The mixed band of Bannocks and Shoshones, like Gypsies, had few possessions. Only Naroyan, their chief, could boast of a chest, but it was crude in comparison. The boy was unused to such luxuries. Although the tepee had no partitions, each occupant had his allotted space as well as a chest to house his belongings. Washakie's lodge was neat and clean, unlike Isha's foul smelling one, which was always redolent of rancid grease and unwashed bodies.

After Tupaku had carefully placed his Medicine Arrow in the chest, he lay trying to convince himself that he was not dreaming. He was so exhausted from his journey and so confused by everything that had happened that he covered his head with his blanket and quietly sobbed himself to sleep.

The next morning he was required to bathe in the river and fast along with the other warriors before going to battle. Washakie directed the ceremony during which his face and body were anointed with grease, then decorated according to his taste. When the ritual was complete, Tupaku was permitted to look at himself in a mirror.

The chief, admiring his handiwork, explained his selection of colors. "White," he said, "is daylight. It come from Dam Apŭ so we can see. Blue is sky and red is sunset, daytime colors. They mean we will fight the Crow and defeat them before night comes again." Then he pointed to the streaks he had painted on his body. "Green is grass. The Shoshone warriors paint their bodies green in summer so enemy cannot see 'em when they creep up on 'em."

Nanagi stood watching in admiration while

Tupaku adorned himself with the ornaments Hanŭbi gave him. Among these was a necklace of bears' claws, showing that he bore a mark of distinction. Other than that, his new attire consisted of a beaded headband and a fresh eagle feather.

"It is well," Washakie remarked with satisfaction. Then he took the boy outside to his waiting horse, the sorrel with long white mane and tail.

A wave of joy swept over the young Bannock when he realized that he was to ride the splendid animal. A pleasant-faced woman, holding the reins, smiled as she handed them to him. He looked to see if Nanagi were watching. Sure enough, there he stood, just outside the entrance of his father's lodge. His childish face was aglow with excitement, and he waved vigorously until his mother led him away from the danger of prancing horses. A runner, who had just arrived, talked with the chief briefly. Then Washakie, beckoning Tupaku to follow, rode through camp as he shouted directions to his warriors.

When the Crows rushed into the valley, they found the Shoshones, with their strategy well planned. Washakie had already directed Tupaku, now bedecked with the chief's warbonnet, to dash forward, while he, stripped down as an ordinary warrior, was to follow. "Go!" he commanded.

The boy desperately clutched his reins with one hand and held high his Medicine Arrow with the other, just as he had been instructed. He had no fear, for he had experienced so much that he could not feel emotion. In fact, he did not have the slightest idea where he was going.

The Crows were in for a surprise. Instead of Washakie's leading his warriors like a majestic chieftain, here came a little chief, so reduced in size, he looked starved. He carried something, a medicine stick it seemed to be, in the form of an arrow, and he rode the chief's favorite horse. Could this be Washakie? Might the medicine stick have caused him to shrink until he resembled a skeleton? Through the careful application of color, the chief had created a successful illusion.

The enemy warriors were terrified, for they believed that the Medicine Arrow held some supernatural power. Disconcerted, those in the front ranks pulled on their reins in an attempt to stem the oncoming surge.

Still Tupaku galloped forward. The confusion he caused among the Crows presented the advantage Washakie had anticipated.

"Drop back!" he ordered. The boy obeyed, while the warriors passed on each side and rode headlong into action with Washakie in full command. Tupaku breathlessly watched the scene, as much as he could see through the dust. He was fascinated by the sound of battle, by the action taking place before him. In the tumult, it was difficult to distinguish one warrior from another. He wanted to help, but he could not tell a Crow when he saw one.

Fighting was soon at such close range that the bow and arrow were of little value. Some of the Indians on both sides began to resort to knives, war clubs and tomahawks. Tupaku saw a warrior grab an enemy by a braid and yank him to the ground. No sooner had he landed than a woman who had followed her mate to battle struck him down with a white man's ax, her only weapon. Her glory was short lived because she was slain with a war club wielded by an enemy warrior.

Washakie, shouting directions, came in view for a moment. His orders seemed to intensify the Shoshones' thirst for victory. The young Bannock was so engrossed in watching the action taking place before him that he was almost caught off guard. An enemy, skirting the hand-to-hand fighting, took a quick aim at him. Instantly, he flattened himself on the back of his horse just as an arrow whizzed overhead. In a flash he let fly one of his own. When he saw the warrior topple to the ground he was not sure whether he or someone else had hit him. Too excited to investigate, he rushed forward to count his first coup. He made an effort to capture the Crow pony as a trophy of war, but it got away. One of the Shoshone warriors, his face painted black to show his animosity toward the enemy, saw what had happened. Without a word, he went dashing after the prize.

The battle was brief but costly for the Crows, who feared to tarry long enough to retrieve their dead. As they disappeared in the distance, the Shoshone women came swarming over the battlefield to gather souvenirs while the old man collected arrows for future use. A dozen or more warriors were injured, but because of the Medicine Arrow there was only one fatality, the woman who gave her life for her people. As a woman, she was not deserving of the honor that would have been accorded a brave.

When the warrior returned with the Crow pony, Washakie was with him. Tupaku was relieved to see the look of satisfaction on his face. Apparently, all had gone better than he anticipated. The warrior, to the boy's surprise, handed him the end of the halter. "Take it," he said. "It is yours. Tupaku and his arrow both good medicine for Shoshone." The pinto was not as big as Washakie's sorrel, but to the boy it looked beautiful; for it was the first horse he had ever owned.

The chief looked down at the Crow at his feet. "Why not scalp him?" he asked. It had not occurred to Tupaku that he was entitled to the honor. Under the chief's watchful eye, he worked with lightning speed because Pariha Ungu had told him that time was of the utmost importance. Pretending that the lifeless Indian was Isha, rather than an unknown Crow, he began gleefully cutting a circle around the crown of his head with the knife Washakie handed him. Raising the edge of the scalp, he gripped it firmly between his teeth. Then with a quick jerk he tore it off. Waving the trophy by the hair, he looked to his chief for approval.

"It is well," he said. Then Washakie and his good medicine returned triumphantly to the village.

When the elders met in council that evening they voted to give the young Bannock the honorary title Tegwatsi (Little Chief) because he led the warriors in battle. A warbonnet, with its ruff of golden eagle feathers reaching to his heals, was made amidst song and ceremony. An incident of the battle was recounted as each feather was added, and two holes were punched in the band above the forehead to signify his valor. He would be entitled to wear the headdress on ceremonial occasions, but he would not again be permitted to go into battle until he had been given a course of training.

Tupaku had experienced so much excitement during the day that he was unable to comprehend the full meaning of his honor, nor was he really sure of his name. He did not even have a feeling of gladness when he was presented with a pair of moccasins with beadwork depicting three mountains.

"Trois Tetons!" Washakie stated as he pointed to the design on the toes. His reference to his beloved mountains by their French name seemed to add to their grandeur. From his French-Canadian trapper-friends, he had acquired a smattering of French along with his uncertain English. Though he had a reasonable understanding of both languages, he seldom spoke either.

Tupaku, instead of being proud of his spectacular achievements, was tired and frustrated. Success had come so fast that he was unprepared for it. Upon his return to Washakie's lodge, he asked for his blanket, the last link with his Bannock life. Hanŭbi, who sensed his attachment for it, said regretfully that she had burned it. Smiling sympathetically, she presented him with another.

He had to turn away to keep her from seeing the tears that rolled down his cheeks in spite of himself. Covering his head with his new blanket, he pretended to sleep, but the beat of the tom-tom and the uncanny sound of the Scalp Dance rang in his ears. He yearned for slumber so deep that it would help him forget the role he was forced to play in this camp of strangers.

When he finally slept, he dreamed that he was a raccoon, digging a hole to the entrance of his underground home beneath the waterline on the bank of a stream. Not even Washakie could find him. It was a pleasant dream, one that lingered with him when he awakened the next day.

5

Why the Bannock boy was unhappy in the Shoshone camp, he did not know. Perhaps it was because the expectation was far different from the reality. He had not dreamed of regulations, for he had always done as he pleased. He could see no way of fitting into the tribe. He was not even sure that he liked the power that Pariha Ungu's arrow had given him. He resented the elders who looked upon him with the same reverence they had for the Medicine Arrow. They considered him something to be watched over and cherished.

He had come to the tribe naked, his Medicine Arrow unadorned. Now Pariha Ungu would not recognize either, they were so fancy. The arrow, in Hanŭbi's safekeeping, was decorated with beadwork. Besides a fresh feather at the end, there was a long lock of coal-black hair that had recently belonged to the Crow Tupaku had scalped.

When the ritual of the Medicine Arrow drew to an end, the boy had one last look at Pariha Ungu's arrow before it was put away in a chest where no one would be allowed to see it except on special occasions. When the lid was lowered, he felt depressed, as if his soul, too, was confined. Both he and the arrow had been free, free to fly through the air like a bird.

Washakie laid his hand on his head and said, "Tupaku is symbol of sacred Medicine Arrow, messenger from Dam Apŭ." Then, followed by the elders, he turned and left the lodge. The ceremony of the sacred Medicine Arrow was at an end.

"You can take off your warbonnet," Hanŭbi told him. She was always reminding him of something. He wished that she would let him alone. Though the broad-framed woman was kindness itself, he still hated her for destroying his blanket. He did not object to the daily bath she insisted upon, for he liked to swim; but he found no comfort in the cedar-scented blanket that he wrapped around himself. Tattered and smelly though it was, the old one was a part of him.

He had further complaint to make against Hanŭbi. He did not like the way she brooded over him and admonished him to eat. No one had ever urged food on him before. In fact, it had always been so scarce that he had never known what it was to have enough. Now that it was in abundance he had lost his appetite. The last food he had been able to enjoy was the pemmican Washakie had given him before bringing him to his village.

He took off his warbonnet, not because the Shoshone woman told him to, but because he wanted it off. Now that the chief and elders had finally gone, he would go out and find some of the boys his size. He did not want to look foolish dressed as a chief. He would meet them as an equal.

Moon-faced Nanagi, who had been watching him

adoringly, lifted the lid of his chest for him. "Little Chief," he whispered in special homage. The young Bannock, unimpressed, began pulling off his finery, which his brother helped him store away. The only item he kept was his breechcloth.

"Your moccasins? You will not wear 'em?" Hanŭbi asked. She had been studying him carefully, as if trying to find the cause of his sullen manner.

Without answering, he ran out the door. Nanagi was at his heels, but Hanŭbi grabbed him and pulled him back.

Tupaku did not know where he would find the young Shoshones at that time of day. Perhaps they might be fishing somewhere along the river. As he went in search of them, he looked forward to the good times they would have. Now that he was no longer responsible for the food for his family, he could enjoy himself as he saw fit.

He found a dozen or more youths in the shade of a cottonwood tree where they were taking part in a game he did not recognize. They stopped abruptly and watched him approach. Not one offered to meet him halfway. Suddenly shy, he wished that he had not come. A disagreeable looking rebel whose name he later discovered to be Pariha Tawa, or Elk Tooth, picked up something from the ground; then he straightened up and glowered at him. "Bannock!" he taunted, as he hurled a rock in his face.

The name shocked Tupaku almost as much as the rock. As the adopted son of the chief he considered himself a member of the tribe. He wanted to cry out that his father and grandfather were Shoshone warriors, but by the time he discovered that all of his teeth were in the proper place, there was no one in sight. Surely the young hostiles were not afraid of him! He did not understand the cause of their flight until he heard his name spoken by someone behind him.

"Tupaku, what happened?" demanded the stranger whose presence must have frightened the boys away.

The Bannock boy, staring at him, wiped the blood from his mouth with the back of his hand. The stocky stranger's hair was parted in the middle, and his braids were wrapped in weasel skin. He did not have a short pompadoured forelock like Isha's, nor did he have a square-cut bang plastered with yellow clay like the warrior who caught the Crow pony. He even looked as if he might belong to some other tribe, though he was short and heavy built like the elders who had been present for the Medicine Arrow ceremony.

"My name is Wŭda Pekanŭ [Kill Bear], your friend," the stranger offered.

"Warrior?"

"*Kay,* Wobin."

The young Bannock was not familiar with the term. "Wobin?" He was puzzled.

"*Ha,* Wobin, Log or guard, sometimes called Big Horse Lodge. A warrior is Oha Mŭpi, or Yellow Nose. You never heard about Oha Mŭpi?"

"*Kay.*" The boy shook his head. Then he stated, "Tupaku will be Oha Mŭpi."

"And get yourself killed!" the stranger exclaimed. It was apparent that he did not consider bravery a virtue. He sat down in the shade and motioned for the boy to sit opposite.

"Why d' you want to be Oha Mŭpi?" he asked.

Won over by his friendly interest, the boy told him, "Because I want to kill Isha and drive out white man."

"Isha? You mean Pia Isha of Naroyan's band?"

"*Ha.* He beats my mother, Mŭatsi."

"Pia Isha is *kesandŭ,* no good, but white man is friend of Washakie. Shoshone not fight white man."

Tupaku was dumbfounded. Not fight white man? Pariha Ungu had not mentioned the friendship between Washakie and the *taivo.* After numerous questions, the boy learned that the purpose of the Yellow Nose warriors was to fight their traditional enemies; that is, the Blackfeet, the Crows, as well as the Sioux, Cheyenne and Arapahoes who were united against them. Priding himself on the sign language he had learned from Pariha Ungu, Tupaku drew the edge of his hand across his forehead, the sign for white man.

"Why?" he asked.

"Because of white streak when he takes off his hat," Kill Bear explained.

Then the boy drew his hand across his throat with a cutting motion.

"Sioux!" exclaimed Kill Bear.

"Why?"

"You find out plenty quick when you become Oha Mŭpi." Kill Bear laughed hilariously, as if it were a great joke. At that moment, Tupaku wondered if he wanted to be a Yellow Nose after all.

In the half day he spent talking with his new friend, he learned a number of things about the people who had adopted him. The fact that Washakie had pledged his word that he would never fight the white man was the most difficult to understand. It was contrary to the teachings of Pariha Ungu. The boy, a disciple of the old prophet, could not reconcile himself to the thought.

He was so pleased to find someone who would talk to him as one person to another that he accepted Kill Bear's friendship wholeheartedly. He idolized the chief, but he also feared him. Besides, Washakie was too busy to analyze the personal problems of his newly acquired son.

Even so, Tupaku was grateful to him for the material things he had given him, beaded clothing and a knife which he said he should use every time he scalped a Crow. It was a single-edged butcher knife which a trader had given the chief in exchange for a horse. Washakie accepted his word that "Green River" stamped on the blade meant the stream in his homeland. He later found that the white man spoke with a forked tongue, for it indicated a Green River in Massachusetts where the knife was manufactured.

Kill Bear made his appearance the next day when Tupaku was watching from a distance while the young braves raced their horses in a war game. They formed two lines, one representing the Shoshones, the other the enemy. In pairs, they dashed out to a gooseberry bush and touched it with a pole as if counting coup. Then they returned to their lines. The tribe counting the most coups in the time allowed won the game, the Bannock learned later.

"Why not join 'em?" the Log asked as he seemed to appear out of nowhere.

"*Kay*." He would not admit, even to himself, that he longed to be accepted, not as a medicine symbol but as a normal boy who would like nothing better than to share in the fun the young Shoshones were having.

"Where is your brown and white spotted pony?" Kill Bear asked. Tupaku had been so involved in the Medicine Arrow ceremony that he had not seen his war trophy since his return from the encounter with the Crows. When Hanŭbi led him away, he supposed that the warrior had reclaimed him. Now he was alarmed by the realization that the prize was his, and he had no idea where it might be.

"No matter. We'll find 'im." His friend assured him.

Along the way, they picked up Kill Bear's horse he said he got from the Nez Perce tribe. It was a splendid creature, with brown shoulders and forelegs and a marked white blanket, splotched with brown raindrops, over his rump and on his upper hindquarters. The spotted pony they found picketed near the stream was small in comparison, but he, too, was a fine animal. With loving care, he would probably fatten up and look better than the blanket horse.

Although Kill Bear was not a warrior he was an expert horseman, one of the best in the tribe. Patiently, he led both animals some distance from camp, where he gave Tupaku his first riding lesson. "Begin by getting love of horse," he directed. "Show you will not hurt 'im. Walk up slow. . . . Stop and do not touch 'im. . . . Let'm put his nose against you. Then speak gentle and stroke his neck. Just a little. Never touch 'im on nose or ear. He will not like it. Give'm something to eat. Handful of grass or anything you think he'll like." He dumped some Indian tobacco into the palm of his hand, then extended it toward the pinto. After sniffing it a time or two, the pony began to eat.

The first day Tupaku proved to his teacher that he, too, was a natural horseman. A week or so later, Kill Bear was giving him and his pony a workout when a thunderstorm broke overhead. A flash, then a loud clap of thunder made it necessary for them to seek shelter.

"See that big cedar tree?" The Log pointed toward the hillside, but the boy had already spied it and was taking off with such speed that he soon left his friend behind. He was racing the elements instead of Kill Bear because lightning always terrified him. He would be safe once he reached the tree, for the Indians knew that lightning did not strike cedars. Little Moon always had a sack of needle-like cedar leaves that she would sprinkle on her campfire during an electrical storm so that her tepee would be safe.

When the Log reached the shelter, he remarked, "Your pony has strong wind. What will you call him?"

"Kitant Niet [Strong Wind]," came the reply.

In the days that followed, Kill Bear taught the young Bannock how to suspend himself on one side of his horse, out of sight of the enemy. Soon he could manage when the animal was running at top speed. His teacher was so proud of him that he had him give an exhibition performance for Washakie.

Tupaku glowed inwardly when the chief said, "*Tivizant*!" It was more than *tsant,* good. It was very good! The boy would not have been so elated had he known that it was his last riding lesson. He had proved himself such an able rider that he no longer needed his teacher, whose services were required elsewhere.

When Kill Bear did not show up the following morning, Tupaku ventured out alone. While spending most of the day on his pony, he kept wondering what had become of his friend. Several days went by and still he did not appear. The strange part of it was that the boy did not feel alone. The youths with whom he had dreamed of playing war games were nowhere to be seen, but he was constantly running across Shoshones, possibly Logs, for their hair was dressed in the same manner as Kill Bear's. There was no question but that he was being shadowed.

At first he thought that they were guarding him to

see that no harm befell him. Then he was convinced that they were watching so that he could not run away. Kill Bear had only seemed to be a friend! He was just another Log sent to spy on him! How stupid he had been to accept him! The realization that he was being treated as a prisoner made him rebellious. He whispered his troubles into the sympathetic ear of Strong Wind, who seemed equally anxious to make a getaway. With his determination to escape came the first real satisfaction he had found in living among the Shoshones. He began to enjoy his food, and he looked upon the inhabitants of Washakie's lodge with new interest.

"Nanagi, if I go away, you can have my warbonnet and beaded jacket," he whispered to his brother. The child, though puzzled, seemed pleased. Hanŭbi, who was standing by, said nothing, but Tupaku wondered if she might have heard. She looked at him strangely.

Thereafter, the guards became increasingly diligent in watching over him. So Hanŭbi had overheard! No matter, he would elude them someway. He would ride into space on Strong Wind's back and never return, his rebellious spirit spoke within him. He was as sure of this as he was that another sun would come riding over the mountains to bring a new day.

6

One morning Tupaku awoke to find a heavy fog hovering over the Shoshone camp. It was so thick that he could scarcely distinguish the nearest tree. Since fogs were rare in the high country, he was convinced that Dam Apŭ had sent it to help him. He raised his face gratefully to the moisture-laden air that would bring joy to the flowers and make grass for the buffalo so that the Indian might eat. If the fog lifted, the world would be flooded with sunshine.

While the women were preparing the morning food, the Bannock with his bow and arrows, his knife and a skin of pemmican hidden in his blanket, walked slowly to the place where he had left Strong Wind grazing the night before. He removed his hobbles and led him to the creek for a drink. Unnoticed, he passed an old woman trying to start a fire with squaw wood she had gathered the day before.

What if Nanagi should miss him and follow? This was unlikely for he was a lazy boy who always slept until the sun was high. He was so pampered that it was doubtful that he would ever amount to much as a warrior. He might be a Log someday, but that would be galling to his father. Trying to stifle the excitement within him, Tupaku stood, waiting impatiently on a large stone while his horse drank. It seemed that he would never stop. . . . The young Indian whispered for him to hurry.

When Strong Wind lifted his head to look at him, Tupaku fashioned his rope into a bridle, threw his folded blanket on his horse's back, and climbed on. Crossing the stream he followed the opposite bank because he knew that the fog would linger in the lowlands. He dared not expose himself to view until he was safely by the last outpost of Logs, who were stationed on high elevations so that they could see as far as possible and so that their signal fires could be observed throughout the village.

His plans worked perfectly. When he rode up on a high point into the bright sunlight, he looked back at the fog, hovering in a gray mist over the valley. Then, feeling that he was safe, he urged Strong Wind forward. A pat on the shoulder and a moccasined heel in his flank were all that was needed to spur him to action. Tupaku laughed hysterically as his pony fairly flew across the prairie. It was the most exhilarating sensation he had felt in his life! Once a trapped bird, he was now free, free to fly to the far ends of the earth.

All day long he rode without seeing any wild life. Late afternoon he came to a spring where he paused to graze his horse on the lush grass that grew around it. After allowing Strong Wind a chance to take a good fill of feed and water, he moved on, stopping only long enough to pry up some *yamba* or wild carrots to go with his pemmican.

When the sun was high overhead next day, he reached a fine mountain stream, an ideal campsite. He could not release his horse to graze for fear he might run away and leave him, so he hobbled him on the grassy bank. The pony shook vigorously to remove the blanket.

"You do not want my blanket, Kitant Niet?" Now that there was no one to hear, he admitted, "No Indian ever had a finer one. . . . It is a great joy to have my horse, my knife and my blanket." He threw the folded article across his shoulder and started wading in the cold mountain water.

Downstream he found a deep, dead water pocket at one side. Tall grass bent gracefully over the margin. It was an ideal place for fish. Sure enough there were two little speckled beauties hiding under its protective covering! Tupaku grabbed one before it could dart away. He cleaned it but did not cook it, for the smoke and the smell of a campfire might reveal his hiding place. It was not the first time he had eaten raw fish, but he had never relished it so much.

With his appetite appeased, he lost interest in fishing, so he began exploring the immediate area. He found that a beaver had felled a large tree which, reinforced with high-water debris, made an enviable dam with water pouring over the top. Above the log, there was an excellent swimming hole. The boy hid his possessions and, after covering his tracks, dived in. He swam until he was exhausted. Then he lay on the bank and looked up into the shimmering leaves of a quaking aspen.

He was thinking how lucky he was to escape when he heard the sound of voices. His heart skipped a beat, for he feared that the Logs might have tracked him. It was worse than that because he recognized the guttural voice of Isha. The marauders, riding upstream, might not suspect his presence, but what about Strong Wind? He was apt to whiny and give himself away when he smelled the other horses. Tupaku could think of nothing worse than for his spotted pony to fall into the cruel hands of Isha. One Eye, he shuddered at the recollection of the horse his father blinded.

He was helpless to save Strong Wind. No need of praying to Dam Apŭ because Isha was such a mean Indian, He would have nothing to do with him. In desperation, the boy called upon the Little People to help him. He was not sure what happened, for he could not see. The sound indicated that one of the Ninimbi might have shot at the Indian while he was removing Strong Wind's hobbles. The invisible arrow, missing its mark, must have hit the horse, causing him to whirl and kick the surprised Indian. Strong Wind gave a piercing squeal, and Tupaku caught a glimpse of him as, with head and tail erect, he raced in the direction of the Shoshone camp.

The boy was overjoyed to think that his pony had managed a getaway, but his elation subsided when he realized that he was once more a Walker and that he might never see Strong Wind again. He was the only true friend he had ever had besides Pariha Ungu. And yet, he dared not cry out because he knew that nothing would please Isha more than to have him at his mercy. Backing toward the dam, he obliterated each track as he went. He slipped noiselessly into the water and hid under the falls. He thought of his dream, the dream in which he was a raccoon. He must have been mistaken, for he now found himself as a beaver, hiding where not even Isha could find him.

A loud voice he did not recognize could be heard above the sound of tumbling water. Someone was blaming the Indian who allowed the horse to escape. Tupaku heard him say, "He was good horse. He belong to Shoshone. One day I see Kamŭ Kaupa ride him."

Isha apparently caught the name, for he shouted back. "Kamŭ Kaupa no good sonabitch! He run away and cause my children to go hungry when I am away and cannot hunt for them!"

Hunt for them! The lie almost brought Tupaku from his hiding place. Isha was like a predatory animal, roaming around the country and doing evil at every turn. Never had he provided for his family.

One of the Indians observed that they were wasting time going upstream in search of the rider of the elusive horse. "He went downstream. Why would he want to go upstream?" He argued to his own satisfaction. His reasoning, which Tupaku failed to hear, seemed convincing to his companion.

"*Aha,* he went downstream," exclaimed another, as though surprised that the idea had not occurred to him before. When the men began to backtrack, there was a sudden movement in the water near the dam.

"Kamŭ Kaupa!" Isha whirled and shouted triumphantly. But it was a large beaver that came swimming to the surface.

"Ho, ho, ho!" His companions laughed heartily. "Pia Isha not know his boy from beaver. Ho, Ho!" Isha could not help smarting under their ridicule.

Even after the voices had died away, Tupaku did not dare come from his hiding place. How did he know that it was not a trick to lead him into the open? . . . Finally, he heard one of the Indians shouting to his companions. "Tracks will be easy to follow. Hurry! All Shoshone might come." Isha and his companions jumped on their ponies they had left near the beaver dam, and disappeared.

The boy, almost waterlogged from remaining submerged so long, hoped that they were right, that the Shoshone would come to his rescue. It no longer mattered if Nanagi dogged his steps or if Hanŭbi admonished him to eat—if only he had a bowl of her hot stew! His skin was shriveled and his arms and legs ached from being in a cramped position so long.

He raced back and forth until he no longer felt numb and chilled. Then he sat down to contemplate his predicament. Banking strongly upon the possibility that the Shoshone might follow Strong Wind's tracks, he told himself that he must not wander far. In the mean time he would explore the vicinity for food. Having no further desire to wade in the water even to catch a fish, he began looking for berries and roots.

A few currants were plump and juicy, but the chokecherries, bullberries and wild grapes were still green. He was surprised by the quantity of fruits of all kinds. The juniper trees were full of berries, while seeds were beginning to form so abundantly on wild rye and prairie flax that the stalks bowed under their burden. The profusion, he knew, was a sure sign that there would be a long, cold winter. All Indians knew this, but Pariha Ungu was the only one who could predict the weather by reading the bones of a wild goose. Maybe he was not as great as Washakie, but he knew better than to trust the white man. After he had eaten, Tupaku rolled up in his blanket and went to sleep. From a branch overhead, an inquisitive owl looked down upon him.

The next morning he lay thinking over all that had happened. He was so quiet that two beavers came from their lair to frolic in the swimming pool. Side by side they swam, around and around, as close together as a harnessed team. Tupaku, responding to an urge to join them, got to his feet; but they darted from sight.

"Do not be afraid of me, Hanrih," he told them. "I am your friend. I have come to live with—" At the sound of his voice, two turtles plunked into the water from a log where they had been basking in the early morning sunshine. "With you and the turtles," Tupaku added.

He swam with complete absence of self-restraint. The movement of his lithe body was as natural as if he, too, were amphibious. With every swimming stroke, his courage mounted, and a determination began to take shape in his consciousness. Though his resolve had weakened when he thought that he wanted Strong Wind to leave tracks to guide the Shoshones to his hideout, he now hoped that he would not. True happiness could be found only in a life of freedom. He could not endure the affluence he found in the Shoshone camp, for he was a creature of the wild. Material wealth meant nothing to him.

His needs were simple—food, shelter and water. Now afoot, his hunting would be limited. He would have to depend largely on fruits and vegetables, fresh now or dried for winter use. There was no one to look after him, to gather and prepare the quantities of food nature had to offer, as there would have been in the Shoshone village. On the other hand, there was no one dependent on him as there had been in Naroyan's camp. He had lost the burden of responsibility which had made his search for food of urgent consequence.

As the days passed nothing seemed to matter. Instead of gathering his winter supply, he whiled away his time, swimming and exploring. He indulged himself in his favorite foods which were now readily accessible. The future could take care of itself.

Even the Sheepeater band of Shoshones would have spurned the shelter he selected, the one he would occupy when the snow came. He found it in a cave-like depression among the rocks. In a small nook on one side, he cached his prizes as he acquired them. By tilting a large, flat stone, he had a lid to his treasure chest where he hid black currant shafts and the bird points and larger arrowheads he was able to manufacture with a deer horn he found on the trail. As the chest was far from tight, a ground squirrel soon made away with the meager supply of dried serviceberries and sunflower seeds he was one day prompted to store.

No matter, he was content to munch balsam roots and nutty textured wild carrots. He enjoyed eating the sweet, inner bark of the cottonwood, the swollen base of bracken and the stems of thistles and cattails, with greens for salad. If food became scarce, there was always the possibility of returning to Washakie's camp when the snowy moons came again. The women would provide wood for the fires and plenty to eat. When the rivers froze over and the canyons became snow packed, that would be the time to sit around Washakie's campfire and hear what he had to say about the white man.

The carefree days slipped by so fast that Tupaku did not realize that summer was on the wane until a chickadee brought it to his attention. The sight of Huchuchi, Little Bird, indicated that snow would be flying before long. The Bannock boy, half asleep, was looking through the leaves of an aspen tree into the branch above him when he saw it staring down upon him from its high perch. Catching his attention, it began to sing. Then it spoke, or was it his imagination? Perhaps he was having a vision, the way Pariha Ungu had when the bear talked to him.

"Why did you run away?" Chickadee asked, cocking its head as if listening for a reply. Tupaku was too surprised to respond. "Why did you? Why did you?" It then twittered as if pleased with itself for knowing the answer. "You want to be free." The word "free" trilled through the air. The boy put his hands over his ears to shut out the sound.

The bird laughed at him. "You would rather not hear what I have to say, but I warn you to listen. You are making a mistake. You are headstrong and do not want to know what is best for you. Turn back and listen to the words of Washakie. He, too, dreamed of a life of freedom when he was young, but times change. Ask Washakie. He knows that freedom is not the answer. It is adjustment to life as it is, not as you would like it to be.

"Do not be deceived by the voice of the past. The buffalo will one day be gone, and the Indian must learn to raise food from the ground. It is futile to resist the white man, for he comes in ever increasing numbers. White men are as numerous as leaves on the trees. If one or all should fall with the snow, more will come with the grass. You should listen to the wise words of Washakie."

Tupaku rolled over on his face, pillowed his head on his arm, and tried to sleep, but he could not. He was disturbed by what Huchuchi had said. If Washakie were right, Pariha Ungu was wrong. The holy man was older and smarter than the Shoshone chief, even if Huchuchi thought otherwise.

7

The Bannock boy was not sure what prompted his desire to find the White-top Wagon Road unless it might have been the words of Chickadee. He wanted to see for himself if the caravans of emigrants were still going in the direction of the setting sun. Pariha Ungu had told him about the gold seekers, and he wondered where the gold might be found. There must be a big tribe of white people somewhere toward the east, maybe as many as the Shoshones. Chickadee implied that there was no way of stopping them. They were like ants, constantly moving forward in the same direction. The little bird was supposed to have superior wisdom, but he could be as mistaken about the white man as he was about Washakie.

Tupaku's sense of direction told him that the trail lay to the south, and that if he would follow the course of the river he would find it not too far distant. He packed his moccasins away with his other possessions in his cache. Then he made sure that all tracks in the vicinity were obliterated. With his blanket folded over his shoulder, his knife at his belt and his bow and arrows on his back, he began his journey.

The stream, after the floodwaters from the highlands earlier in the season had subsided, was so shallow that he could see the gravelly bottom. Bordering shrubbery furnished a protective screen so that no one could observe him from a distance. Though he preferred the sandy sides, much of his trail lay in the bed of the stream, where no tracks could be seen. With his bare feet, he found it easy to cling to the rocks which were only partly submerged. He had fun jumping from one to another. Occasionally one would tilt, but he was on the next before it could send him plunging into the water. When there were no stepping stones, he waded.

As he neared the vicinity of the trail, he determined that he would be more careful. He remembered how the white man's dog had betrayed him. Nothing of the sort must happen again. In spite of his precaution he almost exposed himself to view before he realize it. He was not aware that he had reached the trail until he saw a yoke of oxen and a white-top wagon at a shallow crossing immediately ahead. He rushed into the thicket before he could be observed. Never before had he been so close to the emigrants! With a palpitating heart, he watched while the oxen splashed and the wagon creaked its way to the opposite side.

As soon as the first wagon had crossed, another followed. Tupaku watched breathlessly. He saw men and even little boys on horseback. How he longed for Strong Wind! No matter whether the emigrants were on horseback or in wagons, they chattered constantly.Why was it that the white man did not know how to hold his tongue?

While the wagons were following one after the other, Tupaku saw several Indians ride stealthily into the canyon and take up positions behind a clump of willows, screening them from the trail. He was not surprised when he recognized Isha and several other braves of lesser rank. He feared for his own safety because he knew they were up to devilment. As long as they were concentrating on the wagon train, it was doubtful that they would discover him, though he was not in an enviable position, crouched in the bushes so close to the crossing.

When the lead wagon of a second caravan appeared he saw an old man with his arm around a woman at his side. She had her head on his shoulder. They would not have looked so pleased had they known that Isha was ready to spring upon them. The wagon passed safely. Others came and went, but still nothing happened. The renegades seemed to be waiting for a strategic time to strike.

The driver of the end wagon was a pleasant-faced black woman. At her side sat a little white girl. Could the boy believe his eyes! "Daidŭtsi!" he gasped under his breath. Her hair was like the golden throat of the sego lily and her skin was as fair as its wax-white petals. Judging by the woman's hearty laugh, the girl at her side must have said something amusing.

Two black men, following on horseback, were so lost

in conversation that they lagged behind. It was clear that they were new in Indian country; their position encouraged an attack. Tupaku now realized why Isha and his companions held back. Apparently they had been following the wagon train for some time, and they were watching until it reached a spot where they could cut off the end wagon without drawing fire from the whole train.

A faint breeze fluttered the aspen leaves while the sun reflected on the water. It was a hot day, with mountainous clouds building up toward the west. In all probability there would be a thunderstorm midafternoon. Not that it mattered, for Tupaku had already picked out a cedar tree for his protective shelter. Besides shielding him from the lightning, it had such thick foliage that it would keep him dry regardless of how hard it rained.

Why didn't the men on horseback hurry? The wagon had crossed, but the laggards paused to water their horses. Anyone who knew the country would not have tarried where there was such an excellent chance for ambush. They should have noticed that the wagons ahead had not stopped. Instead of moving on, the end wagon came to a halt on the far side of the stream.

To the boy's astonishment, the *daidŭtsi*, with the help of the black woman, climbed down from the wagon and went running toward a clump of greasewood where the sun brought out the color of a pink lustre pitcher, lying discarded at the side of the road. The girl did not pick it up at once. Startled by something that she did not seem to understand, she paused an instant. She glanced anxiously toward the thicket as though conscious of the hawk-like eyes trained upon her. Then seeing no cause for alarm, she leaned over and picked up the bright object. With her curls bouncing on her shoulders, she ran back toward the wagon, her prize tucked proudly in her arms.

The horses were restless, as if they sensed danger though the emigrants did not. The men rode up to the wagon, where one dismounted and helped the girl back to her seat. The grownups were as pleased as the child over her find. Tupaku was breathless with anticipation, for he knew that the man would never mount his horse again. It served him right. He should have kept up with the rest of the train.

Yelling fiendishly, the braves dashed forth from the timber. They were wise to wait until the men had reached the side of the wagon because they could accomplish their plan with a single effort. Every motion counted, for another train might be along any time. With the small group well organized, each Indian seemed to know what he was supposed to do. There were six in all, working in pairs. The action was so swift that it was difficult for the boy to see all that was taking place and yet he relished every exciting moment.

The first pair attacked the horsemen, while the second began stripping the harness from the team. Meanwhile, Isha and Yŭ (Porcupine), a Shoshone outlaw Tupaku recognized, were setting fire to the wagon.

The man who had lifted the girl to the seat did not have a chance to reach for his rifle, strapped to his saddle. One of the Indians grabbed it and dealt him a heavy blow over the head. When he fell, his attacker shot him with his own gun. The other black man was so panic-stricken that he was unable to take aim before he was jerked from his horse and finished off with a tomahawk. The horses, plunging frantically in an effort to break loose, were held securely. The Indians never stopped yelling from the time they came into the clearing although they could not help knowing that their noise would bring the rest of the train to the relief of the victims.

While Isha and his companions were firing the wagon, the woman had a chance to wield her whip across the bare shoulders of one of the Indians working at the harness. He let out an anguished cry. Before she could hit him again, Porcupine grabbed her. She fought like a wildcat, scratching and kicking, as she was pulled from the wagon seat. She made so much commotion that he silenced her with the broad side of his tomahawk.

The girl, in a state of shock, caused no trouble when Isha lifted her from the flaming wagon. Tupaku, forgetting his animosity toward the white man, had an urge to shoot him as he went by, but that would have been as foolish as arousing the bear. He could not take aim in the thicket. If he had stepped out, Isha's companions would have destroyed him as ruthlessly as they did the emigrants. He watched the attackers gallop away, richer by two hostages, two rifles, two scalps and four horses; and he wondered what they would do with the *daidŭtsi*. She had not screamed as he expected. She had simply allowed herself to be plucked like a prairie flower.

The train turned back only to find the wagon in shambles, the men killed and the woman and girl missing. The hostiles, riding toward the crest of the hill, yelled until they disappeared from sight. The old man from the lead wagon began shouting orders. He flew into a rage when the men tried to unharness their horses and go in pursuit.

"Whatcha aim t'do? Let them Injuns lead y'away from yer wimmen an' children so's they can swarm in an' kill 'em all? Them hills is probably alive with Injuns. Damit! Git in yer wagons an' start movin'!"

Tupaku did not understand his words but he got his meaning. The wagon boss was naturally anxious to get the emigrants to a place of safety, but he would have been surprised had he known that in the raiding party there were only six, and that one of them had stopped behind a boulder while the others had gone over the hill. Armed with the emigrant's gun, he was prepared to protect his fleeing companions.

With one exception, all seemed anxious to comply with the order given by their wagon boss. A man on foot kept running in the direction of the Indians. No amount of shouting could stop him. He must have been crazed by the loss of the girl, for he kept calling frantically. Half stumbling on the uneven ground, he rushed madly on. When he was within range, the Indian stepped from behind the boulder and killed him with a single shot. Then jumping on his horse, he sounded a war cry and galloped over the hill.

The boy felt no sympathy for the man who gave his life in a vain effort to save the captives. He was just one less white man in Indian country, but he was concerned over what might happen to the *daidŭtsi*, in the cruel hands of Isha.

8

Tupaku's venture to the wagon road was so exciting that he decided to make a similar excursion upstream to see if he might find something of interest. While foraging for food, he came upon the broad tracks of a mountain lion. His interest aroused, he followed them to the top of a hill where he discovered the carcass of a fresh-killed deer, lightly covered. Looking around to make sure that he was safe, he hacked off a generous portion with his Green River knife. Loading the meat in his blanket, he slung it across his shoulder and began exploring the country beyond. The unknown intrigued him.

He had not gone far when he observed what appeared to be tepee rings and a cluttered campsite, with a lone lodge standing deserted on the side nearest him. The flap at the entrance, stirred by a breeze, waved him a warning not to come near. It was apparent that the Indians had left in great haste, abandoning many of their valuables. There were stone bowls, deer-horn ladles, mallets and other useful articles scattered around as if of no consequence.

The entire place was pervaded by a deathlike silence which fascinated yet frightened the boy. There was no need for the flap to warn him not to enter the tepee; he was afraid even to glance inside. There might have been a smallpox epidemic. He approached cautiously, all the while studying the ground in an effort to find a clue to what had happened. Without thinking, he leaned over to pick up a hide scraper. Aghast, he dropped it, for lying there beside the sagebrush were the remains of a gopher that the magpies had left.

Now he knew why the camp had been abandoned! He was horrified at the thought of the danger that confronted him. The gopher was an ill omen; it had put a curse on the camp. A gopher could come out of its hole, look at an Indian and cause him to die. Tupaku shook with fright as he recalled how his people had been forced to move from more than one campsite because of the evil *yuavits*. He grabbed his blanket and began running with all his might. The wind, to his relief, was in the right direction to blow the bad medicine away.

On his return he avoided the mountain lion's cache for fear the beast might have returned. He had enough trouble without inviting more, but like the bear it would probably let him alone if he did not bother it. As long as he kept to himself, wild animals paid little attention to him. When he was perfectly still, they would cavort before him as if he were one of them.

Now that he had exposed himself to the bad medicine of the gopher, he felt that he should stay near his base. It would be dangerous to wander far from the beaver dam and the water it held. He would be ill, of that he was sure.

One morning he awoke, aching in every muscle; and he felt as if his body were on fire. Since there was no medicine man to care for him, he would have to suffer for his foolish venture. Crawling to the stream, he sloshed water over his face and body. Then he began chilling. Helpless and sometimes delirious, he lay upon the sand while Chickadee twittered excitedly above him. It was needless for the bird to remind him that he should heed the words of Washakie.

During the boy's intermittent lapses into consciousness, he was afraid that he would never live to see his chief again, and he regretted the trouble he had caused. The chickadee was right about one thing. He had been headstrong. If he should ever have another chance, he would try to obey his chief.

In his delirium he thought that the Logs, instead of Hanŭbi, were forcing food upon him. . . . One morning when he awakened his mind was clear, but he was so weak that he could scarcely lift his hand. He looked about to see if the Logs might actually have been there. It all seemed so real!

There were no tracks, that is, no moccasin tracks. The imprints of horses' hooves were numerous, particularly near the water. A band of wild horses must have come to drink. As soon as he could grow strong, he would go in search of them. Perhaps he could catch one.

Suddenly, he was startled by an apparition which

must have been brought on by his weakened condition. Before him stood Kill Bear, holding Strong Wind's rope. It was a cruel dream when he longed so much to see his pinto! It nuzzled him as if urging him to his feet.

"You're better?" Kill Bear asked, but the boy was afraid to answer for fear that the horse would fade from his sight. Not receiving a reply, the Log continued, "You've been mighty sick. You almost died. . . . You like it here by yourself?" Without waiting for an answer, he continued, "You cause Shoshone much worry. You should be in camp where *Pohakantŭ* can care for you, not have to come here."

Washakie had known where he was all along! His guards had probably watched his every move. He had just thought that he was free! He was bound by circumstance to the tribe. No matter where he might go, they would find him and bring him back. Chickadee was right again when it said that freedom was not the answer, at least not for him. He might as well recognize his bondage and adjust to it, the little bird had told him.

"*Pohakantŭ* fix you up. He want to take you home, but Washakie not let 'im. He said you must come back on your horse the way you went. Then you won't be so quick to leave again."

Tupaku watched helplessly while Kill Bear kindled a fire. Then he feasted his eyes on his pony. Not until he felt the velvety nose against his cheek could he convince himself that he was not dreaming. In no time, the Log had warmed the food he brought. Getting down on his knees, he lifted the boy's head and held the bowl to his lips. There was something strangely familiar about it all as if Tupaku had had the experience before, but it was vague.

"You need someone care for you. It's no good for Indian to live alone," Kill Bear scolded. After the boy had eaten, the Log helped him to his feet. His legs would have crumpled under him if he had not been supported. Each step was an effort, but his friend kept working with him. They finally reached the stream which, to the boy's surprise, was practically dry. He asked where the water went.

"Turtle carry it away," Kill Bear replied. "You rest, then eat some more. We go when you can travel." There was no use for Tupaku to object because he now needed Washakie's Snakes more than they needed him.

When the Bannock boy and his companion rode into camp, word spread from tepee to tepee. The Shoshones' Good Medicine, saying not a word in response to a hearty welcome, went in search of the chieftain's lodge. Indians, crowding around, made way when Washakie came forth, his face shining.

"My son!" He grasped him by the shoulders and looked searchingly into his face, but he neither reproved him nor demanded an explanation. Tupaku said nothing when Hanŭbi came out to greet him, and Nanagi began plying him with questions.

Everyone was jubilant. The young Bannock was too weak to appreciate the significance of the occasion until he was told that in his absence the Shoshones had suffered reverses at the hands of the Crows. Now he knew! His return was more than a family reunion. It was one of the great moments of the tribe, which had recovered its symbol of good fortune. With Tupaku among them, the Indians need no longer fear their enemies.

They could turn their attention, for the time at least, to the ever-present need for food. Their first object would be to put an end to the drought so that rain might come and stop the prairie fires that threatened to drive the buffalo out of their range. The Naroya, a dance given to the Shoshones by Coyote, the trickster, was sure to bring stormy weather. Without further delay, the headman announced the dance.

Tupaku, too weak to participate, watched from the sidelines while it was in progress. There were so many performing that smaller circles were made within the larger ones, with men and women, alternately, joining hands and moving clockwise. As they shuffled their feet, they sang without accompaniment. The second day the dance ended in a downpour. When the headman announced that the Naroya was at an end, the dancers vigorously shook their blankets to drive away the last semblance of the drought. Then, with the women going to the left and the men to the right, they filed to the river to bathe.

Following a feast of boiled vegetables, Washakie called a council of the tribal leaders. Porivo, Chief Woman, was the only female to sit in council, an honor accorded her because she had traveled widely. In her younger days, she had gone down the Big Muddy River with her trapper-trader husband to the white man's camp she called "St. Looie." Now she appeared to be no more than a motionless object as she huddled, waiting for the council to convene.

When everyone was seated, Tupaku found himself in the place of honor beside his chief. After the pipe had been passed around and everyone's heart had been made glad, Washakie arose and addressed his followers.

"My people," he stated, "it is with much joy that we celebrate the return of Tupaku, our Good Medicine. We do not know why he went away. Maybe it was work of Ninimbi. Maybe it is because he not like it here. Whatever the cause, we must keep him with us! I tell you plain."

He turned toward Porivo and said, "Tell my people about Crows' Good Medicine. Why we must keep ours strong."

The chief always stood to address his people, but the woman did not rise. Even so, she held her audience from the moment she started to talk. "The story of the Crow's Good Medicine is well known. Once there was a trapper who called himself Beckwourth, but the Indians knew him as Red Eagle. The Crow claimed him as a member of their tribe, captured when a baby. They rejoiced to have 'im again because after his return they had many, many victories. But, like Tupaku, he did not want to stay. Many misfortunes came to the tribe when he left. They invited him back for a feast. They fed him poisoned food so his spirit would stay with them forever. That is why they are such good warriors."

Tupaku, realizing that the story was told for his benefit, was appalled when a bowl of stew was placed before him. He stared at it in fascination because the implication was clear. As if responding to Hanŭbi's admonition to eat, he mechanically fished out a chunk of meat with his fingers. Before he could reach it to his mouth, Washakie stopped him.

"*Kay*! Do not eat! This is warning to you. Washakie not talk crooked talk. Take bowl away," he ordered Hanŭbi, who stood back of the boy.

While she was obeying his command he continued, "Tupaku has many, many things to learn. First is obedience. Heed word of Porivo. Shoshone, too, will keep their Good Medicine!" With that the council ended.

Dejected, the boy sat while the tribal members filed by. Long after the last one had gone, when the council fire had burned low, he sat. For three glorious days, he had enjoyed the honors accorded him. He had relished all of the attention, and he was prepared to make every effort to adjust to the Shoshones' way of life. Now he was plagued by the realization that his spirit would be shackled forever to the tribe.

9

After the first frost, the weather became mild. There were several weeks of autumn, during which the warriors engaged in sham battles and horse racing. Occasionally a small war party would set out to harass an isolated camp of Platte River Indians: the Sioux, Cheyennes and Arapahoes. The women, meanwhile, were busy laying in a supply of fruits and vegetables which they dried for winter use.

Tupaku, slowly recovering his strength, lounged in the sunshine and stuffed himself with the food Hanŭbi provided. He no longer resented Nanagi. If his brother talked too much, he would turn over on his face and pretend to sleep. The boy was not a bad sort, but Tupaku preferred the beavers for they knew enough to keep quiet. Longing for freedom once again, he would go for a whole day without speaking. As his health returned, so did his wild spirit. He smarted under the knowledge that he was forcibly detained.

A disturbing dream came to him one night. Near a campfire lay the familiar figure of Isha, but this time he was not drunk. He appeared to be gravely ill, and a number of women were caring for him. As soon as the food in the kettle was ready, they took him a bowl, steaming hot. Groaning in agony, he propped himself on his elbow and took several mouthsful. Then he pushed the bowl away. He was too sick to care for food. His moaning grew louder. No one seemed to notice Tupaku. It was as if he were not there, though the scene was clear. Where was Little Moon? He waited a moment. Still she did not appear. It was odd that everyone was concerned about Isha but his good-hearted wife.

"Mŭatsi! Mŭatsi!" the boy called repeatedly, but there was no answer. At last he realized that no one could hear him. Pariha Ungu could, because he had powers no other Indian had. Tupaku ran in search of him. When he located him, he implored, "Tell me, where's Mŭatsi?

The old Indian puffed on his pipe, then answered, "Isha acts sick so evil spirit will not bother Mŭatsi, so she can have a baby. Isha might even die," Pariha Ungu told him.

Tupaku returned hopefully to see if it were true. Though too ill to rise, Isha was calm when Little Moon, carrying a small, blanketed object, came from the bushes. When she reached his side, he jumped to his feet. But it was not Isha, the Bannock, but a big timber wolf that tore at her throat!

The shock caused Tupaku to awake with a start. Something was wrong in Naroyan's camp! His dream was so real that he feared for his mother's life. Grabbing his blanket, he carefully made his way out of the tepee. The night was still. Not even a dog was stirring. If he could just reach Strong Wind unnoticed, nothing could stop him. . . . Luck was with him.

He removed the hobbles, threw a rope around his pony's neck and jumped on his back. He then galloped fearlessly into the darkness. The sound of clattering hooves would arouse the sleeping Indians, but he had the advantage of a head start. It would not be long before he could assure himself that his mother was all right. He had no thought of running away, for he had discovered that was futile. Somehow the Snakes would track him.

He wished that his chief had known about his dream, though he might not have allowed him to leave. His errand was so important that it made no difference what Washakie or anyone else thought!

When the boy reached the Bannock camp, he saw his sister, Kwitawoyo Waipŭ, playing with several other children near his mother's tepee. They rushed forward to admire his horse, with everyone speaking at once. He ignored their questions.

"Where's Mŭatsi?" Tupaku asked.

"Picking berries and watching little white girl."

"She has baby!" he stated emphatically.

His sister looked mystified. "*Ona*? She takes care of white girl Pia Isha got on White-top Wagon Road. Why you think she has *ona*?"

Tupaku ignored her question. "Where's Mŭatsi?" he demanded a second time.

Magpie Woman, refused to divulge the whereabouts of Mŭatsi until he let her ride his pony. He did not like being outwitted by a girl, especially by his sister who was overbearing like Isha. Pariha Ungu had given her the Shoshone name Magpie because she talked so much. Rather than waste time, Tupaku granted her wish. Still he would not tell her about his dream.

"Where's Isha?" he wanted to know.

"He has gone to Fort Hall maybe. He says white man will give him something for white girl. He says he will kill Mŭatsi if she is not here when he gets back."

"Ugh!" the boy grunted in disgust.

When Tupaku and his sister reached the berry patch, they found Little Moon and the fair-haired child, the Daidŭtsi-Who-Became-a-Prairie-Flower. Burdened by his own problems, the boy had almost forgotten her. How different she looked with her ragged dress, straggly hair and badly stained face and hands. Pariha Ungu had once said that all Indians were white at first, but that a mother picked chokecherries and fed them to her children, causing them to change color. He wondered how long it would take for the *daidŭtsi* to turn into an Indian. Her lips and hands were already changing color because of the berries she had eaten.

"Kamŭ Kaupa!" Little Moon exclaimed "How you grow! Tall like Bannock and wide like Shoshone!"

He was so surprised to hear his Bannock name, that he disregarded her flattery. "You all right? Isha not hurt you?"

"Hurt me! Why you ask?" The question did seem senseless since she appeared to be in excellent spirits. He did not tell her of his foolish dream.

After she had admired his horse, she told him about Washakie's generosity. "He send many gifts to me and to children. Before he die, Pariha Ungu tells Mŭatsi is daughter of Washakie. He was glad he took you and named you Tupaku for his Medicine Arrow."

"What'll Isha do with Daidŭtsi?" he asked abruptly.

"Maybe trade for whiskey."

Tupaku looked at the girl, so frail and helpless; and he knew that she was not safe in the Bannock camp. "Washakie likes white man," he told his mother.

"Would he like little white girl maybe?"

"He likes white man," the boy reiterated.

His mother seemed to be making a decision. He could read her thoughts. What if the girl were gone when Isha returned? If he became too abusive, Little Moon could pack his belongings into a buckskin bag and set them outside, and the divorce would be final. He would have no recourse without making himself the laughing stock of the tribe.

"Take the girl to Washakie," Mŭatsi commanded. "He send many gifts to me. Now I give her to him. Tell 'im."

Tupaku, after seriously considering the matter, decided that the risk was too great so he refused.

"Do what I say!" Little Moon was a well-built woman with hardened muscles and a newly aroused sense of power. Was she not the daughter of the chief whose generosity awed Naroyan's entire band?

"Isha kill you if he come back and find her gone. He has spoken. "

Little Moon laughed mockingly. "Isha afraid of Washakie's Snakes. He went away when his braves brought gifts, and he stayed until they left. Mŭatsi will say when he returns that Washakie sent for his little friend and warned if Isha harms his daughter he will come get him with his tomahawk."

The memory of Tupaku's dream haunted him because he could still see the timber wolf at at her throat. He looked at the girl with her funny cloths. Hanŭbi could make her a nice doeskin dress with beads. Hers was as flimsy as a worn-out piece of tradecloth, which would be no protection in the raw winter winds. She looked so forlorn that he wished he had something to cheer her. All he had was a piece of moss agate. "Here," he said awkwardly, as he handed it to her.

Pleased, she smiled for the first time. But there was not the radiance about her that he had observed when she saw the pottery along the trail. Living in the Bannock camp had sobered her and caused her to lose weight. She was so thin she looked as if a strong west wind might blow her away. Unquestionably she would fare better among the Shoshone. Washakie would probably adopt her and spoil her as badly as he did Nanagi.

Little Moon was watching him closely. "Kamŭ Kaupa take little white girl to Washakie?"

"*Aha,*" he replied.

After handing her son some of the jerkmeat the Shoshones had brought her, Little Moon begged him to hurry. By signs she succeeded in conveying the idea to the girl that she was going somewhere. She gave her a comb and a small mirror which had been among the cherished gifts from Washakie. Placing the child on the horse behind her son, she smiled encouragingly.

The kindly faced woman touched the *daidŭtsi's* heart. Not knowing how to thank her, she leaned over, threw her arms around her neck and kissed her. The demonstration of affection, wholly unknown to the Bannock children who had come to stare at her, surprised yet delighted them. When she waved, they responded enthusiastically.

The Bannock camp was not far from the Shoshones' which was then on the South Fork of the Popo Agie. Mountains intervened. Rather than return through the lowlands as he had come, the boy decided on a shortcut through high country which afforded a wealth of beauty. Shimmering gold of the aspens marked the course of the streams, and majestic evergreens dotted the mountainsides. Billowy clouds, in a state of irresolution, cast shadows though the sky beyond was crystal clear. Tupaku, with senses exalted, wished that he knew the words with which he could teach the *daidŭtsi* the joys of nature because to him the world seemed unusually good. He could relax after crossing the Bannock Trail leading to Fort Hall. From then on, it was doubtful that he would encounter Isha.

Daidŭtsi, who had kept her arms locked tightly around his waist to keep from sliding off the horse, also began to relax. Tupaku, alarmed by the possibility that she might go to sleep and fall, wished that he could talk to her. Each time he saw something of interest, he would point it out. There was an elk at the edge of the timber and two moose grazing in a glen.

At one place the high trail skirted a deep canyon. Looking down on a rocky column they saw an eagle's nest with three eaglers just learning to fly. They must have been a late hatch. One at a time, they soared to a pine tree on a nearby bluff. Each uttered screams of fright as it flew through space and returned to its perilous nesting place.

On and on they rode, until Daidŭtsi was completely overcome with drowsiness. Her head slumped against the boy's back, and her arms dropped from his sides. Luckily he was able to catch her in time to keep her from falling. He stopped his horse and placed her in front of him so that he could hold her while she slept.

Daidŭtsi's dependence gave him a feeling of manliness, for he was now her protector. Though he hated the white man bitterly, he could not hate the child with hair as soft as milkweed down. He touched it gently so that he would not awaken her. Then he wondered how long it would be until the chokecherry juice would coarsen it and turn it black. While he held her against him, he could not understand the yearning that swept over him and caused his heart to pound. He had never felt this way toward the great chief nor toward his mother. It was his first experience with young love, and he did not recognize it.

With the sun relentlessly pouring its warmth down upon him, he, too, felt drowsy; but he could not climb down and exercise without awakening the *daidŭtsi.* He rode under a cottonwood tree where he stopped his horse long enough to reach one arm and then the other to the nearest limb and stretch himself.

By late afternoon, his thirst was unbearable. He stopped beside a small brook, and the girl awoke with a start. For a moment she seemed unable to realize where she was. Then she smiled. He slid to the ground and helped her dismount. Flattening himself on his stomach he drank while she watched. Patiently he taught her to cup her hands. Then in sign language he indicated that she was to stay and rest while he went sprinting down the trail. When he returned, he handed her a handful of ripe strawberries. He insisted upon her walking back and forth a number of times before he lifted her onto the horse. Refreshed, they rode into the night.

"Kitant Niet," the boy implored, "do not sleep. Take us to Washakie's lodge." His voice seemed strange, for the altitude had muffled the sounds around him. Even the tread of the horse's hooves was muted. As he rode down the mountainside in the late afternoon of the following day, Tupaku worked his jaws vigorously, allowing himself to hear more plainly. The sun was disappearing amidst a bank of crimson clouds in one of the most vivid sunsets he could remember. The sky overhead was salmon colored as it flaunted its glory.

When they neared camp, the boy thought for a moment that the Shoshones had come out to greet him, but he soon found the cause of the turnout. Men, women and children were watching in awe a phantom in the sky above the village. It was accompanied by screaming sounds. Together, Tupaku and Daidŭtsi sat watching the strange sight overhead. Two hawks were flying close together. One was contesting the right of the other to a long snake, dangling helplessly from its talons. With an unexpected swoop, the one higher in the air dived down on the other and took the twisting object in midair. The screams were more raucous than ever when the first hawk tried to regain its prize. Still fighting furiously, the hawks flew into the sunset. Tupaku was sure that it all meant something. If only he could ask Pariha Ungu! He could explain.

Washakie, with blanket wrapped around him, stood looking sternly at his son. Could he have brought shame by stealing the child he brought to camp? Such a thought had not occurred to the boy, but he was sure from the way the chief looked at him that he was condemned.

The girl, startled by the stranger, shrank against Tupaku, who was unable to find words to defend himself. Even if he had, he would not have been able to use them. The chief, who was slow to anger, was so furious that he upbraided the boy. "Washakie promised to be friend of white man and treat him like his brother. Now my son brings shame to his father. Taivo will blame Shoshone because you go with Pia Isha and steal little white girl."

Tupaku had anticipated reproof or punishment for breaking out of camp, but it had not occurred to him that he would be accused of stealing the child. He protested, "*Kay*! *Kay*! Tupaku not steal her. I found her picking chokecherries with Mŭatsi near Bannock camp. Isha got her on Wagon Road and Mŭatsi send her as gift to Washakie."

"Tell me true! You did not steal little white girl?"

"*Kay*."

The chief, accepting his word, asked abruptly, "Why you run away?"

"Because in my dream I saw timber wolf at Mŭatsi's throat. Tupaku must go see." He did not need to say more; the chief was satisfied.

"Come," Washakie said to the girl. When he lifted her from the horse, she burst into tears. He patted her on the head in an attempt to quiet her. "Hanŭbi!" he called anxiously. The Indians who had been watching made a path for her when she came in response to his command.

"What you call little white girl?"

"Daidŭtsi—just Daidŭtsi." The boy would not admit to his chief that he had given her the secret name Satonzibi (Flower) because she was the Little-Girl-Who-Became-a Prairie-Flower.

When Hanŭbi appeared, the chief said, "Wash the girl and dress her nice. She will be daughter of Washakie. Turn her over to Porivo. She will understand her needs."

When the boy started to lead his horse away, Washakie stopped him. "We try every way to keep Tupaku. We watch over you and warn you. Still you leave and cause us much trouble. You do not know that our people need you? That you are Good Medicine for Shoshone? You want enemies to destroy us?"

"*Kay*!" "*Kay*!" the boy protested.

Big Chief looked searchingly into his face. "Can Washakie trust you? You will promise him true? You will not leave again unless he knows?"

"*Ha*!" Tupaku answered so convincingly that there was no doubt that he meant it. "Kamŭ Kaupa, Bannock. Tupaku, Shoshone, son of Washakie!" His words pleased the chief, who extended his hand in the white man's manner to seal the agreement.

The leaders of the tribe had already found their

places in the council circle when Tupaku seated himself beside his chief and glanced uneasily toward Porivo. This time the council did not directly concern him. Washakie had called it to consider the meaning of the omen in the sky. Each dignitary would be given a chance to express an opinion.

"The omen of the hawks means we will starve when white man takes all our buffalo," said one.

Another thought that the white man would take the land so that there would be no place for the Indians to go. Porivo believed that the red sunset foretold the end of the red man. Little Chief squirmed when someone said that he thought it indicated the Shoshones would lose their Good Medicine. Then it became Tupaku's turn to express himself. "Someone will take Daidŭtsi?" It was a question not a statement, one that could not be answered.

Washakie did not mention the white girl when he gave his interpretation. "First hawk means Shoshone, second Crow. Snake is our Big Horn hunting grounds we have fought over so long a time. Some day it will be taken from us." He was saddened by the prospect. Then he added, "We will see."

10

Washakie's lodge was cozy during the snowy moons that followed. It was chinked around the edge and heated by a lively centerfire. The floor was carpeted with buffalo hides and there were soft, furry robes for beds. No matter how cold it was outside, Tupaku was snug and warm as he slept with Nanagi at his side.

Warm clothing now protected him from the raw winds. The coonskin cap Hanŭbi fashioned had fur inside and the long tail hanging down for decoration. It was a handsome cap. He wished Little Moon had a chance to see it, but he would not ask the chief's permission to return to the Bannocks even for a brief visit. With the snow piled deep in the canyons, he might perish along the way. Anyway, he knew that Washakie would not let him go.

The snowy moons indicated the story telling period for the Shoshones. While men of all ages sat around their fires with nothing to do, their tongues were loosened, and they told endless tales that had been handed down from one generation to another. They usually had to do with their animal kindred. Washakie was one of the best narrators, but when he started talking about the white man Tupaku would close his heart and his mind.

As winter melted into spring, snow made way for buffalo grass and wild fruits and vegetables. It was the time of year Tupaku liked best, a time of promise, of what he was not sure. This spring, his first in the Shoshone camp, he found himself in the unhappy position of being too young and inexperienced to be a warrior, yet not in the same class with the other youths in camp. He still secretly wished for their companionship, but they spurned him every chance they had.

His jealousy reached its peak when he overheard them planning a horse catching excursion after locating a band of wild horses in the upper Sweetwater country. Kill Bear supplied the details. It seems that Pariha Tawa, their disagreeable leader, had discovered the herd and had reported it to the warriors, who were too busy with their war maneuvers for horse wrangling. Tupaku asked if he might be allowed to go with the youths, but Kill Bear considered it too dangerous after the rock throwing incident.

Tupaku was even more restless when they returned with two mares soon to foal. In his presence, they seemed to delight in telling tales of their adventure. They fired his imagination with their account of a black stallion they had tried unsuccessfully to capture. Someday Tupaku would catch him, and he would prove himself their equal if not their superior.

One day when Tupaku and Kill Bear were returning from a hunting trip, they heard a commotion beyond the willows at the edge of the camp. The wild cries were in the uncertain key of changing voices. Unquestionably, a war game was in progress. The boy started ahead to see what was taking place, but the Log stopped him. "Stay back!" he urged.

"*Kay*, you stay! Tupaku will go!" For the first time there was a sound of authority in his voice. His companion looked at him in surprise. "Give me your rifle, Wŭda Pekanŭ!" The urgency of his manner indicated that this might be his proving ground. The Log handed over his weapon, and he watched admiringly when the boy rushed forward alone.

Beyond the willows, Elk Tooth was leading a war game. Daidŭtsi, the hostage, was gagged and bound to a tree. Her eyes were wide with terror while the young warriors sounded their cries and danced gleefully around her. The game must have been planned in advance because the participants were dressed for the occasion, with feather bustles which they had filched from their elders. Their bodies bobbed up and down, and they doubled forward with each trying to outdo the other in his contortions. They were so completely carried away that they did not see Tupaku, who watched them with mounting rage.

Slowly, he lifted the rifle to his shoulder and aimed above them. He would not shoot to kill, but he would teach them a lesson. The sharp report of the rifle brought the War Dance to a halt. The young braves stared at Tupaku, who kept the gun pointed menacingly in their direction. The expression on his face dispelled any thought that he might be a weakling.

"Who planned this?" he demanded to know.

The youths were only too glad to point to Elk Tooth. "We were playing a war game," one of them tried to explain.

"War game?" Tupaku looked toward Daidŭtsi as he slid from his horse. "Very well, we play!" Though he had never taken part in one of their games he would include them in his.

"Pariha Tawa," he addressed the leader, who stood glowering at him, "obey the word of Little Chief. Release the captive!" But the sullen youth did not move. "Hear me! Let the captive go!" Still the young Shoshone did not respond. "Anyone who disobeys Little Chief will suffer," Tupaku stated coldly. Someone untie the captive." Several youths scrambled to carry out his order. "Now bring the *daidŭtsi*."

Two make-believe warriors, one on each side of her, led the girl forward. "Stop!" Tupaku ordered as they neared him. Then he told them to go back. "Daidŭtsi, come!" He beckoned her to come the rest of the way alone. As she did, he noticed that her wrists and ankles had been rubbed raw by the rope. When she reached his side, he stepped between her and the youths. Elk Tooth started to run.

"Stop him!" Tupaku shouted. The boys were anxious to comply, for it was a new experience having a gun trained on them. "Bring him here. He is now my prisoner. He tries to bring grief to your chief by robbing him of daughter. . . . Treat him like you did Daidŭtsi. Tie him to tree!". . .

"Pariha Tawa," Tupaku addressed the culprit, "now you know what it's like to be captive. This'll teach you not to bother daughter of Washakie!" He shot into the tree trunk immediately above his head.

"Now dance!" he ordered the young warriors. "Do not stop 'til I tell you." Again the drum sounded, and the youths danced as never before. Leaving them to their sport, Tupaku helped the *daidŭtsi* on Strong Wind's back and led him toward Porvio's lodge. He was surprised when she spoke to him in the language of the Snakes which the old woman must have taught her.

"Tupaku, if you had not come—how can I thank you?"

Thank him! How absurd! What did she want to thank him for? No Indian would have said that! He had saved her life, not because she was the daughter of a white man man but because she was Washakie's daughter. There was also another reason. He had been strangely drawn to her from the first. By reminding him that she was white, he almost wished that he had not come to her rescue.

"Never leave Porivo's tepee alone!" he said gruffly.

Meanwhile, the war cries continued unabated. Evidently the adults recognized them as amateurish, for no one took the trouble to investigate. Tupaku, knowing that the boys were afraid to stop, took his time returning. The prolonged lesson would be good for them. As he rode along, he kept thinking about the black stallion that had been seen somewhere in the wilds. After he captured him, he would add more horses in his forays as a warrior. He would be able to afford slave wives to do the drudgery so that Daidŭtsi, who would be his favored wife, would have time for the quillwork Porivo would teach her.

He rode up to the place where the young braves had terrified the white captive. For a moment he sat watching. Something told him that he would not need to use Kill Bear's rifle again, that he had won their respect. He let them dance awhile longer, though he could see that they were weary and out of breath.

"Stop!" he shouted at length. "You still want Pariha Tawa for chief?"

"*Kay*," they answered in unison.

"Who you want?"

"Tegwatsi, Little Chief!" came the spontaneous reply. It would have been unanimous had it not been for Elk Tooth, who stood defiantly before him when he was released. His dark look indicated that he would never forgive Little Chief for disgracing him before his followers.

After Tupaku's phenomenal success he should have been happy, but it seemed in no way to quiet his restlessness. Kill Bear, sensing his troubled spirit, asked what was wrong. Usually it was easy to confide in his friend, but this time it was not.

The Log ventured a guess. "You want Coming-of-Age Ceremony? You not know that Washakie's band not have it?" Then he explained that the ceremony known to the Western Shoshones had been discontinued by the Eastern bands. That did not mean that he could not have one if he wanted it. The Log placed his age at around 16 or 17, old enough to have a manhood ceremony if that were what he wanted.

"How you know when—"

"When you feel you not want to play brave but be brave and go on warpath. That is when you come of age."

"Tupaku want to go away. He—"

"And live with beaver?"

"*Kay*. This time want to go on high hill, near Dam Apŭ. Washakie maybe let me go?" The boy looked anxiously toward his companion.

"Ask him."

Talking to the chief was different from talking to Kill Bear, but there was no alternative. He had given his word. Several days elapsed before he found the courage to approach Washakie, who was sitting, smoking by the fire. It was late afternoon, and the women were preparing an evening meal. Holding the bowl of his pipe in his hand, Washakie motioned for the boy to be seated.

"What's wrong?" the chief queried.

"Tupaku not know." There was nothing else he

could say, for he was baffled by his own feelings. All he knew was that he must get away. He longed for solitude so that he could probe his soul, but he was unable to say so.

"How old are you, my son?"

"*Kay shunbana,* don't know."

"You want Coming-of-Age Ceremony?" Kill Bear must have told him.

Tupaku nodded though he was not really sure what he wanted.

"Very well, you'll have one," the chief replied indulgently. "Do not eat after tonight. When sun come again, go to mountain top. There you be near Dam Apŭ. He will watch over you. Four days, you'll fast. Last day, you'll have vision, showing road ahead. When you come back, Pohakantŭ meet you and have purification rite. After that, come to me for moccasins to travel new road."

Hanŭbi appeared, carrying a bowl of stew for Washakie. "Bring one for my son. This night he'll eat with his chief. We have much to discuss."

The next morning the youth climbed to a ledge overlooking the valley where the Sweetwater curves its way eastward through green meadows. In the distance he could see an unusual rocky formation against the horizon. As he gazed toward it, his mind wandered. If only he could talk with Pariha Ungu. Might he be looking down upon him from the spirit world? Could he be guiding him, sharing his joys and sorrows?

The first day the sun was unbearably warm, but

after it disappeared he had to pull his blanket around him for comfort. He wished for some hot food as darkness settled and obliterated the rocky form which had caught and held his attention. He could not see the lights from the Shoshone campfires, which were screened from view by willows and cottonwoods beyond the curve of the river. There appeared to be a black, fathomless pit before him.

On the second day, he continued to center his attention upon the massive rock, and he wondered how there could ever have been a force mighty enough to split it asunder. The longer he looked, the more he wondered what caused it to break from top to bottom. Concentrating upon the single object and speculating upon its significance, he could forget the gnawing hunger that almost drove him in search of food.

At the end of the third day, he prayed. "Tupaku want vision. Washakie not like if Tupaku not have one."

He was so weak from hunger and thirst by the fourth day that he could scarcely endure the privation. Still his gaze was directed toward Split Rock, as he now thought of the object looming up before him. While he watched, he went through various stages of inertia until by the end of the day he was in a trance. The cleft formation had been his focal point of interest so long that it was not surprising, when the vision came, it involved the rock.

The young Indian became aware of a bird, darting through the dusk. Could it be Chickadee again? No, it was larger. It was a nighthawk, sounding its plaintive cry. It swooped toward him several times and finally stopped to rest at his side.

"Why you sound so sad?" Tupaku asked.

"You do not know why nighthawks cry?" Weyavo (Night Hawk) asked.

"*Kay*!"

"Weyavo used to make a musical sound when he flew around in the evening stillness hunting bugs, but no more. One time my grandfather saw a trapper coming over that hill across from us. Suddenly, without warning, a big boulder began rolling directly toward him. No matter how fast he ran, he could not get out of the way. There was only one thing to do and that was to crouch in a hole and let it roll over him." There was a pause.

"What happened?" Tupaku asked, anxious to get on with the tale.

"It did not roll on. It stopped just above the unfortunate trapper, and he did not even have room to turn around in the hole where he was lodged. With no possibility of escape, he became desperate. He knew that he was in the land of the Snakes, so he cried, 'Nŭ-dŭtsowe! Nŭ-dŭtsowe! Help me! Help me!' but there were no Indians near enough to hear.

"The only one who heard was my grandfather, who felt very, very sorry for him. He promised that he would rescue him, and he pushed and pushed but could not budge the boulder. Then he flew to find Mumbitsŭ [Owl], the wisest bird in the country. Perhaps he could advise him. Owl asked grandfather who the mightiest power in the land was, and he answered 'Enga-Kwitsaikite [Lightning].' So Owl told him to go to him for help.

"When Lightning heard the story of the trapper he agreed to come to his rescue, but first he had to gather some clouds. Grandfather darted back to the boulder to reassure the trapper, who kept grumbling until he was hoarse. Grandfather became disgusted, for he had done all in his power to help.

"Finally, there was a roar of distant thunder, heralding the approach of Lightning. Each time there was a flash, grandfather could see that more clouds were gathering; and he could hear the repeated roar of Thunder. Lightning, together with his clouds, kept coming nearer and nearer until he was finally overhead. Then in a blinding flash, he reached down and smote the boulder so hard that one stroke severed it.

"When the trapper crawled out, he stretched himself from being in a cramped position so long. 'My, but I am hungry.' he exclaimed! 'Come closer so I can thank you,' he instructed Night Hawk, who flew toward him. Before grandfather suspected the trapper's intentions, he grabbed him, pulled off his head and feathers, and roasted him for his supper.

"Grandmother, who had been sitting watching all that was taking place, went crying into the night. From then on, all nighthawks have made the same sound, for they have not forgotten the treacherous trapper at Split Rock."

When Weyavo flew away, he left one of his feathers, indicating that Night Hawk would henceforth be Tupaku's "helper." In the years to come, the feather, besides giving him strength and wisdom, would be the most cherished item in his medicine bag.

Tupaku could think only of his vision when the *pohakantŭ* was chanting and making medicine during his purification rite. The shock of cold water brought him to his senses. Wrapping himself in his blanket, he went barefoot to meet Washakie, who handed him a new pair of moccasins and offered him his calumet. Recalling Pariha Ungu's foul tasting pipe, the young Indian was reluctant to smoke. The first puff was different. The bowl contained a pleasant mixture of herbs and tobacco.

When Washakie asked his son if he had a vision, he recounted the story of the treacherous trapper just as Weyavo had told it. The chief sat motionless, in no way indicating his thoughts. When the story was finished he asked Tupaku what he thought it meant.

He was quick with an answer. "It is warning. It means white man will treat Indian same way trapper treated Night Hawk."

Washakie was displeased. "You talk like white man who says only good Indian is dead Indian. There are good and bad white men as there are good and bad Indians!"

The Manhood Ceremony ended with a feast, which Tupaku looked forward to, and a dance he dreaded. If a girl asked him to be her partner, he could not refuse, for if he did he would be killed by a bear next time he went hunting. Pariha Ungu had told him so.

To his relief, two horsemen in ceremonial dress came leading a party of dancers. One of them announced that there would be a general dance in which there were no partners. The festivities began when the dancing party stopped in front of Washakie's lodge where someone started beating a drum and singing. Men and women danced around and around, each by himself.

"Come," said the chief to the members of his family. "Let's dance. We celebrate Coming-of-Age of my son." Soon after they had joined the revelers, the music stopped abruptly. Round one of the dance was over. Then everyone moved to the next tepee, where the rite was resumed. Tupaku was familiar with the dance as it was also popular in Naroyan's camp. As the Indians moved from one place to another the ranks swelled until every able-bodied man, woman and child old enough to walk was taking part. At the first opportunity, Tupaku dropped out and returned to his lodge.

When Washakie went in search of him, he found him sound asleep.

Now that the son of Washakie had attained the status of a brave, it was time for him to return to the Bannock camp and settle his score with Isha. He had waited long enough. When he talked with his chief, he encouraged his going. Early the next morning when he went after Strong Wind, he found Kill Bear waiting for him with a parfleche filled with presents from Washakie to Little Moon.

While he was riding in search of the Bannock camp, Tupaku had time to think about the object of his excursion. He was still belligerent, but so much had happened in the brief time he had spent among Washakie's Green River Snakes that it was difficult for him to have the same feeling toward Isha that he had when he was subjected to his cruelty. It was not that he had weakened in his determination to eradicate him as much as that he had changed his sense of value. What once had seemed all important was now secondary to something that had not occurred to him during his Bannock life. It was so much easier to hold a vision of the black stallion than to conjure a clear mental picture of Isha. In fact, he did not remember exactly how he looked.

Tupaku had some difficulty locating the Bannock

camp, which was not where he thought it would be. It was late in the day when he spotted it tucked forlornly among the cottonwoods at the bend of the river. He was shocked by its ugliness. There was not a new lodgeskin in the lot. He thought of Washakie's handsome lodge with its battle scene painted on the exterior. He would have one someday with prairie flowers painted on the outside for all to see.

As he approached the camp, he found it hard to believe that he had belonged to this band only the year before. Children came running to stare at him. Suddenly he felt foolish. Why had he worn ornamental buckskin and beadwork? After all, he had come on a mission that made ceremonial clothing out of place. He looked around for his mother.

"Kamŭ Kaupa! You not know Mŭatsi?" She had been standing with the others, but she now came forward to greet him. Her hair was chopped off short and her legs and arms had long, partly healed gashes on them.

"Mŭatsi, what happened?"

In her sadness, she had not even noticed his fancy clothes. "You not know?

"Know what?"

"Isha's dead!" He could not believe her, but she must be speaking the truth, for she gave every evidence of grief.

"Dead! What happen?"

"Lightning struck him." When she began to cry, Tupaku was perplexed. Could she actually have cared for the beast? Could she have forgiven him for his cruelty and his failure to provide for the children she bore him?

Washakie must have known. Perhaps that was the reason he allowed his Good Medicine out of his sight.

"Why you slash arms and legs?"

"To let grief out," she replied.

When Tupaku dismounted and handed her the buckskin bag Washakie had sent, she smiled for the first time. He did not notice what it contained, for he was deep in thought. Isha was dead! If Mŭatsi cared for him as much as she seemed to, he was glad that he had not made her unhappy by killing him. He was more grateful to Lightning than the trapper at Split Rock had been.

11

The snows of another winter had melted when a runner came, inviting Washakie to Fort Bridger to talk with representatives of the Great White Father about tribal matters. The chief had been asking for such a council, and the time had finally been set.

On the appointed day, the Snakes in single file began crossing the peaceful Bridger Valley. When the column entered the courtyard, it split, with one Indian going to the right, the next to the left. As the advance guard fanned out each side of Washakie, the chief and his leaders rode forward to greet their hosts. With the exception of Tupaku, everyone seemed to be in a holiday mood. He looked grimmer than usual. In his otter skin quiver, he carried the Medicine Arrow that Washakie had entrusted to him for what he believed would be a great occasion.

Tupaku had been apprehensive from the time he first heard about the white man's invitation. When he asked his chief the purpose of the trip, Washakie had replied, "We'll go to Great White Father and tell him Shoshone own Big Horn hunting grounds and for him to tell Crow to get out!" The explanation sounded logical, but the young Indian could not see the point in going to Fort Bridger to talk about the Crows. Why not settle the matter directly with them?

Washakie, smiling broadly, shook hands with his old friend Blanket Chief (Tegwana Wanŭp), Jim Bridger, and with Broken Hand, Thomas Fitzpatrick, the Indian agent from Fort Laramie. They exchanged greetings in the white man's tongue. Blanket Chief was the first to turn toward Little Chief.

"Well ef it ain't Tupaku!" he exclaimed. "Y'shore are gettin' to look like yer granpappy! Kain't hardly tell y'apart. Fitz, this here's Tupaka I told you 'bout."

When Fitzpatrick extended his hand, Tupaku was reluctant to take it. Though Kopŭp Mo, as the Indians called him, dressed nice and looked honest, he would not be deceived. He was suspicious when the agent said pleasantly, "So you are Tupaku! I have heard a lot about you, and I have looked forward to seeing you and your Medicine Arrow. It is as well known as the Flat Pipe of the Arapahoes and the Medicine Hat of the Cheyennes. I hope someday to have a chance to see it." His words were intelligible through signs.

To Tupaku's surprise, Washakie directed that he show him the arrow. After removing it from his quiver, he held it out of reach of the white man. No one had touched the arrow except Hanŭbi and Washakie since he had delivered it to the Shoshones. He thought how angered Pariha Ungu would have been if the white man had tried to take it, or even looked upon it for that matter. The young Indian had tasted peppermint candy, dried apples and lumps of maple sugar on a previous visit to the fort, but they had failed to sweeten his attitude toward the white man.

Tupaku was half starved when the feast began. After the warriors had satisfied their appetites, they sprawled out on the ground to nap; but he considered it prudent to stay awake and see what was going on. Since the council would not convene until the next morning, he would sit around the campfire with his elders and listen to their reminiscences about fur trading days. He had a good knowledge of sign language, and he would be able to follow every word that was said.

In spite of himself, he was impressed by the geniality of the white man. What was it about him that caused Washakie to talk and laugh in such a friendly manner? Was it because they had so many experiences in common, and there were exciting memories to share? His chief was usually quiet and thoughtful, but now he did not disguise his genuine pleasure. Tupaku wanted to warn him to be on his guard. He should not allow himself to be tricked.

After the morning meal, the dignitaries of the tribe silently filed into the willow lodge for their council with the white man. First, the pipe was smoked. Bridger spoke a few words of welcome in Shoshone, then turned the meeting over to Fitzpatrick, who said in English and sign language, "The Great White Father sends greetings to you, and he wants me to remind you that he has not forgotten you. Many times your chief has asked that he meet him in council. It is too far for him to come, but he has sent me to speak for him. Blanket Chief and the Utah agent at Salt Lake have tried to keep him informed of your wishes. Perhaps you will have an agent at Bridger some day so that you can talk over your problems with him. Until then, Blanket Chief and I will do what we can to represent you."

"Give us our hunting grounds!" one of the elders shouted.

Fitzpatrick either failed to understand or he ignored him. "Since I am the agent for the Sioux, Cheyennes and Arapahoes, the Great White Father has asked me to come here to invite you to the Great Treaty Council to be held at Fort Laramie on the North Platte, the first day of September. It is being called for the Platte River Indians, but you will be honored guests."

"Our enemies!" a voice shouted.

"Fort Laramie in Sioux Country!" another added.

"That is true, but the Great White Father wants all of his children to come together as brothers to discuss your problems with him. He is concerned with all of you. Besides, the Platte River Indians have pledged that they will not cause trouble. I'm sure you will, too."

"A trap!" Tupaku said under his breath. He was thinking of Night Hawk.

The chief gave him a look of reproof.

"My vision showed me not to trust white man. He will destroy—" Washakie was not listening.

"Tegwana Wanŭp, how will we find our way to Fort Laramie?" he asked.

Bridger answered glibly, "I'll guide ya clean thar, an' I'll garntee safe passage to and from. Not that ya need it with Tupaku 'long, but I'll give every warrior that goes a rifle that'll make other tribes set up an' take notice."

A rifle! Tupaku began to brighten over the prospect. Big Chief seemed annoyed. The council had turned into a question and answer session, and he had not been called upon for a speech. Without waiting further, he arose and addressed his hosts, "Washakie is sad because he hoped to have talk with Great White Father at Bridger. We want Crow to get out of our Big Horn country, and we want Blackfoot to stay away from Medicine Mountain and Tetons. They belong to my people. If it is too far for Great White Father to come see Washakie, then Shoshone will meet him at Fort Laramie. We don't want him to have medicine talk with our enemies when we are his friends."

He asked a shrewd question. "Will white man have paper to show who the land belong to—that it belong to Shoshone?"

Fitzpatrick answered frankly. "I don't know where

the boundaries will be, but they will be decided at the council."

"If Blanket Chief show the way, we will go," Washakie promised.

Tupaku, listening carefully, was alarmed over the turn of events. In Broken Hand's statements he implied that the Great White Father appreciated the friendship of the Shoshones and wanted them to come to Fort Laramie so that he could reward them for being such good Indians. He would never forget that Night Hawk came near so the trapper could thank him.

When Tupaku had a chance to get away from his elders, he went in search of Kill Bear, who he found relaxing with his back against the log building. He sat down beside him and began plying him with questions that had nothing to do with the white man's council. "Tell me," he urged, "how'd you catch Black Horse?"

The Log was unprepared for his question. "You come to medicine talk and all you think about is Black Horse!" He was quiet a moment; then he said, "Crease him."

"Crease him?"

Since Tupaku did not understand the term, Kill Bear told him of an experience he had some years before. "That is how I got most beautiful elk I ever saw. He was fine bull, big and strong. And oh, how proud! I watched him graze. He would raise his head often and look at his cows to see if all is well. When one started to stray, he would whistle, and they would come running. They would try to see how close they could get to him.

"I did not want to kill him, but Shoshone must eat. When elk spread out to graze, I took aim with rifle. I not want hole in his hide, so I shoot him high on the neck, that is, I crease him. When he drop, his cows ran to woods.

"I thought he's dead. I straddle him and lifted his head to cut throat and bleed him. You know? He is not dead! He jump up and start running with me holding his antlers. I never had ride so wild. With knife I tried to find vein. I held his antlers with one hand and cut vein with other. He ran, blood gushing from neck. Then he dropped dead with me on 'im. I couldn't walk for long time."

Tupaku was so carried away by the tale that he lost the connection with the horse. Remembering, he asked incredulously, "You mean crease Tupungo?" The idea was appalling. "Little Chief not shoot Tupungo! Maybe hurt him!"

"Remember," Kill Bear told him, "stallion plenty smart, but mares and colts easy to catch in Sweetwater where water's shallow and meadows flat. We line both sides and chase 'em. Even in shallow water they tire quick. When one come out someone jump on its back and keep it going in stream until it give up. Never mind! We figure how to catch Black Horse later."

True to his promise, Bridger provided the warriors with guns. Although Washakie allowed them the pleasure of carrying their new weapons, he wisely held possession of the ammunition until they were a safe distance from the White-top Wagon Road, so that an innocent passerby would not be the target for a trigger-happy young warrior.

Rifle practice began the day the Snakes reached their camp. They intended to master the art of handling their firearms before going into enemy territory. Prior to this, only the chief and sub-chiefs, together with a few of the Logs, including Kill Bear, had guns. In spite of Washakie's precautions, there were several casualties, some deliberate, others accidental.

The first use the chief had for his new weapon was to teach a lesson to his mother-in-law, who had crossed him on several occasions. When the Snakes returned from the fort, he discovered that Hanŭbi had moved his lodge in his absence. He had always determined just where he wanted it placed, but she had defied him twice before. On being questioned, she confessed that her mother was behind the move. Washakie angrily demanded to know where she was.

"She went down river to get wood," she replied fearfully. Then she whispered to Tupaku to follow the chief, who left, enraged. They found the woman chopping kindling with a heavy hand ax.

"Waugh!" Washakie roared at the sight of her.

Like a trapped creature, she stared at him. There was a look of resignation in her faded eyes, as if she were prepared to accept the punishment due her.

"Three times you tell Hanŭbi to move lodge while I am away. You know I like it on highest ground in camp. You want it down by river so you not have so far to go for squaw wood. I warned you, but no good. Now I teach you I am chief!" He lifted his rifle, pointed it at her and pulled the trigger. He glanced briefly but significantly toward Tupaku. Then without the slightest indication of regret, he walked away.

Tupaku looked down upon the woman, lying lifeless across the wood she had so arduously chopped. She should have known better. Upon numerous occasions, Washakie had impressed his followers with the fact that his word was law. Perhaps this was just another lesson. As far as Tupaku was concerned, it was wholly unnecessary, for he had only to look at the scarred face of Pŭshikantŭ to know that Washakie meant what he said. The indelible blow of his tomahawk across the sub-chief's face was put there for all to see.

As the days went by, Tupaku and his young followers devoted most of their time to war maneuvers with an occasional horse-hunting excursion. Only once did they see the coveted wild stallion. He was standing like a sentinel, surveying his domain from a high knoll. After a shrill whinny, he disappeared toward Crow country. The horse hunters dared not follow, though they were fearful that he might fall into the hands of their enemies.

In the early summer, measles struck the Shoshone camp like a plague, with Tupaku one of the first victims. In his delirium he raved about Tupungo, and he even tried to fight the Crows for taking his horse away from him. The disease, running rampant through the tribe, brought great suffering, especially among the young and the very old. Nanagi's case was one of the most serious among the children, though several deaths occurred among the older Indians.

Washakie was brooding at his son's bedside when word came that Blanket Chief Bridger and his Shoshone wife, Rutta, had arrived. When they came into his lodge, he told them what had befallen his people. "Someone put little black stone, bad medicine, in my lodge. I not find it, but know it is here. So much grief has come to me. My people are sick and dying. Washakie can't go to Great Treaty Council."

"Wall, ef that don't beat hell! What's ailin' 'em?" Blanket Chief wanted to know.

"Bad medicine—squaw man says measles."

"Measles!" Bridger exclaimed. "They ain't nobuddy knows more 'bout measles 'an Rutta. Her's took care ov manya case at the fort. Everbuddy'll be fit's a fiddle come time t'go!"

Nanagi lay sleeping in spite of the intonations of the *pohakantŭ* who sat at his side. Bridger was annoyed by his antics. "Kain't see how the youngun kin sleep with alla that thar racket! Why don'tcha make 'im shut up?" he asked irritably.

The chief glanced toward the medicine man with respect. "He make Nanagi live again. When I look in his eyes I see his spirit's gone. *Pohakantŭ* die, too, so he can bring 'im back to life. He die here." With a sweep of his hand, he indicated the prone position which the medicine man had assumed in departing from this life. "He find spirit of my son. Bring it back and place it between his eyes where it belong. When I put hand on *Pohakantŭ*, he come back to life and tell me what happen. I look at Nanagi, deep in his eyes I see his spirit has returned. He's sleeping now, but he'll get well. The older people, I worry 'bout. Some already dead."

The next morning while Nanagi was still sleeping, the medicine man reached under the edge of the child's blanket and found the stone that had brought so much grief to the chief. The black magic could now be cast out, ending his troubles. Washakie rewarded the *pohakantŭ* with a fine horse.

12

The Shoshone camp was in a state of excitement the day of departure for the Great Treaty Council. Dogs that were valued as pets had to be confined to prevent their following the tribe. Better to tie them up and let them howl than to see them thrown into the pot by the dog-eating enemies on the Platte, where dog flesh was considered a delicacy fit for a chief.

Eighty of the most distinguished warriors and their families were permitted to go, but the whole village was in confusion. Those who were not bedfast were doing their part in giving the delegates a great send-off. In spite of their recent illness, women and children were laughing and shouting to each other; and their braves were congregating in their war togs.

The dress parade, which stretched from the chief's lodge to the opposite side of the village, was the final event. While tom-toms sounded, men, women and children fell in line in their proper places, with the Yellow Nose warriors taking the lead. Blanket Chief rode beside Washakie, with Tupaku immediately behind them. Following the women and children came the Logs who, besides serving as guards, must replace or repair broken lodgepoles.

Big Chief checked to see that the line was intact and

ready to move. Every adult was mounted on a good horse. Each warrior, besides being armed with a gun, carried a war club, a tomahawk and his bow and arrows. Tupaku was instructed to carry the sacred Medicine Arrow, which would bring good medicine to the Snakes on their journey.

The Indians, about 200 in the entire procession, circled the village twice so that all might see them in their glory. Nanagi, broken-hearted that he was not permitted to go, wailed pathetically although one of the women tried to console him. Tupaku feared that his father might weaken the last minute and take him, but when the procession passed the lodge a second time, Washakie stared straight ahead as if unaware of the commotion the boy was making.

Blanket Chief had said that notices would be posted and word spread among the emigrants going westward that they would meet a friendly band of Shoshones on their way to the Great Council. He planned to guide them over the medicine road of the whites, the White-top Wagon Road. Unless forewarned, some of the brash emigrants might open fire upon the Indians, who would welcome an opportunity to try out their new weapons.

Tupaku had cautiously crossed the emigrant trail several times, but this was his first excursion along the great roadway, which the Shoshones reached by following Beaver Creek to the crest of the Divide at South Pass. When they met wagon trains, the emigrants pleased by the pageantry, waved and shouted words of greeting.

"*Ahai'i*!" the Snakes responded good-naturedly. They could afford to be in high spirits because they were on their way to meet with the Great White Father, who was generous with his gifts.

The first camp was made on the banks of the Sweetwater. Women scurried about, watering horses, preparing campfires and erecting their tepees, while men lounged and listened to Bridger's droll tales. The fragrant smell of boiling fresh-ground coffee issued from pots over campfires. Blanket Chief's gift had been a 100-pound sack of coffee beans and a mill which perplexed those who tried to operate it. Although Rutta gave a demonstration, they finally resorted to their rock grinders, which had served their people for untold generations. They were slow in accepting all of the newfangled gadgets Rutta had acquired while living at Bridger's fort. The braves washed down their pemmican and jerky with coffee while they waited for the stew to finish boiling in the kettles. The strong odor of wild meat, darkened with age, soon permeated the air and subdued the coffee aroma.

The only diversion of the day was provided by a dozen hungry Cheyennes whose sense of smell guided them to the feast. All communicating was done by signs, which Little Chief followed closely. He knew that the Cheyennes were lying when they indicated that they had become lost from a hunting party. Hunting!

They were probably hunting Snakes, whom they must have been following along the way.

The stew was ready by the time the guests were comfortably seated. Each of the strangers reached for a bowl. As soon as it was empty, he handed it back to be refilled. The serving women seemed displeased, though by devouring the food the guests were showing their appreciation. As soon as their bowls had been emptied a third time, they got up and left without a word to the chief.

"Wall," Bridger spoke at last, "looks as how we might have a round with the Cheyenne. Wonder whar them Injuns left their hosses. They was hongry aw right, but they didn't come here jest to eat. They come to find out how strong we was. I seen 'em eyeing them rifles."

The next morning there were no signs of a hunting party. It was a calm, beautiful day, typical in the high country; but Tupaku felt gloomy.

He kept wondering if there might be trouble with the Cheyennes. He tried to read the expression in his chief's face, but he could not. Anyway, he was sure that Washakie was worried.

The Shoshones, gorging themselves at their morning meal, were told that the procession would not stop again until the setting of the sun. Vegetation was so dry that Bridger cautioned the women to throw dirt over the campfires to prevent a prairie fire. This accomplished, the Indians were on the move.

Toward noon the sun became so hot that Tupaku

longed for a shady spot. He was half asleep when one of the Logs galloped up from the rear with the startling news that the last two Indians who dropped out of line to relieve themselves had failed to return. The entire procession was brought to a halt. Washakie ordered all to remain where they were except a dozen Yellow Noses and a like number of Logs, who comprised his search party. He led out, with Bridger and Tupaku following. They had no difficulty finding the victims, lying on the blood-stained ground. Their scalps had been removed, and their bodies were studded with arrows. Obviously, it was the work of the Cheyennes.

Big Chief was boiling mad. "Find 'em!" he roared. The moccasin tracks led into a wooded sector along the stream. There it was apparent that the marauders had waited on horseback in the hope of cutting off any stragglers. After accomplishing their purpose, they had fled the country. While a *pohakantŭ* went about singing a death song, the women keened loudly over the victims, and Tupaku pondered over the meaning of it all.

Tupaku had no idea that the world was so large. Day after day the Snakes rode eastward. On the evening of the ninth day, Blanket Chief told Washakie that he would ride ahead and give the word that they were nearing the fort. At their usual rate of travel, they would reach it by noon next day. Tupaku wondered what the soldiers' tepees would be like. Would they be made of logs like at Fort Bridger? He would rather die than sleep shut up in a box like that.

The next morning, Washakie changed the order of the march. As the column cautiously approached the fort, the great chief of the Shoshones was in the lead. He was followed by Tupaku and other tribal dignitaries. The young Indian liked the arrangement, for as second in line he had an excellent view of Fort Laramie–the most amazing sight of his life. A part of it was surrounded by a high wall, but the enclosure must not have been large enough because several new adobe buildings had been constructed outside. Each side of the structures and along the river, there was an impressive array of tepees. Tupaku was awed by their countless number, for he had not realized that the Shoshones' enemies were so numerous.

Soldiers and Indians stood watching the approaching column. When Blanket Chief rode forth to welcome the Snakes, some of the women in the encampment to the right of the fort began to wail like timber wolves. Bridger explained that they were "carryin' on" because some of warriors had been killed by the Shoshones during a recent battle.

Suddenly from among the Sioux ranks, a lone warrior, armed with a bow and arrow, jumped on his horse and galloped forth. Washakie stopped and waited, gun in hand. The Snakes shouted defiantly when they saw that the Sioux was flourishing his weapon. Everyone watched breathlessly to see what the chief would do. Another rider, from the direction of the fort, came dashing out to overtake the reckless brave.

Then Tupaku sprang to action. His only thought as he rode forth was that he must divert the enemy so that he would not strike the chief. Instead of shooting at Washakie as the Sioux obviously intended, he aimed at Tupaku, who dropped to the side of his horse when the arrow whizzed overhead. The young Sioux was immediately disarmed by the man from the fort and forced to return to his people, who jeered him for the fiasco.

The Snakes were delighted by Tupaku's unrehearsed move. Shouts arose from their ranks, and they stood their ground until he had returned to his position in the line. Then, more majestically than ever, they resumed their trip toward the fort. There they were greeted by commissioners and soldiers. After the handshaking was over, Broken Hand Fitzpatrick smoked the pipe with the Shoshone chief and his sub-chiefs. Then he directed them to set up their tepees in the places assigned to them, next to the Dragoons.

Ten thousand Indians with a proportionate number of horses presented unforeseen difficulties. It was late in the season and grass was scarce, especially in the over-grazed radius of the fort. Forage for the horses made it necessary to change the location of the Great Treaty Council before it convened. The site selected was on the fertile bottom lands farther down the Platte, at the mouth of Horse Creek. When runners spread word that plans had been changed, the women stoically packed their belongings and moved down the trail.

The procession, the grandest and most unusual ever to take place on the Great Plains, was led by two companies of troops, followed by the commissioners and other dignitaries in special carriages. Then came the Indians, literally thousands of them, ushered to their new location by fewer than 300 soldiers.

As a precautionary measure, the Dragoons were ordered to stay between the Shoshones and their enemies. A conglomeration of dogs of questionable breed fell in line, some dragging small travois behind them. This interested Tupaku, who had never seen dog-drawn travois. It was hard for him to believe that the beasts of burden would wind up in a pot.

When the caravan reached its destination, the various tribes were assigned to their locations; and villages sprang up as if by magic. After their tepees were in order, the Platte River Indian women turned their energies toward making a shelter for the council chamber. Chattering and laughing all the while, they busied themselves although it was the white man's Medicine Day, a day of rest. They made the structure of tanned buffalo hides, lodgepoles and willows.

In the late afternoon when the Sioux entertained with a dog feast, all animosity between the tribes seemed to be forgotten. Tupaku, quiet as a shadow beside his chief, watched two women loop a rawhide rope around the neck of an unfortunate dog. With one at each end, they gave a quick yank, and the head rolled from the body. After that, they threw the dog, hide and all, into a steaming kettle. The mongrels sensed their danger. After several had met their death, the survivors were more difficult to catch. Tupaku secretly rejoiced whenever one made its escape. In deference to their Shoshone guests, who spurned dog flesh, the Sioux also served dried elk meat.

Early the next morning, the American flag was unfurled and a cannon was fired to announce the official opening of the Great Treaty Council. Indians began swarming in from all directions, their warbonneted chiefs in the lead. Tupaku, at Washakie's heels, was proudly arrayed as Little Chief. From the tip of his warbonnet to the end of his moccasined toes, he was elegant. Too bad Nanagi could not have seen him in all his splendor! The chiefs were followed by the blanketed braves. To the rear came women and children. It was a colorful exhibition, with all dressed in ceremonial clothing.

The program began when a white chief asked that the redstone calumet be passed to all of those whose hearts were free from deceit. The long stem of the peace pipe was decorated, while the bowl was filled with kinnikinnick and white man's tobacco. To show their good faith, the commissioners puffed a time or two before handing the pipe to the chiefs, who placed their right hands on the bowl, then drew them to their lips to signify their truthfulness. When Tupaku went through the ritual with his elders, no one questioned his right to appear in council. His warbonnet and bear claw necklace were proof of his rating. Besides, he had distinguished himself in the encounter with the Sioux.

By means of sign language, the Indians understood what was being said. The white men made it clear that the Great White Father, whom they represented, wanted peace. He was willing to pay the Indians for the loss of grass and buffalo they suffered because of the emigrants. At the same time he demanded permission to build forts along the trail for their protection. Each speaker made a point of mentioning the fact that the train bringing gifts had been delayed but that it would soon arrive.

In the midst of the council, proceedings were suddenly halted when a Cheyenne woman and her son came forward. All eyes turned toward the woman who led a horse with a half-grown boy on its back. The white chief who had been speaking called for an interpreter to make her wishes known. She had come, so she said, to present her son to Washakie, who sometime previously had killed his father in battle. According to native custom, the chief was obligated to adopt the boy and raise him with the full rights of a son.

Tupaku did not like the appearance of either the boy or the horse. It looked as if the woman might purposely have selected the oldest and most undesirable nag in camp to present to his chief. It in no way resembled the handsome horses he saw the Cheyennes ride when they gave an exhibition of their might while the women were erecting the council lodge.

The white man turned toward the Shoshone chief to see if he had understood the interpreter's sign language. Washakie, stepping forward, took the rawhide rope from the woman's hand and acknowledged his responsibility with a nod. Then he gave the sullen youth a reassuring smile. Turning toward Little Chief, he said, "Take your new brother and see that no harm comes to him. You understand?"

"*Ha*!" Tupaku replied. As he lead the horse away, he had a premonition of impending trouble.

Washakie accepted Pungo Mia (Walking Horse), as the Shoshones named him for his horse which was too old to run; but the chief refused to smoke the pipe with the Cheyennes because of the sneak attack east of South Pass. This presented a problem no one wanted to tackle until the arrival of Black Robe, the priest known to the white man as Father Pierre de Smet. . . . When the priest had a chance to talk with Washakie, he urged him to forgive the Cheyennes.

"Not 'til they return scalps," the chief specified. Father de Smet made his terms clear to White Antelope, a representative of the Cheyennes, who returned to his camp for consultation. A short time later, he stalked back with an invitation to the Shoshones to join his people in a corn feast.

"We'll return scalps then," he promised.

After the feast, the Cheyennes formed a circle, in

the center of which they placed gifts that were dear to them. In the assortment, there were blankets, dress lengths of colored cloth, knives, tobacco and other items. Tupaku's eyes sparkled when he glimpsed an unusual narrow-bladed knife with a picture of the *Trois Tetons* scratched on the blade. Obviously it had belonged to a trapper.

When the scalps were presented to the grief-stricken brothers of the victims, the Shoshones made no move to accept them. They just sat, eyeing the gruesome trophies. The pipe was again offered to Washakie, who, with arms folded, continued to ignore it. "Shoshone will not smoke pipe or accept gifts until Cheyenne swear they not have Scalp Dance!" he stated flatly.

White Antelope was no less astonished than the priest. How could the Shoshones remain obstinate after all the concessions the Cheyenne had already made? The silence was alarming. An unidentified chief, quicker of thought than White Antelope, stepped forward as spokesman for his people. He assured Washakie that there had not been a Scalp Dance. Whereupon the bereaved brothers embraced their enemies, and the Shoshones, after smoking the pipe, accepted the gifts.

Tupaku's heart sank when he saw Kuna (Driftwood), a Shoshone interpreter who managed always to be first in line, claim the knife he had secretly hoped to own. Little Chief already had reason to resent him because the white man seemed to favor him over

Washakie. When the supply train finally arrived with uniforms, swords and other gifts, there stood Kuna again, at the head of the line. The chief showed his disappointment.

Kuna, son of a fur trader, had been educated in the white man's schools in St. Louis; but he had returned to his mother's tribe. The Indians, who were quick to notice that he had gained favor with the commissioners, began calling him Tavenduwits (White Man's Child); and he soon had a following.

In spite of Bridger's pleas, the Big Horn hunting grounds were given to the Crows. The disputed area between the Absaroka and Big Horn mountains, extending to Wind River, was designated as Crow country. Accordingly, it would include the canyon where the wedding of the waters takes place, where Wind River enters and the Big Horn emerges to flow northward to the Yellowstone. For generations the Shoshones and Bannocks had met there "to buffalo." That was before the Sioux pushed the troublesome Crows westward from the Powder River country.

Washakie sat helplessly watching when each enemy chief signed his "X" to the document. As a guest from the Utah Agency, he was not required to sign, nor was he given an opportunity to express his displeasure. The white man had failed him, but he could not say that he was not forewarned by the omen of the hawks. It was the white man, not the Crow who deprived him of his hunting grounds.

13

With a sad face and heavy heart, Big Chief led his people back to the Bridger country the way the bird flies. It was almost as if there were two distinct columns, with approximately half following Washakie, the rest Tavenduwits, midway in the broken line. The Shoshone chief did not return Bridger's greeting when he rode up beside him. Since Washakie was in no mood for talk, Blanket Chief dropped back to ride with Tupaku.

Leaving the natural roadway along the banks of the Platte, the Indians moved across the flats toward the mountain range where Laramie Peak stood out against the skyline. Washakie had maintained a keen interest in the many landmarks pointed out to him on the way to the council, but when Bridger raised his voice to utter his witticism about being "in this here country every since Laramie Peak war a hole in the ground," he appeared not to hear.

The Snakes proceeded westward toward the foothills. After leaving the main trail, they seemed to be moving toward a protrusion. "See that thar bump?" Bridger asked Tupaku, who was the only one interested in his stories. Little Chief nodded.

"That thar's Squaw Mountain. Y'probly won't believe it, but I'll tell you how it come 'bout. A Sioux squaw an' her youngun got overtook in them hills. She couldn't go no father, so's she set down on a rock an' tried to kivver the little un with 'er blanket. Come night the snow kivered 'em both clean over, and twarn't till spring they found 'em. She war froze solid's a rock, an' she ain't thawed out yet. Thar she sets after all these years."

That night the Shoshones made camp on the Sybille, which Bridger said was named for an old trapper he used to know. The next stop was on the Blue Grass, as he called it. After the Indians had made camp in the shade of some large cottonwood trees, Washakie announced that they would stay over a day or so in order to find food for the long journey. The next morning, the women and children were up early berry picking. The birds had eaten most of the currants, but chokecherries and bullberries were still to be found in profusion near the water. Some of the women began patiently picking chokecherries. Others held blankets under the bullberry branches, while the fruit, now loosened by frost, was beaten off with sticks.

The braves, following the hills to the northwest, crossed the rock divider separating the Cheyenne and Arapaho hunting grounds. Bridger, who pointed it out, explained its importance. Since there were no other Indians in sight, the Snakes did not care whose hunting grounds they were on as long as there was game. They bagged 19 deer and 12 elk before returning to their encampment.

As soon as the women could butcher the meat, there was a feast, following which men and women alike enjoyed a lively game of Hands. Many of the peace offerings of the Cheyennes were used as prizes which went to the lucky ones who could guess which hand held a small bone that was passed among the players. Meanwhile, the braves added zest by placing bets. Before the night was over, many of the white man's gifts, including medals and scrolls, had changed owners.

Breaking camp the next morning, the Indians began their slow climb to the higher elevation and crossed the wide Laramie Plains. In the Medicine Bow region they stopped long enough to replace bows and lodgepoles. After skirting Elk Mountain they turned south toward the north fork of the Platte. Then slowly they ascended the slope at Bridger's Pass and crossed the Continental Divide.

In the foothills of the Sierra Madre Mountains, and in sight of the well-wooded Bridger Pass, an Arapaho war party overtook them. Judging by the condition of their horses, the warriors had lost no time after finding evidence that the Shoshones had been hunting in their territory. Unwilling to risk a frontal attack, the enemy rushed pell-mell into the rear of the column. Before the Snakes were aware of their intentions, four of the Logs were killed. The women and children fled in panic toward the timber, while the rear guard engaged the enemy in battle until the Yellow Nose warriors could come to the rescue.

Weakened by the split in their forces, the Snakes had difficulty holding their ground. Tavenduwits, who lacked the ability to cope with the situation, was hard pressed until Washakie, alerted by frantic cries from the rear, began giving orders to turn back. Instead of recklessly rushing into battle, he stationed his best marksmen at the edge of the trees before any of the enemy had a chance to follow the women and children.

Using the sturdy trunks as their fortress, the riflemen were able to cover the advance of the Yellow Noses whom Washakie lead to Tavenduwits' relief. Tupaku, wishing to experience the thrill of meeting the Arapahoes in open conflict, was disappointed when Big Chief ordered him to barricade himself behind a tree. The chief not only wanted to save his Good Medicine, but he also hoped to give the women and children the added protection of his presence.

The Arapahoes, though suffering a number of casualties, fought on. Finally, Tupaku spotted their war chief, with his feathers laid back like the ears of an angry mule. Taking careful aim, he fired. The bullet struck with such force that the chief's bonnet was knocked from his head before he fell to the ground. Seeing this, the Arapahoes lost all desire for battle. Fearful of losing more of their number, they stopped fighting. Gathering up their dead and wounded, they departed.

During the heat of the battle, Walking Horse, apparently believing that the Arapahoes, allies of his people, would be victorious, had tried to join them.

Tupaku considered it a crazy thing to do, especially on the old wind-broken nag. He could not help hoping that the Cheyenne boy would succeed so he would see the last of him. Walking Horse had not gone far when his horse was shot from under him. Tupaku was amused to see him come scurrying back to safety.

When the Snakes broke camp and prepared to move the next day, Little Chief looked down upon his new brother, who was the only one without a horse. He disliked him so much that he would have been pleased to see him walk the rest of the way. Since his chief had directed him to take care of him, there was nothing that he could do but reach down and pull him up on his horse.

The Indians moved westward, covering mile after mile of barren sage-covered prairie, where only they would have been able to find water. They passed through Bitter Creek Basin, crossed Green River and descended into Rabbit Hollow. Here they stayed over long enough to allow their pent-up energy to express itself in a Pia Pungo, Big Horse Dance, the dance of the Yellow Noses and Logs. Ordinarily the two societies danced separately, but not so on this occasion, when everyone joined in the day long festivity.

While a large tepee was being erected, the headman rode around telling the people what to do. The sides of the lodge, when completed, were raised like a curtain so that those not dancing might see what was going on. The musicians, drums and singers sat back of the enclosure, with the women and children forming an outer circle. . . . At the conclusion, everyone indulged in a feast of wild carrot stew.

From Rabbit Hollow, the Snakes moved in the direction of Church Buttes, below the mouth of Ham's Fork. Then they proceeded toward Black's Fork and on to their beloved Fort Bridger where they planned to meet the other members of the tribe and establish winter quarters.

The first to greet them was Nanagi, now glowing with health. He shouted a welcome. Then he stopped at the sight of the stranger riding on the horse with Tupaku.

"Who?" he wanted to know.

"Pungo Mia [Walking Horse]. Cheyenne come to live with us. Our brother." Thus Tupaku explained the presence of the youth adopted by his chief at the council.

The first snows of early winter had sifted through the cracks in the log walls at Fort Bridger when the delegation of Snakes returned from the Horse Creek Council. With the Big Horse Dance, the prelude to the fall hunt, out of the way, preparations were soon made for the hunting party that was to move into the Big Horn country. Runners had already located the buffalo.

Winter camp was set up about a mile below the fort. Here several interpreters, trappers and traders were already settled with their mixed-blood families. Those in the Shoshone tribe too old or too infirm to make the trip were to be left in the protection of a number of Logs appointed to guard duty. The Indians would be near enough to the fort that they could flee to its stockade for protection if they were threatened by an attack from any of their enemies.

The morning the hunting party was to leave, Tupaku was so excited that for the first time he did not find Walking Horse objectionable. He was relieved to see that the chief had provided him with a pony, for riding double would have taken all of the pleasure out of the excursion. His new brother had only one admirable trait to his knowledge, his interest in horses. He did not know the meaning of truth, and he stole everything he could get his hands on. The day before the time of departure, Walking Horse appropriated his Green River knife, and Tupaku had to struggle with him to recover it. The Cheyenne was slightly smaller than Little Chief, but he was strong for his size. The other youths in the camp shunned him at every turn. They even avoided Tupaku when the two were together.

The Indians were ready to move northward when Enga Kwitsu (Red Buffalo), one of the Logs, came to Washakie with the startling information that the little white girl was ill. "Bad sick. Face hot and talk crazy!" he reported.

The chief would not have been more stunned by news that the Sioux were on the warpath, in which event he would have known what to do. He stood thinking a moment. Then he strode toward Porivo's tepee, with Tupaku and and Red Buffalo following. They found the old woman smoking at the bedside of the fretfully sleeping girl.

"Enga Kwitsu says Daidŭtsi sick. What you say we do?" It was not like Washakie to humble himself before a woman, but he was forced to in his desperation.

Porivo seemed to weigh the matter. Then she replied, "*Ha'a,* Daidŭtsi has pneumonia, bad sick. Porivo knows that white man wants to take little Indian but does not like Indian to take little white girl. Porivo not let white man have her. *Pohakantŭ* make her well."

The muscles in Washakie's strong face relaxed in a faint sign of gratitude. With Tupaku and Red Buffalo at his side, he stood looking down upon the flushed face of his daughter. Although she had learned to speak the Shoshone language, in her delirium she was jabbering in English, so fast that he could not understand what she was saying.

"Satonzibi maybe die?" In his anxiety, Tupaku unconsciously used his secret name for her. Washakie showed no surprise because he knew whom he meant.

"*Kay shunbana,*" the chief admitted. Then he turned toward Red Buffalo whose knowledge of English was better than his. "What she want?"

"She wants Liza. . . . In Naroyan's camp Black Woman, Porcupine's wife, calls herself Liza. He says she good woman, can do plenty work."

"Get Black Woman!" Washakie ordered. "Pay as

many horses as Porcupine asks. Maybe she can help *Pohakantŭ* and Porivo make Daidŭtsi well." With that, the chief left the tepee to join the waiting hunters. He assigned several Logs to the duty of keeping him informed. Those not needed as guards were to accompany Red Buffalo on his important mission.

When everyone was ready to move, Big Chief paused long enough to lift his eyes and direct a few words to the Supreme Power. "Dam Apŭ, help Enga Kwitsu find Black Woman and make Daidŭtsi well. Guide us on the surround so we will have plenty buffalo for food and lodgeskins to keep our people warm when snowy moons come."

Tupaku did not speak, but in his heart he carried a prayer for Daidŭtsi-Who-Became-a-Prairie-Flower.

The Snakes had no fear of encountering the Crows who, runners had reported, were engaged in a hunt of their own on Crazy Woman Creek. But time was precious. They must make their kill while the enemy was elsewhere in order to prevent the hunting grounds from turning into a battlefield. The Shoshones had come to buffalo, not to lift scalps.

A'a Kopŭp (Broken Horn) cautioned the young hunters to follow his instructions because a false move might have serious consequences. After being informed that a large herd was coming to the river, the Indians took up positions in the ravines and behind the willows so that the unsuspecting creatures would not see them as they neared the water. No one was to make a move until Broken Horn blew his whistle, the signal to charge. The wind had already been found favorable.

When a runner slipped into the ravine where Washakie and his headman had taken up positions, Tupaku listened carefully to his report. The buffalo were coming steadily forward, a line as far as the eye could see. Few of the Indians had guns. Even those who had been armed by Bridger preferred the bow and arrow so that they could more easily identify their kill.

"Signal from top of hill when they near water and bunch up," Broken Horn instructed the Log who rushed back to his post. Little Chief, looking at the Cheyenne, wondered how he could be so calm. He was glad that the day before the two of them had branded their arrows—his with a miniature arrowhead and the Cheyenne's with a crudely drawn walking horse. They would have no difficulty identifying their kill if they were among the fortunate.

When Tupaku had almost given up hope, the Log signaled Broken Horn, who sounded a loud blast with his whistle and galloped forth from his hiding place. The whole country suddenly sprang to life with Indians, whooping, frenzied huntsmen, bent on the single purpose of annihilating the herd. Before the surprised animals were aware of their danger, they were completely surrounded. Some tried desperately to break through the encirclement of galloping horses and shouting Indians, but their efforts were futile.

Others stood, bewildered, only to be slaughtered. The noise, the dust, the animal smell would linger in Tupaku's memory.

He saw a shaggy bull lower his head and make for him. Whirling his horse, he escaped the plunge of his horns. Then he shot an arrow back of his left front leg. He feared that it had not sunk deep enough to prove fatal, for the bull was still on the fight. Before he could charge a second time, he dropped to the ground. Little Chief, pausing to investigate, found that the bull was dead. The deeply embedded arrow had apparently reached his heart.

In the feverish pitch of excitement, Tupaku rode on. There would be time enough to claim his kill after the surround was over. He shot an old cow next. But he would not claim her because she was not worth mentioning in council, not after his fine kill! When he returned to it, there stood Walking Horse, boasting to Washakie that he had made the kill.

Tupaku, jumping from his horse, rushed over to inspect the arrow with which the animal was felled. Though he knew from the feather that it was his, it had a crudely drawn walking horse on the shaft. He was baffled, for he was sure that he alone had made the kill. How had it happened? Could Walking Horse have pulled out his arrow and inserted one of his own? This would have been impossible, for it was so deeply embedded that it could not be extracted without butchering the animal.

There was only one explanation. While the two were

branding their arrows, the Cheyenne had put his mark on one belonging to Tupaku, who had not noticed. Walking Horse, after finding that the shaft sticking from the side of the still bore his brand, had taken advantage of the situation and had claimed the honor—one he could boast of the rest of his life.

The Bannock wanted to shout, "Liar." But how could he prove that the Cheyenne had not made the kill? Too infuriated to trust himself to speak, he jumped on his horse and galloped toward camp. He had tolerated Walking Horse's lies and thievery, but this was more than he could abide

---

Meanwhile, trappers, traders, Indians and half-bloods sat around at Fort Bridger and hoped for news regarding the daughter of the chief. Mariana, the Mexican wife of Louis Vasquez, Blanket Chief's partner, had urged Porivo to bring the patient to her living quarters. There the child slept in a conventional bed the first time since her capture.

"Milk ole Red reglar so's the youngun kin have all the milk she kin hold," Bridger instructed Rutta before leaving with his traps. He had bought a Jersey cow from an emigrant so that Washakie's daughter might have fresh milk daily.

The *pohakantŭ* assigned to the task of doctoring her spent his full time at her bedside, where he prepared potions and chanted incessantly to the annoyance of

Mariana, who had little faith in him. Although the Indians gave him the credit when the fever broke and the child passed through the crisis, Mariana insisted that her recovery was due to the loving care of Rutta and Porivo.

Daidŭtsi was convalescing when a runner came with the glad news that Red Buffalo was returning with Black Woman. The girl impulsively threw her arms around Porivo's neck and kissed her repeatedly. The old woman asked several questions in her broken English, which was sometimes so confused that it was hard to understand. Would Tuwaipŭ (Black Woman) want to take Daidŭtsi away? Would she try to take the daughter of Washakie? She asked questions so rapidly that it was hard for the girl to follow, but she got the idea of being taken away.

"*Kay*!" she protested. "Liza and I will live with Shoshones!" How could she explain that Liza had cared for her from the time of her mother's death, soon after she was born. Her spicy gingerbread was better than Indian bread; she was the best cook in all the world. The Shoshone women had been kind to her. She had loved them from the first because they had dark skin and motherly fingers, which reminded her of Liza. Now that her old nurse was coming to her, she was aglow with anticipation.

The next day Black Woman arrived. When the heavy gates to the stockade were opened, she and Red Buffalo rode into the snow-covered courtyard. She made a strange picture to the unbelieving eyes of the girl, who had never seen her on horseback. She appeared to be just another Indian woman, wrapped in her blanket.

Daidŭtsi watched impatiently from the window while she dismounted and Red Buffalo led her toward Mariana's quarters, which were always the center of activity. When the door opened and the two captives faced each other, no words could have expressed their joy. Porivo, Mariana and Rutta stood silently looking on when Black woman's blanket enveloped the child, and she kissed and cried over her.

"Yo all look like little Injun!" Black Woman declared as she held her at arm's length so that she could have a good look at her. "Yo done growed like a weed, an' yo haiah and skin done changed collah. I would not know you 'ceptin' foh you eyes an' yo voice. What they done t'you?"

"I am Daidŭtsi, daughter of Washakie," the girl replied with a twinkle in her eyes. Black Woman's laughter was so contagious that the other women joined in. Suddenly, the child was reminded of their presence.

"Liza, these are Poriva, Rutta and Mariana, my friends—no, my people!" she exclaimed warmly. "Porivo and medicine man make me look like little Indian so white man will not take me."

Although the buffalo hunt had proved rewarding

for the Indians, Tupaku returned to Fort Bridger with bitterness in his heart. He would never feel anything but hatred for Walking Horse, who had cheated him out of the glory of his first kill. If only he had not promised Washakie that he would protect him! He wished that the Snakes had not killed the boy's father in the first place. Then the woman would not have had an excuse to inflict her son on the tribe. No doubt she wanted to get rid of him. There was no question but that he was making every effort to cause all of the trouble he could. Tupaku recalled that he had not wanted to go to the Horse Creek Council in the first place, that he feared a trick. His fears were confirmed when the white man gave the Shoshone hunting grounds to the Crows. Now the Cheyenne was a persistent reminder of the unhappy event.

Once at the fort, Tupaku lost no time hunting for Daidŭtsi, whom he found in Mariana's spicy smelling kitchen. He did not recognize her at first glance. He thought that a black woman was braiding an Indian child's hair.

"*Ahai'i*!" she greeted him. Seeing the puzzled look on his face, she asked, "You don't know me?"

"Daidŭtsi!" he exclaimed. Then he recalled the time he saw her picking wild fruit with Mŭatsi. "Chokecherries finally turn you brown! You are little Indian now!" He was glad, for she no longer looked cold like the snow that covered Squaw Mountain.

14

The Snakes said farewell to their friends at Fort Bridger as soon as the first indication came that the snowy moons were on the wane. Washakie was anxious to return to the Wind River country, where wild game was abundant. When a break in the weather occurred, he guided his people northward to the confluence of Little Wind River with the Popo Agie, one of his favorite campsites.

To Tupaku it was like returning to his homeland, for he, too, loved the rivers and the rugged mountains towering above the valley. When the Indians were settled, he would organize the young braves for a horse hunt along the Sweetwater. They recognized him still as their leader, but he had lost some of his popularity because of his association with the young Cheyenne.

Tupaku had not seen the black stallion in almost a year, but he had not forgotten him. With a pang of sadness, he often speculated upon the whereabouts of the splendid animal. He was sure that the Crows must have captured him by this time. As fond as they were of horses, they would not be apt to let one so fine slip through their hands. Perhaps some day he might see him on the battlefield. There was no question about recognizing him.

Washakie, who favored the horse hunting plan, insisted that Kill Bear go along. No one seemed to mind, for he was such a good horseman. Tupaku was pleased because he had seen little of him since the Cheyenne joined the tribe.

"What about Black Horse?" Kill Bear asked.

"*Kay shunbana*! Crow probably have 'im."

"You say he has blaze face and white hind feet?"

"*Ha'a*!"

"Crow not have him. I saw him after we come back from Bridger."

Tupaku let out a whoop that brought the young braves running.

"Black Horse!" he shouted. "We thought Crow had 'im, but Wŭda Pekanŭ has seen 'im. He not with Crow! . . . But how we catch 'im?" he asked Kill Bear. "Drive 'im into Sweetwater?"

"*Kay*! I told you before, he is too smart. He will not let you get close. He is wildest horse in country. Shoshone and Crow try to catch him, but no use."

Little Chief could talk of nothing else the entire way to Split Rock, where his attention was diverted by the familiar landmark. Although he recalled every detail of his vision, he did not mention it to the young braves. He did not want to discredit Washakie, who continued to have faith in the white man. Before returning to his blanket, he asked Kill Bear once again how he would go about catching Black Horse.

The Log was thoughtful a moment. Then he said, "It is plenty dangerous, but only way I see to get 'im is to ride among the herd bareback. Lay low on horse so black stallion not see you. Have rope in hard knot 'round pony's neck, with slip loop on other end. Get noose 'round stallion's neck. Keep tight 'til he chokes down." Tupaku, following each word of advice, was undaunted when Kill Bear added, "More than one try, but no one catch phantom horse."

Phantom, was he! So the Indians had come to accept him as that! He was as real as the rocks, the ground, the sky! When the hunters rode over the hill northeast of Split Rock, they looked down upon a clearing just in time to see a sorrel stallion go in among a herd of horses and cut out a mare. Little Chief watched spellbound when he saw the horse of his dreams come from beyond the trees to contest the daring deed. With his ears laid back and his teeth bared, he charged.

The sorrel, alert to his approach, was ready for the challenge. As the two came together, sniffing and squealing, the fight was on. The mares raised their heads from their grazing and looked curiously toward the drama taking place before them. Several younger horses, with heads and tails erect, raced about in excitement. Rearing, striking and biting each other savagely, the well-matched stallions waged their battle.

Tupaku, without a word to anyone, tied a firm knot in the rope around Strong Wind's neck and made a slip loop at the end, just as Kill Bear had instructed. Bareback, he flattened himself on his pony and made his way toward the fighting horses. It was a reckless thing to do, and yet they were so intent upon their fierce struggle that they were unaware of his presence. If only he could get his rope around the black's neck, his ownership could not be contested! Both horses were squealing loudly when he reached them. At that moment, the sorrel took a vicious hold on the black's withers, causing him to jerk his nose into the air. In a flash, Little Chief slipped the rope over his head.

By now the other braves had arrived. They made every effort to catch the sorrel, but he whirled, and with a last murderous kick, thundered away. The young Shoshones followed. Tupaku, with Black Horse on the end of his rope, was joyful when he wheeled his pony to take up the slack. Strong Wind, unprepared for the jolt, was almost jerked off his feet. Tupaku fully expected the black to attack with his vise-like jaws, but he was too involved with the rope, which he fought with vengeance. He braced his four feet and pulled back.

The rope had slipped to the small part of his neck, just back of his ears; and it was pulling over the top of his head. His nostrils, dilated, showed the red membrane within, while he wheezed and fought for breath. He then lunged forward, loosening the rope. Little Chief quickly urged Strong Wind ahead to tighten it again. After drawing back and plunging forward repeatedly, Black Horse finally settled down for a last desperate stand, his haunches nearly touching the ground. His eyes were set and glassy, and he quivered in every muscle while he labored for breath.

When the rope tightened and he finally choked

himself down, he fell heavily on his side, his body lathered with sweat. Tupaku was so frightened when he was no longer able to hear him breathe that he gave him slack. As soon as the horse had regained his wind, he was again on his feet and trembling from the ordeal. Much of the fight had been taken out of him. Tupaku began working him toward a lone sapling.

Kill Bear, who had been watching, anticipated what he had in mind and was ready. He tossed his rope over the black's head and dallied the end around the tree several times. Then he tied it as high as he could reach so that Black Horse would not pull his head down. Little Chief turned Strong Wind around and took the rope from his neck.

"When the sun is high tomorrow, Black Horse will be broke to lead. Then you can ride 'im." Kill Bear spoke with satisfaction, while he assured himself that the rope was securely tied.

"Black Horse, you are worth all the buffalo bulls in the Big Horns," Tupaku spoke gently. "I'm your friend. Not hurt you." He kept talking softly as he came nearer. Then he turned away. Could he believe it? The horse took a step in his direction. Tupaku stood still, his heart hammering.

When Black Horse took another step, Little Chief tingled with excitement. What was it Kill Bear had said? "Wilder the horse, easier to tame 'im unless he's outlaw." Black Horse was no outlaw! The greatest thrill of Tupaku's life came when he felt the horse nuzzle him. It was all he could do to keep from shouting, he was so excited. Very slowly, he began rubbing Black Horse's glossy neck.

"Never touch horse's nose or ears," was another thing Kill Bear had told him. Before Black Horse realized what he was up to, Little Chief had slipped the nose band of a hackamore over his muzzle and had fitted the headstall back of his ears. Kill Bear, untying the rope from the tree, snubbed the horse to his saddle horn. Tupaku then mounted Strong Wind, and together the two Indians took the stallion to the stream. Since he had been without water so long, they allowed him to drink only a little before pulling him away. He must not be permitted to founder.

"Wŭda Pekanŭ, I ride him now?" Tupaku asked excitedly.

"Slip from Strong Wind's back on 'im and see." When he did, Black Horse made no effort to unseat him. With a horse on each side, he had little freedom of action. Since the two Indians did not allow him to break into a run, the chances of his bucking were slight. On and on they went, three horses abreast. Black Horse was nervous at first and twitched under the feel of the rider, but the farther they went, the more accustomed he became to his weight and the soothing sound of his voice.

When Tupaku rode into camp on Black Horse, the Indians turned out to admire his splendid catch. No one could ever again say that Black Horse was a phantom!

15

Except for the large-scale encounter with the Crows at the time Tupaku came to live with the Shoshones, both tribes seemed to avoid a showdown to settle their claims to the Big Horn hunting grounds. It had now been more than a year since the white man specified on his paper that the land was Absaroka or Crow territory. Still the Shoshones had no thought of relinquishing their prior rights.

Numerous scares and infrequent skirmishes had thrown their camp into temporary turmoil. The Crows, satisfying their craving for horses, had at various times run off a number of head. Washakie's warriors, going in pursuit, would attempt to recover their loss. If they were unsuccessful, they would usually attack an isolated camp of Utes to the southwest. Compensated for their loss, they would return to their campfires to boast of their accomplishments. It would not be long until the vengeful Utes would make their appearance. This had become the pattern of their warfare.

Little Chief still hoped that the time would come to teach both tribes a thing or two. He was sure that it had, when a band of Crow warriors appeared one day early in the summer. Sending a spokesman ahead, they rode fearlessly toward the Shoshone camp, then in the Big Horn Valley. Washakie's warriors jumped on their horses and rushed to his aid. Women and children, in a state of panic, scattered to the cutbanks along the river where they hid. They wailed so loudly that had the Crows been conducting a raid they would have had little difficulty locating them.

Kak Yorandegin, Flying Crow, who was the son of a Shoshone mother and a Crow father, was the go-between; for he could speak both languages. He came forward to explain the unprecedented visit. "Big Robber want to meet Washakie for medicine talk," he said while the warriors of both tribes stood measuring their opponents.

"What he want to talk about?" Washakie demanded impatiently.

"*Kay shunbana,*" Flying Crow responded.

"Tell him Crow are enemy of my people. We not welcome 'em. This our land, and we want 'em out!"

Several of the Shoshones shouted their defiance. Why did Big Chief not order an attack? Tupaku was convinced that the enemy could easily be defeated.

When Flying Crow returned from delivering the message, he said, "Big Robber still want medicine talk."

There was an ominous hush when both chieftains rode forward with their interpreter. Washakie, with his peace pipe and his gun was ready for any eventuality. It was his first direct encounter with Big Robber, the respected leader of the Crows. The two eyed each other coldly.

"What you want?" the chief showed his impatience.

"We come to tell you never again come into Big Horn hunting grounds. Great White Father say it belongs to Crow. We say so, too. Stay away!"

"It belongs to Shoshone!" Big Chief was furious, but still he did not make a move.

Big Robber began taunting him. "Chief of Green River Snakes coward and old woman! He not fight even for hunting ground!" As if the whole purpose of the medicine talk had been to insult Washakie, the Crow chief turned and raced back to his warriors.

"Waugh!" Washakie roared in rage. Then shouting orders, he and his warriors charged the enemy who, to Little Chief's disappointment, did not put up a fight. The anticipated engagement turned into a horse race with the Crows so far in the lead that the Snakes succeeded only in driving them out of the country.

The episode did not add to Washakies' popularity because the Shoshones felt that he had fumbled a good chance to conquer the enemy. Subsequently, some of his warriors went to the side of Walkara, the Ute war chief who had begun to harass the settlers. Elk Tooth, whom Tupaku had not forgiven for terrifying Daidŭtsi, was among the number.

Big Chief was saddened by their defection because Walkara was also the enemy of his people. The thought seemed to burden him more than the insult Big Robber had hurled at him. Tupaku, sitting beside him at his campfire, could sense his mood. When he spoke, he did not mention either the Crows or the Utes.

"Walking Horse bother lately?" he wanted to know.

Little Chief shook his head. There was no need of burdening him with an account of petty annoyances. He would probably do nothing about them anyway.

"Walking Horse talk crooked and take credit for what he not do."

Tupaku's heart jumped. Could the chief have known about the buffalo bull the Cheyenne claimed to have killed? He had an uncanny way of finding out what was happening.

"We have much trouble in this life," Washakie told him. "Dam Apŭ watches to see how we do. It make us *tsant* or *kesandŭ* (good or bad). We must always do what we think's right. You promise to take care of your Cheyenne brother no matter how bad he treat you. Washakie, too, promise not to fight white man. No matter what happen, we keep our promise!"

Throughout the stormy summer, the Utes rent their vengeance on the settlers in the Salt Lake area. At the same time, they showed their animosity toward the Eastern Shoshones who would not join in their venture. The two tribes were more antagonistic than they had been the year before. The Ute agent had felt that it was necessary to buy a carriage to convey Walkara and other tribal leaders safely through Shoshone country on their way to the Great Treaty Council. He preferred to remain on his home grounds where he could raid the Shoshones, who were weakened by Washakie's absence.

Unable to interest the Utes in the proposed trip to the Great Treaty Council, the agent had abandoned his idea and had given each a suit of clothing and other gifts. Then he arranged a peace council between the Utes and the Shoshones who were left in the Green River region. It resulted in an agreement on only one issue—the settlers. Both tribes had a chance to air their grievances against the white man for driving them from their fertile valleys and making use of their soil and their timber. Their resentment against the encroachers brought temporary harmony between the two tribes. It might have lasted had it not been for the capricious Walkara, under whose leadership the raids against the Shoshones gained tempo.

In one of the major Ute forays during the summer following the Great Treaty Council, ten Snakes were killed. Again there was an exodus of warriors. Several angrily packed up and went to Tavenduwits' camp. The next day four left for Bannock Creek to align themselves with Ka-tat-o's band of Shoshones. Three more left the following day to join Chief Taghee's Bannocks. Wŭda Mo (Bear Claw), the Shoshone war chief, threatened to quit the tribe if he were not allowed to take action against the Utes; but Washakie remained firm.

Tupaku was alarmed because the Snakes, who

were constantly threatened by their enemies, could not afford to continue to lose their warriors. Washakie finally called a council to discuss the matter.

"We go ten sleep to Fort Laramie to have medicine talk with white brothers," he told his elders. "We should do as much for Ute, our red brothers. Walkara is *kesandŭ*! Ouray, Ute chief, friend to Shoshone. He try, like Washakie, to have peace.

"Can Washakie help if Tavenduwits attack emigrant? Is he to blame for what Pocatello does? Ouray not control Walkara any more than Washakie control Tavenduwits and Pocatello. Great White Father has office at Fort Laramie for Platte River Indians. He also has office in Salt Lake where White Chief Brigham talk medicine with Shoshone, Bannock and Ute. Washakie will go to Salt Lake and ask White Chief to make Walkara behave."

Tupaku was bitterly disappointed for the Great Treaty Council was still fresh in his memory. Had Washakie forgotten the treatment he had received from the white man? He could not understand. Big Chief was no coward. Had he not proved on numerous occasions that he was fearless? Right or wrong, Tupaku craved action. Why could the chief not see that his peace policy was doing as much to wreck the tribe, as the white man had done by splitting the Shoshones into factions?

Washakie concluded his remarks by stating, "Big Chief Brigham help." Then he began to issue orders to those whom he named to make the trip. At sunrise they would leave for the white camp. The trek to Salt Lake, with its promise of the inevitable white man's gifts, was preferable to forced idleness at Wind River.

Tupaku would not forget the month he and his people spent camped on the outskirts of Salt Lake City while the white chief tried to get the unpredictable Walkara to come to the council. The Snakes did not mind the delay, which gave them ample time to make a first-hand inspection of the white man's camp. There they found much to marvel over while they enjoyed the beef given to them by the Saints. They roamed the streets, and they investigated everything they saw, even to some of the white man's "big boxes," which they did not hesitate to enter, to the consternation of the occupants.

Wire, which Tupaku saw for the first time, enclosed the gardens behind the houses; and irrigation ditches, carrying water, formed a network of rivulets. It was his first chance to observe the Mormon's scientific method of farming. Amazed by its magnitude, he remarked to his chief, "White man plenty smart to make water go where they want it." But he was not as favorably impressed by the plow. "Why does he turn grass upside down?" he asked.

"Taivo does not hunt buffalo for food," his chief explained. "He must raise what he eats from ground. Indian will have to when buffalo all gone."

When Washakie and Walkara, followed by their retinue of dignitaries, took their places each side of Brigham Young, Tupaku noticed that they exchanged hostile glances. They had come for a medicine talk, but neither indicated any friendliness toward the other. Little Chief was bored by it all. Why did Washakie not use his tomahawk to teach the undersized, dark-skinned Walkara a lesson the way he did Scarface? One blow would make the Ute chief behave.

The Mormon leader looked uncomfortable with his wide, white collar riding above his dark brown worsted suit, though he made a striking contrast to the buckskin clad chieftains. His smooth-shaven upper lip exposed a broad mouth, drooping slightly at the corners; and his fluffy sideburns terminated in a flowing beard. Tupaku wondered how he would look if there were no hair on his face.

Everyone waited for the governor to make the first move. After thoughtfully looking from one bonneted chief to the other, he called for interpreters. Then he began by asking the chiefs if they wanted peace, to which they nodded.

"Walkara, take a vote of your followers and find out if they do, too." When the Ute war chief took the vote, one hand went up, then the rest.

"Washakie will now do the same."

After Big Chief called for a show of hands, all went

up immediately but Tupaku's, for he still hoped there might be a showdown with the Utes. One look from Washakie was all that was needed for him, too, to conform. By the time the pipe had been replenished several times, the Utes were in such an agreeable mood that they voted unanimously to allow the white man to settle on their lands.

"Let me beg of you—never fight again!" The Mormon leader pleaded during a sermon on brotherly love. "Live peacefully with one another and travel freely in each other's country. The Mormons will trade with both tribes as long as you are friendly."

Washakie invited the Saints to Green River, but he did not extend the invitation to include his beloved Warm Valley at Wind River, which was still free of the white man. When the Shoshone chief agreed to settle his claim against the Utes for nine horses to be delivered at Fort Bridger at an unspecified date, the Ute chief seemed contrite. "Walkara is crazy to fight Washakie, white man's friend. He now be good."

For a time it looked as if Walkara might be true to his promise, at least to the Shoshones, for he was too busy trying to eliminate the white man to bother with them. In his endeavor, he had the support of several Shoshone bands, but Big Chief spurned his overtures.

Frustrated by being unable to uproot the settlers, Walkara forgot the nine horses he had promised the

Snakes and gradually returned to harassing them. Before he could do more than steal a number of their horses and and make accusations against them for similar offenses, he died of natural causes, thus bringing an end to the Walkara or Walker War.

The bellicose chief was buried in the Utah mountains. Thrown into the pit with his body were the remains of two of his wives who had been killed so that they could accompany him to the spirit world, along with ten horses, ten blankets and ten buckskins. Two live prisoners, a Southern Paiute boy and girl, were placed in the rocked-up cairn on top and left to perish.

The war chief who succeeded Walkara was more friendly toward the Shoshones, who could now turn their attention in the direction of the Crows. Washakie would show then that the Big Horn hunting grounds belonged to his people regardless of the white man's paper! He would chase them out, just as they had been chased from the Popo Agie, the headwaters of the Big Horn River, many years before.

16

The great Shoshone chief, hunched in his blanket, sat staring into the flickering fire. He would take a well-timed draw on his pipe just often enough to keep it going. Otherwise, he was motionless, his hands idle, his gaze fixed. He was oblivious to everything around him as he seemed to probe the depths of the flames for a solution to his problem. What had become of his allies? It had now been many days since runners had been dispatched to the scattered bands to ask their help in a battle that was to end all battles with the Crows and drive them forever from the Big Horn hunting grounds. Not one chieftain had responded.

A withered old woman, who had spent the night periodically darting into the lodge with her hands full of sticks, tripped over a sleeping dog in the shadows. Losing her balance she almost fell into the flames. The dog, letting out a yelp, skulked out of her way when she dropped her load with such force that glowing embers flew in all directions. Tupaku shifted his position, but his chief seemed unaware that anything had happened. He was sick in body and spirit.

One of the scouts had brought word only the day before that the Crow in great numbers were preparing to move southward, and they would soon be pitching their tepees in the contested region. This meant that the long anticipated showdown was near at hand. Where there should have been jubilation, there was despair. The warriors were not brandishing their weapons and offering supplications to Dam Apŭ. The valley was not reverberating with war cries. Instead, there was silence, not broken by a single tom-tom.

The morning fires had already been kindled when a dog at the edge of the camp sounded a warning. Another picked up the alarm in a higher key. One here, one there joined in until there was a discordant clamor, an unmistakable sign that someone was entering the village. Evidently it was not an enemy, for the camp was well guarded.

The rider did not stop until he had reached Washakie's lodge, where he swung from his horse and entered unceremoniously. He had come with the glad tidings that Taghee, chief of the Bannocks, was on the way with 100 of his best warriors. He, too, had a grievance, for the Crows had killed a number of his people on the Bannock Trail when they were on their way to the Yellowstone country. Now he wanted to help push them out so that the Bannocks and Shoshones could hunt in peace. Taghee was coming! The news seemed to bring the chief to life. He rushed from his lodge to start giving orders.

By noon, the village was in a turmoil. Mirrors, signal fires, criers and gossips had broadcast the news of the approaching Bannocks until there was not a single person in the encampment who was not informed. Had

Taghee's entire tribe been coming there could not have been more excitement.

The unsuspecting Crows, snuggled in their warm blankets at their temporary camp on Owl Creek, did not dream that by the time the sun came over the hills they would be completely surrounded by the Yellow Nose warriors of Washakie's band. As darkness was being routed from the valley, the Shoshones and Bannocks were taking their positions preparatory for the attack. After riding as near as possible, the young braves dismounted and crept cautiously toward the camp. Meanwhile, Washakie and the more seasoned warriors, poised for action, remained with the Logs who were holding the horses in reserve beyond a clump of willows to the south.

Bear Claw, in command, stationed Taghee and his braves to the southwest with instructions to block the Black Mountain Trail. A more decisive battle could be waged in the open country than in the mountains, where sniping could go on indefinitely. No attempt would be made to stampede the enemy's horses, grazing a short distance from their camp. This was not a horse stealing expedition but the most important battle the Shoshones had ever been forced to fight. It was more than a battle for territory; it was a struggle for existence.

The Yellow Noses, their bodies splotched with war

paint, were scarcely discernable as they hugged the earth, nearer and nearer the enemy camp. Every stone or shrub was a fortress and every depression a rifle pit. Little Chief, flat on his stomach, lay watching an old woman, who was the first to emerge from the tepees. As others followed, he realized that their keen eyes might detect the Snakes, waiting to strike when the men appeared. Hungry dogs, unable to catch their scent in the morning stillness, scampered at the heels of sleepy-eyed children who came next. Then there appeared a wizened old buck, who looked vaguely toward the women who had disturbed his slumber, before heading for the brush.

Little Chief's shot, aimed at his midriff, was the signal for the battle to begin. At the sound of the sharp report of the rifle and at the sight of the yellow-white puffs of smoke, dogs began barking frantically. Naked warriors, startled from their blankets, rushed out to see the cause of the confusion. Some were shot down; others dived back into their tepees to fire from beneath. The camp was chaotic. The sound of shrieking, screaming women and children was met by the Shoshone war cry which seemed to spring from the ground. Above the tumult, the warriors could be heard shouting at each other. The air reeked with the smell of gun smoke.

If only the Crows could be subdued before they reached their horses! Bear Claw shouted orders, but his voice was lost in the din. The guards and night herders, hearing the sounds, rushed to the aid of the hard-pressed camp. Driving a wedge into the encirclement, they made it possible for the warriors to reach their horses. Several of the ponies reared and dropped from under them, but most of the Crow warriors managed to break through and dash madly from camp. They were obviously trying to draw the Shoshone fire away from their women and children.

Several of the relief were killed in the process. When Walking Horse leaned over to scalp one of them, Little Chief shouted, "*Kay*!" He was brave! Follow them!" He pointed toward the fleeing Crows. Jumping astride a pony that had belonged to one of the victims, he also went in pursuit. Washakie and his men, coming at top speed, were unable to stop the Crows, who were rushing toward Black Mountain. Once on the trail, they would gain access to the rugged country beyond.

The Crow pony Tupaku appropriated could not compare with his Black Horse, which one of the Logs brought him. The time lost in changing mounts was soon made up, and he was in the thick of the battle by the time the enemy reached the base of the mountain.

In spite of all that Taghee's Bannocks could do, the Crows broke through their lines and forced open the main trail as they poured through to the rugged terrain beyond. Their rear guard, suffering several casualties, blocked the way until their warriors had reached strategic positions. Then they disappeared up the trail. It would have been suicidal to follow because they were well armed. Little Chief could not help admiring their daring.

The Shoshone and Bannock leaders held a parley to plan their next move. The encirclement had been effective long enough to inflict an undetermined number of casualties, but not one had counted on the bravery of the herders and the guards. So far, the enemy had outmaneuvered both Bear Claw and Taghee, the latter in particular by gaining access to the mountain trail. Instead of trying to seal off the entrance, he should have had his warriors line the sides of the trail as the Crows were now doing.

The only solution to the problem was for the Snakes to skirt the mountain and head off the Crows from the opposite side. Washakie, who was familiar with a hazardous, abandoned trail, led the contingent. Taghee, remaining at the base of the mountain, was convinced that the Crows would eventually try to fight their way back to their camp. It was unlikely that they would abandon it along with their women and children.

If Washakie's plan were successful, the enemy would be hemmed in; for the only way the Crows could come down the mountain with their horses was by the trail they had used. The Snakes, who found the going hard, spent the rest of the day tediously working their way to the opposite side, which they reached by nightfall. Without stopping, they quietly wound their way up the mountain, almost to the top, where they decided to tarry until daylight.

Big Chief told Tupaku about a natural fortification halfway down the main trail—one he had used many years before in a battle with the Blackfeet. He was sure that Big Robber was aware of its value and had put it to use. While Tupaku listened to his account, he wrapped himself in his blanket for a short rest. He did not intend to fall asleep, but when he opened his eyes, it was dawn. Big Chief, who was calmly seated at his side, was eating pemmican. He seemed unmoved though it was the second day of battle, and the Snakes were far from victory.

"It's not safe to ride closer," he said to Tupaku. "Go with warriors and stir Crow from hiding. I stay here 'til needed. Do as Bear Claw says."

Before the sun had a chance to take the chill from the mountain air, the Shoshones had fanned out on both sides of the main trail and were creeping down the slope. Midmorning they encountered several Crows, who were searching for roots and berries to satisfy their hunger. After a brief hand-to-hand struggle, the Shoshones wiped them out; but they did not fire a shot for fear it might alert the warriors farther down the trail. Proceeding cautiously, the Yellow Noses were determined to take the fortress at all costs. Tupaku, after crawling out on a precipitous ledge that afforded a view of the inside, could see the enemy holding a council of war. On a rimrock above, a sentry stood watching down the trail. Apparently it had not occurred to him that anyone would come from the top.

Tupaku wormed his way closer and lay waiting

until the most trusted warriors had caught up with him. When all was in readiness, he signaled Bear Claw, who killed the sentry and directed his men to rush the stronghold.

When they jumped into the open fortress, the Indians mingled in a confused mass. The tomahawk and knife were the only weapons they could use in such close quarters. Tupaku, pitted against a powerful warrior, found that he had met his match. They were still struggling fiercely after the rest of the resistance had been wiped out. During the melee, the Crow chief and several of his warriors managed to escape. Spurred on by the realization that the Snakes had scored a temporary victory, Tupaku, with a supreme effort, wrested the knife from his opponent. Before he had a chance to use it, a Yellow Nose finished off the Crow with his war club.

Exhausted, Tupaku felt his legs give way beneath him. He had not realized that he was wounded. . . . Weakened from loss of blood, he was in no condition to go with Bear Claw when he proceeded to attack the Crows farther down the mountainside. After a while the Shoshones were pushed back to the fortress, where they found Washakie anxiously fretting over his son, whose wounds were not serious.

The third day a Crow attack on the fortress was repulsed, and the battle reached a stalemate. The original enthusiasm on both sides was beginning to wane. The Shoshones, who were sure of ultimate victory, could starve the enemy into submission, but they yearned to return to their tepees. As they sat in council in their crude, rock-walled fortress, Bear Claw commented, "Too bad to kill any more Crow. They are brave." He spoke with respect.

"We're no nearer victory than we were first day," Washakie affirmed. He was thoughtful a moment. Then he asked, "Where is Flying Crow [Kak Yorandegin]?" The Indian was migratory, sometimes with one tribe and then with the other. For some reason he had chosen to align himself with the Shoshones in the present conflict.

"Kak Yorandegin!" The name passed from one Indian to another until the scout was located. Washakie, with Tupaku at his side, sat quietly waiting until he appeared. When Little Chief saw Flying Crow, he relinquished his place and motioned for him to be seated.

"Big Robber with Crow?" Washakie asked.

"*Ha'a*!" replied the scout.

"Tell 'im we not want to kill any more of his people. We kill enough. Washakie and Big Robber will have duel to find out who own Big Horn hunting grounds! If Washakie win, Crow must leave and never come back!" It was the biggest gamble of his life.

"Let me—" Bear Claw urged.

"*Kay*. Washakie is chief of Shoshone, Big Robber of Crow. It is for us to settle. . . . Go, Flying Crow!"

Tupaku pondered the matter. Of course Big Robber would agree since he was a much younger man. And yet, if Big Chief had the sacred Medicine Arrow, he could win. But he did not have it. He had decided to leave it in the protective custody of Hanŭbi rather than run the risk of losing it in battle. Had the Gros Ventres not lost their Sacred Pipe to the Assiniboines and the Cheyennes their sacred Medicine Arrows to the Pawnees? Tupaku would be medicine enough!

The two chiefs met on an exposed level so that all might see. Both had witnessed more than one duel between the trappers, but it was an unusual way for Indians to settle a quarrel over territorial rights. Warriors on both sides watched in wonderment.

A Frenchman would have deplored the procedure, as there was neither palaver nor handshaking. On one side, there was stalwart Big Robber, saddened by the losses he had sustained. On the other there was a bitter chieftain who would not concede that the hunting grounds belonged to the Crows. This was his long-anticipated time to right the wrong that had been done to his people at the Great Treaty Council.

Basil, master of ceremonies, asked of Washakie, "You have second?"

"*Kay*! "

"You?" he directed his question to Big Robber. When Flying Crow explained what he meant, he shook his head.

"What weapon you choose?" Basil asked Washakie.

Tupaku was shocked when he held up his Colt revolver. There was a murmur among the warriors of both tribes. They had expected a tomahawk or a lance, not a firearm.

"Washakie will settle the matter with the white man's weapon the way it should have been settled with his paper!"

Basil made his own rules. First, he stood the two chieftains back to back. Then he attempted to work out his communication problem. Flying Crow was the only one who could help in such an emergency.

"Flying Crow, Big Robber understand if I count in Shoshone?"

"*Kay*," was the answer.

"Then I'll just say, 'boom' for each step. After tenth "boom" I'll say, 'fire,' in English. That mean they are to turn and shoot at each other. Make sure Big Robber understand."

Both factions held a brief conference. When they seemed satisfied, Basil stood at attention.

"Ready! . . . Go!"

As he began to count, there was complete silence on the part of the onlookers. Never had they witnessed anything like this!

"Boom! Boom! Boom!" It was like the rhythm of a clock striking the hour.

After the tenth "boom," Basil cried out, "Fire!"

The weapons clicked in unison when the two chiefs whirled to face each other. Washakie, untouched except for a single feather shot from his warbonnet, again cocked the hammer of his revolver, but it was unnecessary. Big Robber was dead.

While the enemy rushed for cover, Bear Claw called out, "One shot and we wipe you out!" But the Crows were leaving in such haste that they did not have time for an interpreter.

A half-blood taunted the Shoshone chief in English as he dashed by. "Damn you, old man!" he screamed. Then he lost himself among the Crow warriors.

Washakie was infuriated, but he would have his revenge!

"Old man!" he stormed. Bending over the lifeless body of Big Robber, he ripped open his buckskin shirt. Making a quick incision on the left side, just above the navel, he reached into the rib cage and tore out the Crow's heart. Holding the blood-dripping object high above his head, he shouted, "Washakie carry heart of younger chief on lance at Scalp Dance!" He would not scalp him; he had been a brave warrior.

"Follow them!" Bear Claw called to Taghee, who went in pursuit of the Crows who were dashing toward a butte five miles away. They were obviously trying to draw the Shoshones away so that the main body of their warriors could reach camp, but Bear Claw was at their heels.

The Crows, on arriving at their base, tried frantically to gather up their women and children, but their tepees and other belongings had to be abandoned to the conquerors. After stripping the camp of all desirable spoils of war, the Shoshone victors returned to their village to celebrate. Among their captives was sunny-faced Ahwaipŭtsi, Little Crow Woman, who would later become one of Washakie's wives.

Taghee, meanwhile, was chasing the first contingent of Crows, who, after reaching the butte, climbed its steep sides and contented themselves by rolling stones down on their enemy. The Bannock chief decided to wait until morning to rout them. As darkness settled, he ordered that fires be built in order to keep watch. At the top of the butte, a shrill voice started singing a death song. The Bannocks bided their time. Instead of being able to return to the Shoshone camp for the Scalp Dance, they had to put up with the weird sound of the continuous singing. When morning came, they would wipe out the Crows.

The next day, they were the ones who were surprised. When they reached the top of the butte, which was thereafter to be known to the Shoshones as Haimbi

(Crowheart Butte), they found that the wily Crows had fled. The only one who remained, the one who had spent the night singing a death song and occasionally rolling stones down upon them, was a woman who had followed her mate to battle. When he was killed, she was glad to sacrifice her life to demonstrate her grief. During the time she was singing, the Crows were lowering their horses and themselves with rawhide ropes over the back of the butte, an unbelievable accomplishment.

The woman screamed for Taghee to kill her, but he put his hand on her head and said, "*Kai*, you are brave!" He took her as a trophy of war.

17

With the Crows effectively driven from the Big Horn hunting grounds and the Utes more friendly than they had ever been, the Green River Snakes could turn their attention to the Platte River Indians. The young warriors were anxious to add to their glory, but more important than that, Bear Claw wanted to keep them in trim to ward off the possibility of an attack. When the war chief passed the pipe, he named the mighty Sioux as the object of his forthcoming expedition. Washakie had already given his approval for his two strapping sons, Tupaku and Walking Horse, to take part. Both had proved their bravery at the recent Battle of Crowheart Butte, as the encounter would be remembered.

They were arrayed in their paint and feathers for the warpath when Daidŭtsi and Tsanapui Pavish (Pretty Weasel) entered Washakie's lodge. At the sight of the ferocious looking young warriors, the white girl stood aghast.

"You not know them? They're Tupaku and Walking Horse!" Pretty Weasel spoke admiringly.

Daidŭtsi looked from one to the other. Then she rushed toward Tupaku and earnestly asked, "Why you fix up like that? You going on warpath?"

"*Ha'a*," he answered.

"Why—why?" The question resounded among the Indians. Why? It was the first time such a question had been put to a warrior. Why did the sun shine? The question could not have been more absurd. No one ventured an answer.

Washakie, returning just in time to hear her, tried to explain. "To prove his bravery."

"He not need to prove it! We know he is bravest in all the tribe. He rides, he hunts and he shoots better than anyone. Why he have to go and get himself killed to prove what we know?" Although her words embarrassed him, Tupaku was nonetheless pleased that she should be so concerned over his welfare.

There was no need of Washakie's trying to convince the white girl of the necessity of warfare. It was too complex. All he could do was to reassure her. "He well trained. He come back."

The next day, Daidŭtsi and Pretty Weasel stood watching the grand parade held before the raiding party set out. The sensitive daughter of the chief still was not reconciled to the idea of Tupaku's needlessly risking his life. She could not appreciate the glory of battle or the pride of a warrior over a fresh scalp, because the horror of the attack on the wagon train had left a deep scar on her memory.

"Look!" Pretty Weasel nudged her. Warbonneted

Bear Claw was followed by Tupaku, the picture of pride, on Black Horse. He was staring straight ahead as if unaware of the two girls watching him. Pretty Weasel had to raise her voice so that she could be heard above the clatter of hooves and the jangle of war paraphernalia. For an instant, Little Chief turned. Looking directly into the upturned eyes of Daidŭtsi, he smiled broadly and lifted his hand in a farewell gesture.

"Tupaku see only you," Pretty Weasel cried. "He never look at me. I'm older and better formed. You are straight little stick!"

Pretty Weasel had developed into early womanhood from the arduous tasks to which she had been trained. Daidŭtsi, on the other hand, was as carefree as she had been her first day in the Shoshone camp. The Indian girl, now aroused, continued to speak spitefully. "You white girl and not understand. You should be proud when he goes to battle, but no, you want 'im to stay in hole like gopher. I want him and will have him!"

"But what about Otter Man?"

"Panzukŭ!" Pretty Weasel hissed in disgust. "He is coward. He spends his time among the pine trees playing his flute when he should be on warpath. He'll never be chief—not even Yellow Nose. I'll not have him!"

After the warriors had circled the camp and had

made sure that everyone could admire their pageantry, they galloped away, singing a war song. When they were out of sight of the camp, they slowed down so that their horses might be fresh for the long journey ahead. The enemy was reportedly five sleeps away. Each day Bear Claw sent out scouts who were familiar with the country to select the campsite for the night and to report on any enemies they might find. The other Logs in the war party kept watch in case of an attack.

Tupaku, who was even more eager than he had been on the surround, thought the scouts would never return on the fourth day. He fondled the precious gun that Blanket Chief had given him and fretted impatiently. The calmness of the Cheyenne maddened him.

Late in the afternoon of the fifth day, a runner came with a report that a small encampment of Sioux had been located in the valley along Poison Spider Creek. By midnight, the warriors had again bedecked themselves for battle and had removed the hobbles from their horses. Haste was necessary because they must reach the enemy camp before daylight in order to take up positions in readiness for the attack. Tupaku and Walking Horse knew that the first to arrive on the scene would have the best chance to steal horses or count coup. For that reason, they begged to go with the 15 Yellow Noses Bear Claw picked for decoys.

"We attack when sun appear," the war chief stated. "Enemy follow to ambush. We ride out and surprise 'em."

Tupaku, while wishing to distinguish himself, realized that Bear Claw was a great warrior and that it was for the good of everyone that he spoke. Walking Horse, on the other hand, was so headstrong that he did not listen to what was being said. When the chief led his decoys up a hill overlooking the unsuspecting Sioux, he gave a last warning to be careful and stay in the timber until he sounded his signal. Walking Horse, paying not the slightest bit of attention to him, obstinately rode into a clearing where he could be seen by the enemy.

"Come back!" Bear Claw ordered furiously. "Sioux see you and kill us all!"

Walking Horse refused to move. "Let 'em see us!" he shouted, as if trying to make himself heard by the enemy. "We came to draw 'em out, not to hide in timber!" he retorted.

Disregarding his own safety, the war chief rode toward him, his hand uplifted. Even though the young rebel was Washakie's son, he struck him across the head with his rawhide rope. "When Wŭda Mo say come back, he mean it!" Walking Horse ill-humoredly led his horse back into the timber where the warriors were waiting for the proper time to spring their attack.

According to one of the Logs who had daringly crept up to the camp during the night, the Sioux had been feasting following a successful hunt. After gorging themselves, many had fallen asleep, even some of those who should have been standing guard. It was an ideal time to strike.

From their hiding place, the Snakes observed two

herders driving about 40 head of horses from camp. Bear Claw, after watching them a moment, ordered the decoys to attack. Little Chief and the Cheyenne had such swift steeds that they soon outdistanced the others. Black Horse, snorting in the excitement, took the lead. He was as keen for action as his master.

The Sioux were so frightened that they abandoned the horses they were driving and sped back toward camp. One escaped, but Washakie's sons headed off the other. This was the chance Walking Horse craved, a chance to touch the enemy and add to his personal glory; for he was jealous of Little Chief's superior rating. Riding close, he struck the Sioux from his horse with his tomahawk and counted the first coup. Tupaku counted the second after the enemy had hit the ground. Then the two young warriors whirled to join the decoys who were driving the horses away. Tupaku, who loved horses more than the glory of battle, spied the finest pinto in the bunch. He threw his rope around its neck so that everyone would know that it was his.

By this time, the entire camp was aroused by the whooping Indians. The startled Sioux, rushing out to see what was taking place, unhobbled the horses left in camp. Then at top speed, they rushed forth to meet the enemy.

To his credit Walking Horse furnished the delaying action so that the Yellow Noses could make their get-away with the stolen horses, which they drove toward the Snakes who remained in hiding. The Sioux rode on, little dreaming what was in store for them. Although they shot at Walking Horse several tires they did not score a hit.

When they reached the ambush, the Shoshones rushed into the open. The Sioux, armed only with bows and arrows, were surprised by the gunfire. During the combat which followed, Tupaku shot one of the Sioux through the neck and counted the first coup on him as he toppled to the ground. When Walking Horse rushed up to further his honor, an arrow grazed his head. This so infuriated him that he caught up with his assailant, disarmed him and knocked him from his horse. Then he whipped out a knife and scalped him while he was still alive. This was the first scalp taken during the foray.

The enemy, not wishing to have more casualties, stopped fighting, quickly gathered up their dead and wounded and returned to camp. When Walking Horse started in pursuit, Bear Claw called to him. "Come back! Battle's over!"

The Cheyenne again disregarded him. Galloping on, he kept firing at the retreating Sioux. A few minutes later, he returned with an arrowhead stuck in his thigh. He was groaning loudly. When Bear Claw removed it, he made no comment. The enemy had spared him the necessity of dealing out further punishment.

The Shoshone casualties amounted to three,

slightly wounded. The foray was unquestionably a success since several of the enemy were killed and an undetermined number wounded. The Snakes captured 64 horses.

The Cheyenne was impatient to reach home to boast of his bravery, but the war chief insisted that they return as they left, in a body. The details of the battle were not to be discussed until they could meet in council and publicly count coup. Then each would have a chance to verify his bravery and boast of his accomplishments. Everyone agreed except Walking Horse, who showed his displeasure. Making an excuse to drop out of line, he let the others pass. Then he skirted the procession and dashed ahead. Bear Claw saw what he was up to and called, "Come back!" but the Cheyenne ignored him.

"Walking Horse!" Tupaku yelled at the top of his voice. Then he looked toward the chief.

"Stop him!" Bear Claw commanded.

Instantly, Little Chief dashed in pursuit. He called repeatedly to his brother, then shot above his head. Still the Cheyenne rode recklessly on. Suddenly his pony stepped in a badger hole and fell. Walking Horse, thrown clear, was badly shaken in body and spirit. He sat on the ground and stared at Little Chief, who reproved him severely.

"Fool!" Tupaku lashed out at him. "Washakie say obey your war chief. Bear Claw punish you. Enemy punish you. Now see what you—"

They both looked toward the helpless horse, floundering with a broken leg.

When Tupaku raised his gun, Walking Horse cried out, "Brother, do not shoot!" But the bullet was intended for the horse, not the Cheyenne.

"I shoot brave war pony, not old woman!" Tupaku retorted contemptuously.

The returning warriors decided to let the rebellious son of the chief get back to camp the best way he could. Tupaku watched them ride by without a word. Suddenly, he realized that he could not leave Walking Horse afoot so far from camp. While his behavior was disgraceful, he was still Washakie's son.

"Ashŭraba Kak," Little Chief called to Spotted Crow who led the pinto he had claimed as a trophy of war. The Snake stopped and looked at him. "Give new pony to Walking Horse. The son of Washakie not return to camp on foot."

18

Jim Bridger's personal problems with the Mormons began when he armed the Shoshones for their trip to the Great Treaty Council. Two years later he eluded a posse of 150 select men sent to arrest him for trading guns and ammunition to the Indians. When members of the Green River Mission arrived at Fort Bridger they found the old squaw man gone and the fort occupied by a number of ferocious looking mountain men. Consequently, they went downstream 12 miles to build an agricultural station, Fort Supply.

The Shoshones learned of this in the spring from Basil, who had spent the winter with the Saints. While there he taught them the language of his people. Meanwhile, he acquired a surprising amount of information which he gave to Washakie on his return to camp. He told him that the Shoshone land from the Platte River to Salt Lake was included in Deseret, the vast Mormon empire. Also, he mentioned the Black Book, the *Book of Mormon,* that the Saints planned to bring to him. They would send teachers, and they wanted them to marry daughters of chiefs and sub-chiefs so that they all might be brothers.

Tupaku, listening, was alarmed by the implication. What if a missionary, as Basil called the white teacher, should come to claim Daidŭtsi? She might be attracted to him since she, too, was white. He must talk to Porivo and make sure that when the white man came, she and Black Woman would not be in evidence.

Washakie was not disturbed by the news Basil brought. Though the Mormons and the Snakes had little in common besides plural wives, the chief was on the friendliest terms with Brigham Young, whose farming methods he admired. He had watched him till the soil, irrigate Salt Lake Valley and raise food where only a few seasons before sagebrush and cactus had grown. When Basil told him that the Saints were going to teach the Indians how to farm, Washakie commented, "I hope my people will learn how, but I don't care for it myself."

Big Chief received his first callers from Fort Supply a few days later. Even though Basil told him of their proposed visit, he gave no indication of it when four strangers rode up to his lodge. He stood with Tupaku, just outside, and he watched as they came toward him. With arms folded, he showed no sign of welcome until they dismounted. Then he shook hands with them and directed two of his wives to take care of their horses. After this formality, he invited the strangers to enter his lodge.

Hanŭbi immediately spread robes for their comfort. When the white men were seated, Washakie asked,

"Why you come?" Before they could answer he cautioned, "Do not talk crooked talk."

The sandy-bearded missionary, who said his name was James Brown, answered bravely in the language Basil had taught him. "We are your brothers."

"Ugh!" Tupaku expostulated.

"Our Father, the Great Spirit, sends us to say that He wants peace between His Indian and white children." There was a pause.

Peace! What did the hairy-faced stranger mean? Washakie had never been known to harm a white man. Surely he could do battle with his enemies!

"Washakie not fight the *taivo,*" the chief stated with dignity.

The Saint's well rehearsed approach was leading nowhere, so he tried again, this time in sign language. "We come to tell our brothers that before many more snows the buffalo will all be gone. We do not want them to starve. We would like to show them how to live as the white man does. We will teach them how to build houses and raise cattle and grain, to raise food from the ground."

"Food!" Washakie picked up the word. "My children like white man's sugar. You have little bit to give 'em?" The Saints handed over all they had.

Without a word, the chief accepted their gift, which he handed to Hanŭbi, who was standing back of him. She immediately divided it among the children clustered around her. Big Chief indicated that he wanted his guests to follow him outside. There he stood looking into the distance. "Shoshone will meet in council to hear what white man has to say after sun goes to rest."

James Brown, the white chief, glanced at the large watch he carried in his pocket. Sunset would be in about two hours. "How will you get word to your people?" he asked.

Clutching the edge of his blanket firmly, Washakie turned and pointed toward an elevation behind which the sun was sinking. Although nearly blinded by the brightness, the Saints could see what appeared to be smoke from a campfire on the summit. They had noticed a single column of smoke when they first entered the valley, and they had speculated upon the possibility of a forest fire.

As they watched, the smoke disappeared. Then small cloud-like puffs arose at intervals. Suddenly it became apparent that through some mysterious device the chief was not only receiving but also sending messages to the signal post. The white men were puzzled. Washakie, who had been standing with his back toward his guests, turned toward them and satisfied their curiosity by showing them the mirror with which he had been signaling.

"What do smoke signals mean?" asked one of the white men.

"Sacred medicine," Washakie evaded.

During the white man's dinner hour, the Indians came streaming from all directions. While only a favored few could sit in the council ring, there were no restrictions upon the gathering of the masses. Women visited pleasantly while they kept fires burning and prepared the feast which always followed an important council.

When the guests and tribal dignitaries were seated, Washakie stood to give his opening speech. Meanwhile each councillor held a hand over his mouth to signify that he had nothing to say to the white man, that Big Chief alone was their spokesman.

"My people, White Chief says he sent by Dam Apŭ. He's his Father, too. Our white brother want peace, and he plan to do many things for our people. Washakie smoke pipe with white brothers. Hold up hands, those who want to smoke with him."

First one hand and then another was raised, somewhat reluctantly. The chief, disregarding his usual democratic procedure which recognized majority rule, ignored the fact that those who had raised their hands were few in number. Even Tupaku, who had made every effort to conform, sat silently staring before him. He was thinking of what Basil had said about the missionary's wanting to marry the daughter of a chief. His only comfort lay in the fact that Daidŭtsi had not reached puberty and was not old enough to be anyone's wife. That would not prevent Washakie, in accordance with his policy of brotherly love, from presenting her to the white man. Had he not given one of his Indian daughters to an old man in the tribe despite her wishes?

When the pipe reached Tupaku, he held it a moment. Then looking toward Washakie to make sure he could see that he was going through the ritual for his sake, he took a brief puff and passed it on.

Again Big Chief spoke. "Our friend say he come to help. He talk Shoshone. Basil taught him. He tell what he hopes to do."

Tupaku was puzzled when the white chief asked everyone to bow his head. Why did he pray downward? The Indian lifted his eyes toward the sky. Could it be that the white man's Supreme Power lived in the earth? Was that the reason he turned the sod upside down?

Following the prayer, the white man kept talking. When the Indian prayed he would pause for meditation. How like the *taivo* to launch immediately into a lengthy discourse!

"My brothers," the missionary was saying, "I bring a message of greetings from our chief, Brigham Young. He is a good friend of Washakie, and he is interested in helping you. Some day there will be no more buffalo, and the Indian must learn to raise his food so he will not starve." He spoke at length, outlining the Mormon program for aiding the Shoshones. In conclusion, he said, "Some of our missionaries might want to marry your good daughters. Their children would be educated so that they could read and learn more about God, or Dam Apŭ as you call him."

"No!" one of the elders shouted. "We not give daughters to white man, but we trade Indian girl for white girl."

Washakie, with his natural diplomacy, settled the

matter. "White man look around. If he find Indian girl who will go with him, it is well." Then he added firmly, "But Indian must be able to do same in white camp." With that, the council closed. Tupaku was relieved to see the missionaries leave the following day.

When the Snakes returned to Green River during the summer, they were surprised by the air of permanency about the settlement at the Ferries. Log buildings now took the place of the tepees where the squaw men had lived with their Shoshone, Ute or Paiute wives. In the saloon, Big Chief was fascinated by the games of chance. With his Good Medicine at his side, he watched gamblers shuffle their cards as large amounts of gold changed hands. Never had he seen anything to equal the white man's *puwi* (money) which he considered better than his system of barter.

Late afternoon he, Tupaku, and several other tribal leaders wandered into the ferry office, where a number of fifty-dollar gold slugs on the captain's desk caught his fancy. "Washakie want little piece of white man's *puwi,*" he stated at length. The officer looked at him in surprise, for it was obvious that he did not know what he was asking. Then smiling indulgently, the captain fished a coin from his pocket and handed it to him. Even though the chief did not know the value of that either, he was convinced that he was being treated as a child—that the white man was making a fool of him!

He hurled the piece of silver to the floor and stalked out. The great Chief of the Shoshones was insulted, and he intended to find James Brown, the missionary chief who had visited him, and tell him so.

His indignation mounted as he searched for the Saint, the only white man in the settlement he felt he knew. Basil, his interpreter, had remained too long at the saloon to be of help. By recalling the name of the white man, he was finally able to locate him. Brown was at the riverside, where he was swimming cattle across the stream for a number of emigrants. He was too busy to be bothered, but one glance at the irate Indian made him forget the cattle floundering in the deep water. The chief's stony face was devoid of a sign of greeting, and he made no offer to shake hands. Tupaku and the accompanying warriors merely glared at the missionary.

In his passionate anger, eloquent words seemed to spill from the chieftain's mouth. "This is my country—the country of my fathers!" he shouted. "They drank this water. Their ponies grazed these bottoms." He waved his arm in an all-inclusive gesture. "Here our mothers gathered deadwood for their fires. Buffalo aplenty came here to drink and graze. Now all are killed or driven away. Grass is gone by the white man's horses and cattle, and no dry wood."

After conjuring a picture of the past, he paused to survey the scene before him. Then he continued, "Sometimes when our young men, tired and hungry, come to white man's camp, what does he do? He calls 'em damned Injuns and kicks 'em out! Our young men, heap mad, want revenge. They say they will kill every white man they see, but I always tell 'em not to cover the land with his blood. Washakie's warriors never killed a white man!"

He looked at the missionary in disgust. "Now I see that the *taivo* is selfish. He loves only himself and his *puwi*. He has big bag full he got on my land, and he will not let me have little bit. . . . Washakie is on warpath, I tell you plain. At sunrise tomorrow, we will wipe out every white man this side of that water!" With a brush of his hand he gave emphasis to his threat. "When sun comes again, you see! My warriors, heap mad, will wipe 'em all out!" His vow never to harm a white man was for the moment forgotten. Tupaku was as surprised as the missionary.

Big Chief mounted his horse and called back to the speechless Saint, "Good-bye, you tell 'em get out of my country and not come back!"

With feathers fluttering, the Indians returned to their camp on the Big Sandy.

The badly frightened missionary lost no time spreading the news of the threatened attack. When the captain heard of the threat, he belatedly offered to send a fifty dollar gold slug as a peace offering to the enraged chief. The Indians had obtained a quantity of the white man's liquor, and although the captain offered another fifty dollars and a good horse to anyone who would attempt a reconciliation, no one was willing to risk his life. The white men worked until dawn moving their families and their personal property to the opposite side of the river, where they made preparations for an attack.

At sunup, Washakie, Tupaku, and a half dozen warriors returned to the Ferries. The chief was quick to appraise the situation. He seemed fascinated by the frightened men, women and children as he sat quietly on his horse and watched the confusion in the white man's camp. Then he dismounted and turned to James Brown, who had come forward to meet him. As they shook hands, Washakie said, "Tell 'em to go back. We not want to harm 'em. We are their friends."

19

The following summer, the Shoshones gave the Blackfeet further reason to fear their chief by dealing them a humiliating defeat on the Snake River. Their number badly depleted, the enemy fled northward. The Shoshones, still painted from their victorious battle, dared not tarry; for the ferocious Blackfeet were capable of regrouping and counterattacking with the aid of other bands. Ever cautious, Washakie's Indians immediately broke camp and started south.

Their first encampment was on one of the headwater tributaries of Green River. Here, with darkness overtaking them, they quickly made camp in order to celebrate with a Scalp Dance. While a dozen or so musicians stood beating their hand drums, the women taking part lined up in a row with the fresh scalps on the end of sticks. Dancing toward the men, who kept their original position, they stopped just before reaching them. Then they walked back to their starting point to wait for the next song. The process was repeated time after time.

The women were dismantling their tepees when a runner brought news that several white men were approaching camp. With the warriors still keyed up from their battle with the Blackfeet, it was a bad time for white visitors to make their appearance. Washakie immediately dispatched Tupaku and ten young braves to receive them.

This was the first time Little Chief had been given such a responsible assignment. Since Washakie well knew Tupaku's attitude, he was either testing his loyalty or trying to find out if his feelings toward the white man had changed. The warriors, still with their paint and feathers, made an impressive appearance; for they had "green" scalps dangling from their bridle bits.

It was foolish of the white man to ride straight into an Indian camp without first sending an emissary. Basil had paved the way for the missionaries who came to visit Washakie once before. The white men this time had, in addition to their saddle horses, a four-horse team and wagon. Tupaku, noting the anticipation with which the Cheyenne viewed the oncoming horses, gruffly reminded him that the white man was Washakie's friend. He feared that he might be unable to restrain him.

"We have plenty fun," one of the braves suggested. "Let's make 'em think we're on warpath, but we'll not hurt 'em." Not even Tupaku could object to that.

With a word of warning and a war whoop, he led out. The small caravan continued to come fearlessly onward. As the warriors closed in, Little Chief recognized the bearded white chief as James Brown, whom he had not seen since the incident at the Ferries. He rode up and offered to shake hands, in an effort to impress the braves with the fact that he intended to extend the hospitality of his friendly chief.

The missionaries, after being scared half out of their wits, were relieved by his cordiality. But when they started asking questions, Tupaku placed his hand over his mouth and pointed to the camp. Without a word, he escorted the white men to his chief.

When Washakie had greeted his visitors, he said, "We leave. Come. We'll hear what you say. We've defeated Blackfoot in battle. Now we must find safe place for women and children before they come again." With a wave of his hand and a shout to his men, the chief soon had his Indians on the move. The Logs, fanning out on each side, combed the land for food as they went. Rodents and small animals were bagged while the hungry Indians moved forward into the upper Green River Valley.

In the late afternoon, camp was made in a well-shaded location near the stream. The chief's lodge was soon pitched, and robes were spread for the guests. A centerfire was built, and the councillors filed around to their places after silently shaking hands with the white men. Several of the Indians, going through the formality, were cold in their greetings as they stared suspiciously at their visitors. Only Washakie and Porivo seemed genuinely friendly.

When all was quiet and each was in his place, Washakie opened the meeting. "Tell us what you want to say. Tell it straight!" When the spokesman for the missionaries pulled a letter from his pocket, the chief was impatient to know what it said. The letter was from Brigham Young, promising lasting friendship as well as seeds and tools to till the soil. It also told about the *Book of Mormon* that would teach the Indians many things about Dam Apŭ and what He would do for His children.

After the white man had finished interpreting the message, he presented the Black Book to Washakie, who opened it and studied its pages carefully. He turned it sideways and upside down, but still he could not derive any meaning. Without question, it was the strangest gift the white man had yet offered. Unable to fathom it, he closed it and spoke sadly. "Good for white man. No good for my people." He then handed it to Tupaku, who glanced at it and, without a word, started it around the council circle. As it made its round, the elders took turns expressing themselves.

One old warrior protested, "Shoshone cannot eat the Black Book. Give us food!"

Another shook his head and retorted, "No good. Warriors need gun powder!"

Washakie listened carefully as each expressed his dissatisfaction. Then he arose and angrily denounced his people. "Fools!" His voice shook with emotion. "Fools--all of you--fools not to understand! White man, our brother, has come to warn us. But we are deaf! We have no ears to hear! He wants to teach us many things. He has his Black Book that would tell us what we should know, but we cannot read what it says. He wants to teach us its meaning. But no! We are blind and cannot see the light he brings. We can make bows and arrows, but the *taivo's* mind is strong. He can make this," he held up his precious revolver, "and this watch my white brother gave me." He passed it around so all could listen in awe to the tick of it. "When it is night, he can tell when it will be day. When there is no sun, he can tell the time. This is because the face of Dam Apŭ is toward him, and His back is to us. But if we had eyes to see and ears to hear, after some moons, He would quit being mad at us. He would turn his face to us."

When Washakie finished, there was silence. Then he spoke to his son, "Tupaku, Washakie want you to go with missionary and learn to read his book. You come back and tell its meaning in words we understand."

The surprised young Indian, for an unexplainable reason, wanted the Cheyenne to go with him. Whether it was because he did not trust him out of his sight or because he was beginning to show an interest in the *daidŭtsi,* he was not sure.

"Tupaku want Walking Horse to go, too."

"*Kay*!" retorted the Cheyenne, who stood behind the councillors. The life of the white man as he understood it had no appeal, and he did not hesitate to say so.

Washakie turned to scowl his displeasure. Walking Horse had been involved with Tavenduwits' band during the summer in an attack on a wagon train. Consequently, he was already in disrepute. "Walking

Horse stay here where I can watch 'im," the chief stated. "If Walking Horse ever harm white man, Washakie kill him!" There was no doubt that he meant it. The Cheyenne did not respond.

Big Chief turned toward Tupaku. "Go, my son, and learn way of the *taivo*. Take Basil, for he talk their language. Find out what missionary can teach. Then come back. You maybe bring Shoshone good medicine so Dam Apŭ be pleased with us."

Little Chief was stunned by the responsibility of his assignment. Nothing could have been more unpleasant to him at the moment than the thought of having to live in the white man's camp. If the missionaries forced him to stay shut up in one of their big, log wickiups, he would die. Then he thought of Daidŭtsi. Had she not learned to live the life of an Indian without complaint? Surely he could stay with the white man long enough to find out how to read the Black Book.

The sound of the flute penetrated the night stillness. Otter Man had not given up the idea that Pretty Weasel might succumb to the magic of his love call. His only reward so far had been a perfection of his art, for, though lacking in bravery, he was second to none in the field of music. When the last lingering notes died away, the camp was quiet. The missionaries, who had brought their tent, had pitched it next to the chieftain's lodge. A good idea Little Chief thought, no one would bother them there.

For some reason he could not sleep. His mind was troubled by the thought of his prospective trip to the white camp. As he lay looking up at the stars, he wondered if Washakie might again be testing him. Further tests were unnecessary. He would do anything his chief asked, even to going on the proposed journey.

Black Horse, picketed near his head, stood sleeping. A wonderful accomplishment Tupaku thought, for a horse was in a position to start moving without having to flounder to his feet. Strong Wind was out with the herd. At daybreak, he would go after him and give him to Daidŭtsi. He would not tie him in front of her door to woo her, for she was too young. His spotted horse would be an out right gift because he expected nothing in return. The gentle pony would be ideal for her, and perhaps she would not forget him, with Strong Wind as a reminder.

He heard a twig snap. Though the night was clear, he could not distinguish the object in the shadow of the tree.

"Tupaku," someone whispered.

"Daidŭtsi!" he exclaimed. He dragged his blanket as he went in search of her. But when he reached the girl he found that it was not Daidŭtsi but Pretty Weasel.

"Why you come?" he asked gruffly in his effort to disguise his disappointment.

"You going with white chief?" she asked anxiously.

"*Ha'a,*" he replied. He had no desire to discuss the matter.

He could feel the softness of her young body as she pressed against him, while she clutched his arm possessively. More aware of the pine scent of her clothing than of the meaning of her words, he half listened to her plea.

"Take me with you!" she implored.

He did not love Pretty Weasel, but he accepted her without hesitation. His promise was formality enough to make her his wife.

The next morning when Tupaku reached Porivo's fire, he smelled the aroma of hot bread and coffee. Without waiting for an invitation, he entered her tepee and seated himself at the old woman's side.

"Where's Daidŭtsi?" he asked.

"She's gone with Black Woman to the river. They return soon." She looked at him keenly. "You go with white missionaries?" It was the same question that Pretty Weasel had asked, but this time he gave a more thoughtful answer.

"My father says so. Porivo, is he still testing me to see if I've learn lesson in obedience? Doesn't he know—"

"He's not testing you. He send you to learn white man's road. It's only way for us. You not know how powerful the *taivo* is. They are many more where white man come from. Washakie's oracle warned him not to resist or he be crushed. His people be sent to Indian Territory."

"Indian Territory! Where's that?"

Porivo checked to see that the bread was browning properly before she answered. "It's on low prairie land beyond Great Plains. White men plan to put all Indian tribes in camp, so they can take their land. Shoshone die without mountains and buffalo. Oracle says Indian days numbered. Washakie think so, too. He not save us from our fate, but if he stay friendly maybe Taivo let us keep little piece of our land. That's his only hope. That's why he try so hard to please."

"Taivo!" Tupaku hissed contemptuously. "I hate Taivo! Washakie should not allow any to come to our country! Weyavo, my helper, show me not to trust 'im!"

Porivo got to her feet and went to the back of the tepee. There she picked up an object which she presented to the young Indian. It was a pipe bag with an elaborate porcupine quill design embroidered on it.

"Here," she urged. "When you go to white man's camp, carry peace pipe, not gun. Remember you're Washakie's son. Be proud." Voices indicated that the girl had returned, but Porivo had time for one more word of advice. "Learn what you can!"

When the *daidŭtsi* and her nurse entered the tepee, they were laughing and talking in the language of the white man. Tupaku had never seen Black Woman when she was not in a jovial mood, except that day when she was captured.

"*Ahai'i*!" the girl greeted him. "You eat breakfast with us?" That had not been the object of his visit, but the smell of the food had already convinced him that he should stay.

"*Ha'a,*" he answered.

"Hep yosef, Mistah Chief," Black Woman urged.

The bread was light and fluffy, unlike the Bannock bread his mother used to make. He ate until the last crumb was gone. Then he came to the point of his visit. "Daidŭtsi," he said to the girl. "I go with missionaries. Washakie says to. I give Strong Wind to you."

She looked at him in disbelief.

"I not need him with Black Horse. Strong Wind gentle, nice for you.

She clapped her hands in delight. "You give 'im to me to keep?"

"*Ha'a.*" When they stepped outside and he handed her the lead rope, he was unable to find anything further to say, so he turned toward Black Woman. "Take care of Daidŭtsi and Strong Wind while I'm gone. I'll return with the grass."

For a moment he thought that the girl would burst into tears. Instead, she caressed the horse, and then turning toward Tupaku, she flung her arms around him and kissed him fervently. Both women laughed at her unrestrained display of affection. But when

Tupaku walked away, his heart was heavy. Why could it not have been Daidŭtsi instead of Pretty Weasel who wanted to go with him?

When he returned to his tepee, the one Big Chief had given him following the Manhood Ceremony, he found the Indian girl waiting. She had her few possessions loaded on an old horse her father had given her. She had asked nothing of Little Chief, not even a pony to carry her and her belongings on the journey.

20

The Mormons and their Indian companions, Tupaku, Pretty Weasel, Basil and his family, made a strange procession as they moved across the sagebrush flat. Little Chief did not like the way the white men traveled, all in a bunch. There would have been less chatter and more time for thought had they gone Indian file. The missionaries had so much to say that there was little opportunity to meditate. Somehow there was comfort in having Pretty Weasel along, for besides sharing his blanket, she could prepare his meals and keep his tepee in order.

One of the white men was speaking. "Who is that following us?" he asked. Tupaku had not been aware that anyone was, but he turned to see. "Otter Man," he answered, as if that alone were sufficient. The musician was not playing his flute when he rode up. Instead, he carried a bow and arrow. It was the first time Tupaku had seen him armed. Perhaps he had been out rabbit hunting. There was no one more harmless in the tribe. He passed Basil without a word and rode up beside Pretty Weasel, who seemed annoyed by his presence.

"Where you going?" he asked indignantly.

"Go back to pine trees and play flute! You not need to know!" she taunted.

"You'll not go with Tupaku. You belong to me!" he shouted, crazed by jealousy. Then, to the consternation of everyone, he swiftly lifted his bow and arrow and shot her. He watched in fascination as she fell to the ground.

"Waugh!" Tupaku roared like an enraged lion. Before Otter Man even looked his way, he whirled his horse, grabbed the guilty Indian and bore him to the ground. After dealing him a swift blow with his tomahawk, he stood, trembling with rage. The missionaries were awed by the swiftness of Indian justice.

"Basil, help tie bodies on horses," Little Chief directed. He did not speak their names because he did not want their spirits to return in the form of ghosts to haunt him. Every Shoshone knew that the spirit lingered several days and that if the name were spoken during that time the ghost would appear.

"What will you do with them?" one of the missionaries asked.

"Bury 'em between rocks so wolves not find 'em—their horses, too."

"Their horses! But they are not dead!"

"They will be." The white men were baffled. Apparently they had not heard of the Shoshone concept of the spirit and the ghost. They did not know that unless the Indians destroyed everything of importance that had belonged to the deceased, he would come back in ghost form to claim his property.

When Tupaku and Basil started to lift the bodies onto the horses, one of the missionaries made a suggestion. "Why not put them in the back of the wagon. We can make room."

The Bannock agreed, though no Shoshone had ever been known to be carried to his grave in such fashion. As the bodies were laid out in the wagon box, Otter Man's hand limply touched the girl. Could Tupaku believe it? Although the Indian was unquestionably dead, there seemed to be a faint smile of contentment on his face, as if his soul were at peace with Pretty Weasel whom he was unable to win in life.

When the delegation reached Bridger Valley, Tupaku looked once again in the direction of the old fort. He wondered what became of Blanket Chief and his family, if they were still in "Mizzour" where he had said he planned to go. Little Chief was not quite sure where Mizzour was, but from what Blanket Chief had said, it must be a settlement of some sort at the month of the Big Muddy River. The white tribe had a camp there, his friend had told him.

As he crossed the fertile valley, Tupaku noticed that a change had taken place. Water, from he knew not where, was flowing through a network of irrigation ditches. He recognized them, for he had seen them when the Shoshones went to Salt lake for the peace council with the Utes. Some of the industrious

Mormons were cutting native hay in the meadows, and there were even a few grain fields.

The greatest surprise of all was the old fort. Like busy beavers, the Saints were transforming the whole appearance of the place. They were hauling loads of rock for a wall to replace the wooden pickets, and they were burning lime in a nearby kiln for the buildings under construction.

Tupaku resented the bustle around the fort. It was quite different from the easygoing atmosphere of the past. He was glad when he found that this was not to be his destination. The log wickiup at Fort Supply that the missionary had described would not be as foreboding as the cold stone of the new walls at Bridger. How Blanket Chief would have hated them!

On their arrival at Fort Supply, the Saints tried to discourage the Indians from pitching their tepees in the courtyard. They told them that they would be far more comfortable in the building where there was enough room for all. Without bothering to argue, Basil told his wives where he wanted the tepees pitched—in the courtyard. The Saints, seeing the futility of saying more, raised no further objection. When weather permitted, Tupaku slept under the stars, where he seemed better able to think.

He called John Logan, the teacher assigned to him, "Captain John." He was a tall, thin, bleached-out young man, who looked as if a summer in an Indian camp might be good for him. He spent too much time poring over books and too little exercising out-of-doors. And yet, he had a way of winning friends, even a Bannock. Logan could read and write the white man's language, but Tupaku felt sorry for him because he was so ignorant of the ways of the Indian. Besides he knew little or nothing about the country. He did not know what any of the signs meant, and he could not foretell the weather. As the days went by, Tupaku took pity on him. While he was supposed to be learning the white man's tongue, he was trying to teach Captain John the many valuable facts that he had learned from Pariha Ungu.

They conversed in Shoshone since Logan had a fair command of the language. It was hard enough to get the spoken word across to the Indian, but a formal education was out of the question. Tupaku would not sit inside a building long enough to concentrate on a written assignment.

"No one can teach that Indian to read and write!" Logan complained to his fellow missionaries as they sat at supper one night. "I just wish someone else would try! I have been working with him all of this time, and he can't or won't even write his name. I'll be attempting to explain something, and I'll think he is listening; but he will start talking about something completely aside from the point. You can bring him in side, but his mind stays out with the beavers and the turtles, and I don't know what else. He knows more about nature and animals than a biology professor. Sometimes I wonder who is teaching whom. He has taught me far more than I have been able to teach him!" He pushed aside his untouched plate.

"I have been wasting my time. I've worked hard to gain his confidence. The way things are now, I might even lose that. Today I would have had to nail him to his seat to keep him. When I glanced out the window to see what he was up to, he was riding out the gate. I have no idea where he is now. He hasn't come back. He could be at Basil's gorging himself on jerky. He would rather have that than roast beef and potatoes!"

"I suppose we could lock the gate and keep him in," one of the Saints offered.

"No!" James Brown laid his fork on his plate and turned toward Logan. "That would make him more rebellious than ever. We know how he feels toward us. The only reason he came is that the chief told him to. We must win him through patience and kindness. He would make a good missionary if we could capture his loyalty the way Washakie has. John, quit trying to teach him. Convert him. You can speak his language. What does it matter if he can't read and write? He can talk, convincingly, too. Why, he has made a naturalist out of you. Now it is up to you to make a missionary out of him!"

"You don't know the smoldering hatred inside him.

He is still a disciple of Pariha Ungu, although he has learned a certain amount of restraint from Washakie."

"Nevertheless, I think you can do it, John. Let him conduct the lessons. He is a born leader. Win his trust and friendship in every way you can. Tell him that he has visited among the white men during the winter, and you would like to go home with him and spend the summer. My guess is that when you no longer pressure him you will win him over enough to accept you and perhaps the faith. Next summer you could live among his people. You might even marry a daughter of the chief and settle there. You could do much for the church."

"I have no desire to be a squaw man!" Logan protested.

"Wait and see. You might change your mind."

As soon as the classroom teaching was discontinued, a burden seemed to have been lifted from the young Indian's shoulders. His spirits soared, and he enthusiastically put the white man through a course in physical training. No matter how bitter the weather, he would take him ice fishing, or riding through the raw winds into the nearby hills.

Captain John chose what he hoped to be the right moment to break the news of his intended trip to the Indian camp. Tupaku had finished telling him about the Sun Dance in which he planned to take part during the coming summer, but he was not sure just when it would be.

"I would like to visit your people and see the Sun Dance," the Saint said wistfully.

Tupaku was pleased. "Washakie like you come see him. Do you good to stay with Indian. Then you not look so sick," he said with his customary frankness.

Tupaku sat talking with Basil at his campfire that evening. "Captain John want to go home with us," he told him.

"When?"

"In spring."

The older Indian was slow with his reply. Then he said emphatically, "Basil not go 'til he plant his crop."

"Crop!" Little Chief exclaimed. "What you mean, crop?" So the Mormons had been converting Basil to the idea of farming while Captain John had been trying to teach him how to read and write.

"*Ha'a*! Washakie want me to learn so I teach our people."

"But he not want to farm."

"*Kay*, he is too old to change ways. He's wise enough to know Indian must learn. He want me to teach our people how to do it."

Tupaku was dumbfounded. It had not occurred to him that the trip to Fort Supply might have a two-fold purpose. He hoped that Basil would do a better job of learning than he had done. He was still unable to read a line in the Black Book, as hard as he had tried.

When the cold in the mountains was driven out by the warm suns of spring, Tupaku and Captain John, his companion, no longer his teacher, spent many hours exploring the countryside. Usually the Indian talked about nature, if at all. It was rare for him to mention religion.

One day after the missionary had seemingly aroused Tupaku's interest, he felt that the time was ripe for his conversion. He told him that the Indians were the "lost children of Israel." Upon their acceptance of the faith, they would turn white.

"White!" It was the most revolting bit of information that the young Indian had ever heard! "You mean we change color?" He was incredulous. Was that what Washakie meant by Dam Apŭ's turning His face toward the Shoshones?

The missionary nodded.

"Tupaku not want to be white!" he stated emphatically. Why should any Indian want to be when Indian ways were superior to everything he had found in the white camp? He was ready to go home and tell his chief, but both Captain John and Basil prevailed upon him to stay until they could accompany him. The three would return to camp together as they had planned though the friendship which had been so carefully nurtured by the white man was now in the balance.

Tupaku became impatient as the days went by, but Basil stubbornly refused to leave until his crop was planted. The Saints would irrigate it for him, and he could return in the late summer for harvest. Little Chief, watching the strange agricultural process, decided that he would rather starve than farm for his food. The strip of ground the Mormons turned over to Basil was plowed, planted and the seeds had sprouted when the sub-chief announced that he was ready to return to Wind River.

21

Long before reaching Warm Valley, Tupaku and his companions could hear the disturbing beat of the drum, the shrill, piercing sound of the eaglebone whistle and the monotonous chant of the Tagŭ Wŭnŭ, the Sun Dance. Little Chief regretted that he had been delayed by Basil's farming operations because he had hoped to return in time to take part.

He listened sensitively to the rhythm of the music as he observed the beauty of his homeland. He had never been so aware of its magnitude, though the scene was as he had left it. There were long stretches of waste land and high plains, dotted by sagebrush, cottonwoods and prickly pear. The fertile valley was separated by a clear stream which was boarded by stately greasewood and bushy willows. To him the mountains in the Wind River Range, with their jagged rocks and scattered evergreens, were more majestic than those in the Bridger region although the snow-clad Uintas, the mountains of the Utes, could be seen in the distance.

Tupaku's heart swelled with pride while he looked upon this land of his people. No wonder Washakie preferred the serenity of Warm Valley to the Green River country, which was so overrun by white men. He recalled that his chief had invited the Mormons to Green River, and they had come in ever increasing numbers to form a permanent settlement. He had not mentioned Wind River. Tupaku suddenly resented Captain John at his side. Why had he brought him? The white men had no right in the land of the Snakes!

The sound of the music became more and more distinct as the small party neared the Indian village. Along the way, they encountered a number of Logs, who, greeting Little Chief and Basil, stared at the white man riding beside the son of the chief. They did not say a word, for Tupaku was the Shoshone's Good Medicine. This was not altered by the fact that he wore the absurd dress of the white man, a cotton shirt and homespun trousers, which the Mormons had given him. His two black braids proved that he had not renounced his people.

"What's that?" Captain John pointed toward a forked upright, standing alone on the prairie. "It looks like a cross."

"It's Center Pole where Tagŭ Wŭnŭ held some other time. Two prongs at top mean Indian have two roads to travel, right and wrong."

"Which is also true of the white man," Captain John affirmed. "Let's hope we are on the right! . . . When was the first dance held?"

"Long, long ago, buffalo bring first vision of dance to Shonip Gani [Grass Hut]. Washakie remember when second vision come to Oha Mo [Yellow Hand]. He often speak of him."

The air, fresh and pure from a recent flash storm, was filled with the spicy smell of sage, bruised by hailstones.

"*Ahe-Yai-Yai-Yai.*" The sound carried plainly.

A sleek-feathered magpie, feasting on a dead jackrabbit, was startled by the nearness of the intruders. Emitting a raucous squawk, out of keeping with its handsome appearance, the black and white bird soared gracefully to a nearby tree. It scolded repeatedly as it walked along its sturdy perch.

Tupaku and the white man rode side by side in silence, while Basil and his family straggled along in the rear. Tupaku, who had looked forward to the return to his people, was beginning to worry. How would he be received? Would Washakie feel that he had failed him? Would he, along with the rest of the tribe, wish that he had not brought the *taivo*?

Then his thoughts turned to Daidŭtsi, and he wondered if she might have grown up in his absence. When he left, she was like a young bud, just waiting to blossom. He hoped that she had not chosen her mate as Washakie said she would be allowed to do, for he had felt that she belonged to him from the time he rescued her from the cruel hands of Isha. Pretty Weasel, who had lost her life through her love for him, had briefly satisfied his physical need, but he would never have sought her. She came to him of her own accord to offer him her unselfish devotion. Had she lived, she would have made life more comfortable. Besides, she could have helped Black Woman with the heavy work so that Daidŭtsi could be spared unnecessary hardships.

The horses, tired from the long journey, walked slowly, their pace matching the mood of their masters. The two packhorses, carrying gifts for Washakie, stumbled wearily in the heat. Captain John ran a finger around his soggy collar. Dressed impressively in his black suit, he did not remove his coat though perspiration drooled down the back of his neck, under the gold-brown hair that fell to his shoulders. With a flip of his hand, he raised his tresses so that the air could get under them. As he did, he turned to find Little Chief staring at him.

"Why do you look at me like that?"

"'Tupaku think fine scalp lock," he responded frankly. When he saw the horror on the white man's face, he added, "Stay close to Basil so you not lose it."

As the air continued to reverberate with the chanting sound, a change came over Black Horse. He lifted his head and whinnied loudly. The music seemed to quicken his breath and change his gait. He was impatient to cover the ever shortening distance separating him from home. Could he have smelled the other horses or remembered the once familiar country?

Little Chief could no more explain it than he could analyze his own feelings. The pulsing, throbbing music seemed to arouse the dormant blood in his veins. It was as if the primitive song of the Tagŭ Wŭnŭ had struck a responsive chord. Overcome with emotion, he peeled off his shirt and lithely jumped to the ground to kick off his trousers. He pushed them aside with his foot. Then naked, except for his breechcloth, he jumped on his horse and galloped away without another word to the surprised missionary.

Basil, who was wise to the ways of the young Indian, rode up to the *taivo* and asked, "What'd he say?"

"He said for me to stay close to you so no one will lift my scalp!" the white man answered with a shudder. "Basil, have I lost my friend?"

The sub-chief looked at him squarely. "You never had 'im."

Kill Bear, who had received the vision of the dance, was its leader. He had directed "The Hunt," the first phase of the three-part ceremony, to find a handsome buffalo head to hang on the Center Pole. Then he had lead in the prayers during the four days of preparation in the second part, "Making-the-Ground-Sacred." Once this was done, he had directed the volunteer dancers to bathe and purify their bodies and minds before entering the last part, the "Dance-of-Thirst," which was in its third and final day when Tupaku returned.

The dancers, gaunt from lack of food and water,

were mechanically going through their routine, their muscles flexing to the beat of the drum. Their eyes stared straight at the buffalo head high on the Center Pole, as, with a limping step, they moved their weary feet forward and backward, to and from the Center Pole. The prayers they breathed were projected through the eaglebone whistles held in their mouths, while they shook breath feathers attached to their little fingers.

Captain John, with Basil at his side, was conspicuous as he stood watching the pageant since he was the only white man present. Out of respect for his red brothers, he stood with hat in hand. When the music stopped briefly, all eyes were upon him. Tupaku, making his way to his side, had regained his composure; but the coldness in his voice and manner indicated his lack of friendliness. "Come," he directed.

Logan, who had been standing uncertainly at the entrance of the brush Sun Dance lodge, followed him inside. The Bannock led him to Washakie, who was seated on the ground next to the musicians who had been singing and beating the large ceremonial drum. Little Chief's introduction was short. "Captain John," was all he said.

Washakie looked at him intently. Then he shook his hand and motioned for him to be seated. Turning toward his son, he said, "I hope you come back to dance in Tagŭ Wŭnŭ for our people, to bring good medicine." He did not disguise his disappointment.

"I not get here in time, . . . but Walking Horse?" He

looked toward the stall where the Cheyenne rested momentarily.

"Walking Horse not dance for our people. He dance because he is *kesandŭ*. Now he want to be *tsant* because he want Daidŭtsi for wife."

"Daidŭtsi!" Tupaku was stunned. Gentle little Prairie Flower the wife of the fiery Cheyenne! Impossible! Had Washakie forgotten she was white! Why should Walking Horse, who hated the white man enough to defy his chief and attack a wagon train, want her?

Seeking an answer, he looked searchingly around him. Where was she? He caught his breath when he spotted her, sitting next to Black Woman. She was wearing a white doeskin dress with many pieces of jewelry. It was not the manner of her dress that attracted him as much as the appearance of the girl herself. There was a fine-featured sweetness in her face and an unusual softness in her hair. Before Porivo and the medicine man started applying Indian paint to her skin and vegetable dyes to her hair, he had thought of her as a sego lily. Just as the lily stands apart from the other flowers on the prairie, so did she, even now that she was no longer white. There was about her the radiance of young womanhood, for she had miraculously matured in Tupaku's absence. Catching his eye, Black Woman flashed him a gleaming smile, but Daidŭtsi did not look his way.

He turned toward Washakie. "Daidŭtsi? You let—"

"She decide for herself. Many horses offered for her,

but I say white man not sell his daughter. Washakie not either."

Tupaku glanced again toward the girl, who still avoided his gaze. When Black Woman gave her an obvious nudge, she looked at him and smiled shyly. Tupaku tried to convince himself that this was the child he had brought from the Bannock camp. The name Little One did not fit her, for she was now a full-grown young woman. He thought of the omen of the hawks and his fear that someone might try to take her away. Someone still might. He turned to find Captain John staring at her in admiration.

A wave of jealousy swept over him. Except for his violence toward Otter Man, he had not experienced such a strong feeling toward anyone since the day he vowed he would kill Isha. Why had he been stupid enough to bring the white man to camp? What if Daidŭtsi were to fall in love with him? He could be considered handsome from her point of view, though to him the missionary still looked sick. Might his fair skin and black suit cause her to yearn for her people? Although she had never been treated as a captive, might she seek through him a means of escape?

Four stockily built musicians, sitting around the ceremonial drum, began beating vigorously and singing in their booming voices. The noise was deafening, as the dancers, refreshed by their brief respite, resumed their performance.

Tupaku knew all of the participants, but he paid little attention to any of them except Walking Horse, who made an impressive appearance with his wide shoulders and tall, muscular body. True he was doing penance for his misdemeanor, but more than that, he seemed to be making an impression on Daidŭtsi. Tupaku watched as her eyes followed him back and forth. Although he tried to read her expression, she had lived too long with the Indians to give herself away. Why did she look at Walking Horse instead of at him? Had she already made up her mind? Had he in some way won her affection?

Tupaku's thoughts were thrown into further confusion when a crier announced that the Tagŭ Wŭnŭ was at an end. The faith of the Shoshones in Dam Apŭ, residing somewhere at the top of a high mountain, had been renewed through the media of the buffalo and the eagle, which meant worship and peace, respectively. Many gifts were presented to the dancers before they were led away for a bath and their first food.

Before the ceremony had ended, the participants had raised their eyes toward the rising sun and had prayed directly into it. Its life-giving rays were now beginning to warm the earth and give light for the activities of a busy day. Tupaku, tired from his long trip, strode to Washakie's tepee, wrapped himself in his blanket and proceeded to nap. When he awakened, his chief was sitting at his side. Washakie must have aroused him, for he said, "This, my son, is day of feast. You forget?"

"Feast? I had no part in Tagŭ Wŭnŭ!"

The chief was annoyed. "Feast for all my people.

It's feast of rejoicing. Young men dance the Dance-of-Thirst to please Dam Apŭ. Someday he look on us like on white man."

"Turn us white?"

"*Ha'a,*" the chief replied.

Tupaku was now convinced that Washakie had sent him to the white camp to prepare him for such an event. Thoughtfully, he wrapped his blanket around his loins and started toward the river. On the way, he encountered Daidŭtsi and Black Woman, returning from their secluded bathing spot. Black Woman, with her customary good nature, bade him a pleasant good morning, but the girl merely glanced toward him.

"Daidŭtsi." He stepped in front of her. "Why you not speak? You not remember Tupaku?"

"*Ha'a,*" she said softly, nothing more.

Black Woman was quick to remind him that as a suitor he had no right to speak to her. She was no longer a child, but a 14-year-old maiden, who by Shoshone standards had reached marriageable age. If he could not talk to her, to whom could he talk? He must find Porivo. His heart raced with the realization that Daidŭtsi had not chosen her mate. Black Woman's insinuating glance and the girl's self-consciousness gave him reason to believe that she might look upon him with favor.

Walking Horse made a sudden appearance from behind a tepee. Likely he had been there all the time, waiting for a glimpse of the girl. Little Chief was sure that he had overheard the conversation because of his dark look. He tried to brush by without a word.

"Walking Horse—"

The Cheyenne wheeled and glared at him. "Why you not stay in white camp? Why you bring Taivo?" he demanded. Tupaku could not answer a question he had already asked himself. He, too, knew that the white man had no business in Washakie's camp. "If he take Daidŭtsi, I will—"

"I not think of Daidŭtsi as white girl!" Tupaku protested. "She always one of us. White man was my friend. Now—" He could not bring himself to admit that he, too, had a bitter feeling toward the missionary, who had become his rival.

"You make trouble when you bring Taivo. Walking Horse hates 'im!"

"It's not good for brother to hate, even white brother." Little Chief found himself repeating a lesson he had learned from the white man. Captain John would have been pleased by his statement, for it indicated that his efforts had not fallen altogether on barren ground. Tupaku still tenaciously despised white men in general, but his vocabulary had been modified to exclude the word "hate" through the constant advocacy of brotherly love. His ingrained bitterness remained constant, but his outward expression of feeling was held in cheek by the change

Washakie and the white man had wrought. He had seemingly reverted to his primitive state, but he had learned the meaning of restraint.

When Tupaku went to Washakie's lodge, he found the chief showing Captain John his trophies. As he displayed each gruesome scalp, he told with pride the tribe from which it was taken. He proudly boasted that there was not a white man's in the lot. Colorful quill embroidery, intricate beadwork, perfectly formed arrowheads, spears, war clubs, knives and guns, for the most part, comprised his possessions. Among these was the sword which had been given to him by the Great White Father at the Horse Creek Council.

As Little Chief stood watching, Washakie showed the white man his most cherished prize, a hide painting of the Battle-Where-Boy-Take-Scalp, as he referred to the Crow battle in which Tupaku wore his warbonnet. "My son always good medicine for Shoshone," he declared.

Tupaku interrupted. "My father, I want Daidŭtsi for wife."

"Have you spoken?"

"*Kay,* Porivo say she'll choose."

"Choose?" Captain John was unable to disguise his interest.

So the white man wanted to be classed as a suitor!

Tupaku was quick to accept the challenge. Reckless from his meeting with Daidŭtsi, he was willing to gamble. "Porivo say we wait outside her tepee tonight 'til moon rise above mountain. She come outside and pick one she want."

"We?" Captain Johns' face flushed. While he might have hoped to marry a daughter of the chief, he had not planned it this way. "I have no wish to enter the contest."

He turned toward Washakie to protest, but the chief closed the subject by stating, "Daidŭtsi my daughter. She choose for herself." He then arose, slammed down the lid of the chest and left. The two young men stared angrily at each other.

"You did this to make a fool of me!" Captain John accused. "I have no desire to be involved in your love game."

Word spread quickly among the Indians who had gathered for the feast. This night the daughter of their chief would choose her mate. Though the process was irregular, excitement ran high, for the known contestants included a Bannock, a Cheyenne and a white man.

Tupaku, entering the spirit of the occasion, enjoyed the white man's discomfort. His love had been fanned to a pitch he might never have known had it not been for the contest. He realized that the Indians were betting heavily on the outcome, but few would place their bets on Captain John.

Tupaku was not flattered when he discovered that the wagering was about even on him and on Walking Horse. Had Daidŭtsi been encouraging the Cheyenne during his absence? Might she have given him and others of the tribe reason to believe she cared for him? Little Chief recalled the way she watched him during the time he was taking part in the Sun Dance. He had either gained popularity during the past year, or else Tupaku had lost his rating by going to the white camp. The year before, no one would have wagered a breath feather on Walking Horse.

When the moon, as large as a ceremonial drum, appeared behind a lone pine tree at the top of the mountain, Daidŭtsi, dazzling in her beaded doeskin dress, emerged from her tepee. Tupaku watched breathlessly as she came forth to claim the love of her life. She made a stirring picture. Her face was radiant, her smile mysterious. No word was spoken as Little Chief stood waiting between the bewildered white man and the impatient Cheyenne. When Daidŭtsi reached him, she placed a talisman, a love charm, in his outstretched hand.

"*Ha*!" he exulted, recognizing it instantly as the piece of moss agate he had given her the day he found her in Naroyan's camp. She had not needed Strong Wind after all as a reminder. Wrapping his blanket protectively around her shoulders, he held her close.

"Satonzibi—Prairie Flower," he whispered so that she alone could hear.

"I thought you never come back!" she chided.

Musicians started beating their hand drums and singing while Indians of all ages and sizes danced riotously. Those who had lost in the betting rejoiced with the rest. Captain John, with Basil at his side, stood watching the abandonment of the scene, and Walking Horse disappeared in the shadows.

22

John Logan, in utter defeat, sat staring gloomily at Basil's campfire the next day after the jubilant occasion. He would not have known what to do had it not been for the sub-chief who had remained faithfully at his side. Now with Basil elsewhere, he felt forsaken. When an Indian woman placed a bowl of hot stew before him, he ate mechanically. Perhaps Basil was even then discussing his stay with Washakie.

When someone sat down beside him, he did not bother to turn to see who it was. Startled, he heard Walking Horse speak his name.

"Captain John."

Logan looked at him. Could it be that the Cheyenne wanted to be sociable, now that they had both been rejected?

"Want to go home?" the Indian asked.

While Logan had no desire to stay, he did not relish the possibility of risking his life by making the journey alone. He was slow with his reply.

"Walking Horse, why do you speak to me?"

"Want to know. Want to go home?" he persisted.

Logan, remembering the way Tupaku admired his scalp lock, replied, "I should leave, but why do you ask?"

"Walking Horse be your guide."

"Guide! I thought you did not like the white man."

"Walking Horse like white man's horse."

"You may have my pack horse if you take me safely to Fort Bridger."

"No want pack horse. Want saddle horse damn bad."

"Very well." Logan was in no position to bargain, for he knew that neither Tupaku nor Basil would accompany him. With the animosity that was being shown him, he did not dare remain until the latter made his proposed trip to Fort Supply to harvest his crop.

Later in the morning, the Saint had his final conference with Washakie. "My friend, I return to my people," he told him.

"It is well," the chief replied as he smoked his pipe and stared toward the mountains.

The Mormon was disconcerted. Was this the same friendly chief who had taken him into his lodge to show him his trophies of war? Was this the chief who, a few years before, had thawed out the frozen feet of a fellow Saint on the breast of one of his women? Many stories had been told in Salt Lake to prove his devotion to his white brothers. Now he was unapproachable, his remark a form of dismissal.

"Chief Washakie, do you have a message to send to Brigham Young?"

"Tell him Basil learn to farm. He teach my people." The Chief made no reference to their spiritual needs. The effort expended by the missionaries had been for naught. Logan thanked Washakie for his kindness and bade him farewell. It was obvious that the white man was an unwanted guest in the Shoshone camp.

As soon as Tupaku learned that the missionary was planning to leave, he came in search of him.

"You go alone?" he asked.

"No, Walking Horse is going with me."

"Walking Horse!" Tupaku exclaimed.

"Yes, he will be my guide. Two rejected lovers!" Logan tried to make light of his predicament. Then he extended his hand. "I have not had a chance to congratulate you." When Tupaku shook hands with him, a faint smile flickered across his usually inscrutable face.

Walking Horse had little to say as he guided the white man toward Fort Supply. His statements, though infrequent, were enlightening. He readily admitted that he was under pledge to both Washakie and Little Chief that he would see that no harm came to Logan. Should anything happen to the missionary along the way, the Cheyenne would pay for it with his life.

Logan soon tired of trying to make conversation, so

he lapsed into silence as he studied the surroundings. Since they were not following the same course they had taken in going to Wind River, there were no recognizable landmarks. The missionary was fascinated by the cloud shadows that were like vast scatter rugs on the wide expanse of prairie. They seemed to stand still while billowy, parent clouds churned overhead. Sometimes he would ride into a shadow. Then abruptly he would be in the bright sunshine again.

At one point in the journey, his attention was attracted by a coyote some distance ahead. He was running confidently under a low flying sage hen, but he made no effort to jump into the air after it. He kept going at the same speed. The Saint soon found the reason for his assurance. The predator, aware that his prey could fly only a short distance, was timing his action so that he would be on hand when it dropped exhausted to the ground. Finally, he was rewarded for his wisdom and patience. If the Saints ever converted the Shoshones, they would have to have the patience of a coyote.

The Saint's and the Cheyenne's throats were parched by the time they reached Green River, where they flattened themselves on the bank, splashed water on their faces, and drank from the refreshing stream. No wonder this was the favorite location of the trappers and traders for their rendezvous during the fur trading period! The river, reflecting its verdant valley, was like an oasis in the surrounding desert.

In the distance, the snow-capped Uinta Mountains

formed a jagged skyline. They seemed to be a mirage, at right angle to the Rockies. Somewhere, Logan had heard they comprised the only mountain range in North America running east and west. He wondered.

After leaving Green River, there was little to break the monotony of the journey. The missionary would be glad to reach the hilly country lying west of the fort, for he planned to return to Salt Lake. Scrub oak and greasewood would be preferable to the seemingly endless stretch of wasteland, covered by dwarfed black sage. The country was bleak and depressing, but the silence of the Indian was worse. If he would only talk and quit staring in that maddening manner!

The Saint's patience snapped. "Stop it!" he blurted. "Stop looking at me like that!"

Walking Horse glanced away, then back at the white man. "Want to know?" he asked vaguely.

"Walking Horse, if you have anything to say, in the name of heaven, say it!"

"*Ha'a*." The Indian had to grope for words. "You think Daidŭtsi pretty?"

The Mormon had no desire to express himself on the subject of another man's wife.

"Why?" he evaded

"Would she be. . . . pretty in white camp if—"

"Walking Horse what ails you? Are you still moonstruck?"

The Indian ignored his question. "You ever hear of white girl in Shoshone camp?" he asked.

"Why, er—yes. I remember hearing about one. As I

recall, some of the Saints tried to find out, but—"
Logan was beginning to comprehend. "Was Daidŭtsi the girl?" "She does not look like the others, come to think of it. Her eyes are blue and her hair, tight as it is braided, tries to curl. No wonder they took her for a white girl. She must be part white."

"*Kay.*"

"Well, she looks it."

"She's all white!"

The missionary was stunned. "My God! If I had known—" Although there was little that he could have done about it, he said, "I'd have tried to rescue her."

"Rescue?" It was the Indian's turn to be surprised. "What? She's not prisoner."

"I should have said I would have tried to return her to her people.

"She's with her people."

"You speak in riddles, Walking Horse. Why do you tell me this unless you want her returned to her family?"

"You not want her?" The Indian was incredulous.

"No! She is Tupaku's wife."

Walking Horse could not understand. "You not want me to bring her to you?

"No!"

The crafty Cheyenne thought a moment. Then he asked, "White Chief at Salt Lake want her?" Obviously, he wanted to be the instrument of her delivery and the recipient of the reward.

"Walking Horse, may God have pity on you for betraying your brother. Let me tell you that I and the rest of the Saints despise you for it. Do not come to the white camp to bargain."

Now on familiar ground and in sight of the fort, Logan stepped from his horse. Before handing the reins to the Indian, he said, "I want to know what you plan to do with him. It must be important for the horse to be worth more than my scalp."

"Walking Horse trade for knife."

"Knife! Surely you know that no knife in the world is worth a horse."

"This is."

"It must be cast in bronze," Logan declared, but the Indian did not know what he meant.

"It belong to Tavenduwits."

The white man stood watching the Cheyenne mount his horse and lead his own in the direction of the Tavenduwits' camp. What could he be up to? What ever it was, Logan was convinced that it was not good.

23

In the fall, Tavenduwits, with his two young recruits, Elk Tooth and Walking Horse, made his appearance in Washakie's camp. His excuse was that they had come to visit. Both he and Elk Tooth had relatives there, and Walking Horse was still Washakie's son though he chose to live elsewhere.

Tupaku, studying the three visitors, could not help thinking how much they were alike. They were even dressed the same in their plain buckskin suits and faded blankets. Of the three, the Cheyenne made the best appearance. He was taller, lighter complexioned and cleaner than his stocky companions. He was even-featured and handsome. From the admiring glances the young maidens cast toward him, he seemed, also, to have more charm. No one liked the looks or the smell of Elk Tooth, and Tavenduwits was too old to arouse their interest.

The guests had apparently learned that the tribal elders had planned a buffalo hunt, and they had come to take part. The day before the hunting party was to leave, a runner brought word that Ar-ra-pine, Walkara's successor as war chief of the Utes, wanted to sue for peace. The message was strange because the Shoshones had considered themselves at peace with the Utes since they heard of the untimely death of Walkara.

The runner, who brought Ar-ra-pine's message, mentioned 15 horses the Snakes had stolen from the Utes. Washakie looked accusingly toward Tavenduwits, who did not respond.

"Ar-ra-pine want Washakie come or send Tavenduwits to Salt Lake for medicine talk. Big Chief Brigham says so, too," the runner explained.

Washakie thought a moment. He was not one to deviate from any plan, no matter what it was. He was going on a buffalo hunt, and as Little Chief and everyone else in the tribe knew, neither Big Chief Brigham nor the Great White Father in Washington would be able to make him change his plan.

"Tell him Washakie goes to buffalo. My people hungry. Tavenduwits one he want to see. Washakie talk with Walkara, Tavenduwits with Ar-ra-pine."

The chief turned toward his son. "Tupaku, go with Tavenduwits. You be Shoshones' good medicine at council."

Little Chief's stay in the missionary camp had been such a failure that he could not understand his father's wanting him to go, but he did not mind missing the hunt. With Walking Horse and Elk Tooth along, it would not have been enjoyable anyway. He still felt bitter toward the Cheyenne for claiming his kill on his first surround, and he had disliked Elk Tooth since the rock throwing incident.

When Ka-tat-o (Stays-at-Home), chief of the Northern Shoshones, joined Tavenduwits at Salt Lake, there were about 300 all told in the Shoshone party. After accepting provisions of food, fuel and hay from the Saints, Tavenduwits, Ka-tat-o and Tupaku went to see the Indian agent. There the crafty Tavenduwits made it clear in the white man's tongue that he knew Congress had made large appropriations in the spring for the purpose of giving presents and making treaties with the Indians. His ability to read and write put him in a good bargaining position.

He complained, "White man make roads through Shoshone land and travel in safety. He use our grass and drink our water. We not receive anything, but white man give gifts to other tribes."

Presents, including robes, shirts, tradecloth and beef were forthcoming. After Tavenduwits' successful trip to the agency, he turned to the press. As a result, the Shoshone-Ute stay in Salt Lake City was given full coverage by the *Deseret News*.

The day before the scheduled treaty council, the Shoshone tribal leaders, with 60 warriors, went to the Governor's office. There they had been led to believe they would find Ar-ra-pine and his delegation. When they neared the Tabernacle, they were met by a Ute messenger who told them curtly to stop where they were. The Snakes paused in surprise, then started toward the Deseret Store. Opposite the store they met the Utes, who were well armed and mounted. Their faces were painted black to show their animosity. The Snakes, in contrast, had complied with the usual custom of going to a peace council unarmed. Their interpreter went fearlessly forward to protest to the Utes.

"Put guns away," he ordered. "The Snakes come unarmed." As the hostiles dismounted, they sullenly placed their guns against the wall.

When Ka-tat-o stepped forward proudly, he held up his heavily decorated peace pipe, which he offered toward Dam Apŭ. He said loudly, so that all might hear, "This is weapon Ka-tat-o fight with. Northern Shoshones want peace."

"Washakie want peace, too," Tavenduwits stated. "He send Little Chief, his Good Medicine, with me. He hope he be good medicine for council."

Though Ar-ra-pine was not present, one of his elders stepped forward, and the other chiefs and warriors followed. When one of the Utes held out his hand, Tavenduwits ignored it. Instead, he raised his hands toward Dam Apŭ. The Ute did likewise. Then they both lowered their hands to the ground. When they straightened up, they looked each other in the eye, following which they shook hands and embraced. The other delegates went through the same ritual.

White men, women and children, watching the show with pleasure, were friendlier than they had been when the Shoshones met Walkara. At that time, the children had scattered like snowbirds at the sight of Indians.

After the Utes had passed down the line and had greeted all of the Snakes, they adjourned to Union Square, where the second part of their ceremony took place. There they formed two parallel lines, facing each other. Ka-tat-o and Tavenduwits passed down the enemy line as they presented the pipe to each Ute. While he was allowed to smoke as long as he liked, he was not permitted to touch the pipe with his hands.

After the two Snakes had finished, two of the Ute chiefs went through the same procedure. Following this tedious ceremony, the members of both tribes mingled freely.

On the morning of the council, the Snakes again went to the Governor's office to locate their adversaries. Believing that all was going well, they were in high spirits as they went down the street. When someone started singing a war song, they all joined in. To their surprise, the indignant Ar-ra-pine rushed out of the Governor's office with his interpreter.

"Stop!" he ordered. "Ar-ra-pine not like you sing war song," he stated.

The Shoshones stopped at once.

Ar-ra-pine soon recovered his temper. When the interpreter introduced Tavenduwits, he not only shook his hand but he also embraced him. After discovering that Tupaku was the son and representative of Washakie, the Ute chief greeted him in like manner.

Ar-ra-pine, who had called the council, presided. He asked all of the Indians present to raise their hands toward heaven as a token of peace. Then the Utes knelt while their chief, a Mormon convert, prayed. The Snakes looked on in wonderment at the kneeling Utes. The prayer was so long and inclusive that Tupaku, who had learned to bow his head while living with the Saints, looked up to see if any of the Utes might have turned white. Perhaps the Black Book did not mean that they would turn white all at once.

During the council proceedings, Tupaku was reminded of the time he wished that Washakie would settle his differences with Walkara with a tomahawk. There had been an issue then because the Shoshones were at war with the Utes. This time Tavenduwits had stolen some Ute horses. Why all the to-do? Tupaku could not see why Washakie's Shoshones, or Ka-tat-o's either, should be involved. Anyway, Tavenduwits agreed to return the horses.

At the conclusion of the council, Brigham Young delivered a lecture on brotherly love, which was so inspiring that the two tribes decided to start out right by joining forces in a buffalo hunt along White River. While plans were being made for the venture, Tupaku thought over the facts that might interest his chief. In the first place, he must tell him that Ar-ra-pine was different from Walkara. Big Chief could be assured that he no longer need fear the Utes.

24

On his way back to Washakie's camp, Tupaku accepted the invitation of Tavenduwits to stay over night with him. During the trip, he had found him to be a man of firm convictions, especially regarding the white man, though he was half white. His reasoning reminded Little Chief of his old friend Pariha Ungu, the holy man in Naroyan's band.

He liked to discuss the Indians' problems with Tavenduwits, but to his surprise he would sometimes find himself arguing as Washakie would, in the white man's favor. He realized that some of his original hatred had turned into smouldering resentment. Perhaps his naturally antagonistic nature, as much as anything, accounted for his talking in defense of the white man.

He certainly had no love for him, and yet he was beginning to see that Washakie's theories were realistic. He was aware that the white man would inevitably take over, and no amount of rebellion on the part of the Indian could prevent it. He had not forgotten the words of Chickadee, which he quoted to Tavenduwits as he sat at his fire before retiring to his blanket.

The sub-chief scoffed. "If all Indians had banded together instead of fighting each other, they could have run white man out long ago. Washakie pat him on back and call him brother. That's worse than fighting. Make more come. While Indian sound war whoop and fight each other, white man take over." Tupaku had to admit there was truth in what he said, but he did not agree that the Indian would accomplish anything by committing depredations against the emigrants and the settlers.

Tired from his long journey, he slept late and missed sharing the morning meal with his host. Consequently, he did not meet the members of Tavenduwits' household. A woman, whom Tupaku took to be one of his wives, brought Black Horse when he told his host that he must be on his way.

As he mounted and turned to leave, his attention was attracted by a young woman vigorously chopping wood behind the tepee. As he sat watching her, he was impressed by her sure, swift strokes! Since the weather was unseasonably warm, her arms were bare. He could see her muscles ripple as she lifted the ax. Her waist was slim, her body well rounded and her bare legs tapered but firm. Her face would have been attractive had it not been for her unpleasant expression. She attacked each stick as if it were a personal enemy.

He thought of the asset a strong girl like that would be in any household. Black Woman was getting old. Though she had tried to perform the duties of an Indian woman without complaint, she was far better as a cook than as a woodsman or camp mover. She had never really learned how to erect a tepee properly.

Daidŭtsi, who had mastered the art of beadwork, needed to keep her fingers nimble. He did not expect her to do the many tasks that were performed by Indian women.

The girl chopping wood was an answer to his needs. She would make a good slave wife. If she saw him, she gave no indication. She continued to chop with precision.

Tavenduwits, stepping from his tepee, found that his guest had been detained. "My daughter," he explained.

"I give you two horses for her."

"Three already offer for her."

"Three then."

"*Kay*. Four and she's yours. She make good strong squaw. Do plenty work, but she have temper like wildcat. You tame Black Horse?"

Tupaku nodded.

"He fine animal. Maybe you tame my daughter. Pucho [Blue Beads] we call her."

The girl looked at her father with fire in her eyes. Obviously there had been trouble between father and daughter, but it was no concern of Little Chief's.

"Four horses," he agreed. "Send two braves; they bring horses back. How soon Pucho be ready?"

"Get belongings," her father commanded. "You not make Tupaku wait."

The girl threw down her ax and ran to the tepee without saying a word to her father or to her new master.

Blue Beads thrust her possessions into a buckskin bag with vengeance. She had reason to be angry with her father, who had done everything he could to encourage Elk Tooth. She despised him as intensely as she loved Walking Horse! The latter had spurned her for another. Her only consolation lay in the thought that he would return to her.

Tavenduwits spoke the truth when he said that three horses had been offered for his daughter. What he did not say was that Elk Tooth, who had made the offer after a lucky gambling streak, had lost the horses before they could be delivered. No matter how many horses he could offer, Blue Beads had vowed she would hack him to pieces with her ax before she would be his mate!

As she rode along in the wake of her master, it was hard for her to realize her good fortune. She did not know Tupaku, though she had heard of him. He was the son of Washakie, who was the richest chief among the Shoshones. No doubt his son was rich, too. He had not hesitated to meet her father's price. To her knowledge, she was the first girl in the camp who had brought as many as four horses. That in itself was comforting, though she wondered why Walking Horse had not returned with her father.

As they covered the miles, the girl kept looking at Little Chief, riding directly in front of her. He had not so much as addressed a word to her, but she did not mind. Why had she not noticed how handsome he was? She had never seen anyone so carefully dressed. His ceremonial clothing was ornately decorated with beadwork. She wondered who had the patience to make it. She would rather chop wood than bother with beads!

Tupaku had wide shoulders, and he was tall and muscular, more like a Bannock than a Shoshone. The farther they rode, the more infatuated Blue Beads became. She was now Little Chief's wife, she gloated inwardly. She, too, would have fine clothing, and she would be highly respected by all the tribe. She would bear him children, and they, in turn, would be sons of a chief.

By the time they neared the camp, her heart was singing. She was the wife of a famous man! She was ready to give of herself and her love.

When Tupaku reached his tepee, the one with prairie flowers painted on the outside, he jumped from his horse and affectionately greeted the young woman who ran out to meet him. Blue Beads, unprepared for the scene, sat astride her horse and watched in dejection. She had not thought of his having a wife, yet in her jealous heart she had to admit that the girl was beautiful, dressed in her finery to please her mate! Blue Beads, realizing that she was nothing more than a slave wife, stared doggedly.

After the two had finished their greeting, they turned toward her. "Pucho," Little Chief explained. Then with his blanket around his wife and a happy smile on his face, he guided her into the tepee.

Black Woman stepped up to take the horse, while Pucho alighted and unhitched her travois. Tears of anger ran down her cheeks as she gave her bundle of belongings a vicious kick.

The black woman watched unsympathetically. So Tupaku had brought a slave wife to share his blanket! Her bitterness did not last. That night she heard the girl, heartsick and lonely, sobbing while Tupaku and Daidŭtsi, on the opposite side of the fire, were unmindful of her in their happiness.

With a low, exultant laugh, Tupaku drew Daidŭtsi to him. Funny little girl with face like an Indian and body as snow white as the awesome beauty of the Tetons! Some hungry eyed French trapper, crazed by longing, had given the fantastic name, the Tetons, the breasts, to the majestic peaks. Though three in number, they suggested to his wild imagination a seductive giantess, reclining with breasts uplifted. How cold and unattainable such a creature would be compared with Daidŭtsi, who was warm and yielding under Tupaku's blanket. He had never ceased to marvel at the wonder of her.

Such supreme happiness as the two had found together could not last. Of that he was sure. Just what would happen, he did not know, but nothing ever lasts for an Indian. The beavers that first brought the white man to the Shoshone country were almost extinct. The buffalo, which from the beginning of time had furnished food, clothing and shelter would some day be gone. Then the land—

Contented and temporarily at peace with the world, Little Chief was almost asleep when Daidŭtsi asked, "You see Captain John?"

"*Kay*, he's in California."

"California!" the girl exclaimed in a whisper so that she would not disturb the other occupants of the tepee. "That's where my father was taking me. California," she repeated the word softly. "I wonder if he might see 'im."

"*Kay shunbana.*" Tupaku did not tell her that her father was killed at the time of her abduction. "I see your people in Salt Lake."

"My people?"

"*Ha'a.* Taivo." He could not keep the bitterness from his voice. Sensing his antagonism, she whispered, "You're my people! What does color of skin matter? It's heart that counts. You, Liza and I all have skin of different color. We talk different, but our love is the same."

Throughout the winter, Black Woman and Blue Beads gathered sticks and chopped wood for the fires in the tepee. They tended the horses and prepared all of the food that was eaten in the household.

Meanwhile, Daidŭtsi and Tupaku enjoyed the cozy

warmth of the fur-carpeted tepee. He placed wide strips of buffalo hide around the edges to eliminate floor drafts, for he had not forgotten the time she had pneumonia. If she had the slightest cold, he was quick to go to the medicine man for a specially prepared remedy of beaver grease and herbs. The other women in the tribe were jealous of the thoughtfulness and devotion he showered on her. He alone knew of his constant fear that she might be taken from him.

Blue Beads made every effort to attract him, but he could see no one but Daidŭtsi. He was especially proud of her soft, silken hair and he would have her unbraid it so that he could enjoy its fine texture. Blue Beads was consumed with jealousy when he stroked her tresses.

Biding her time, the vengeful girl found a day when she was alone with Daidŭtsi in the tepee. Without warning she attacked her. She seized her by the hair and screamed, "You white woman! Go back where you come from!"

Caught off guard, Daidŭtsi was stunned for a moment. Then she began fighting with all her strength. She kicked and scratched, but Blue Beads held firmly to her hair until Black Woman returned and separated them. When Liza told Little Chief what had happened, he gave his slave wife a horse and ordered her to return to her people. He was so anxious to get rid of her that he sent an escort to make sure she reached her destination.

Upon her return, Blue Beads was greeted enthusiastically by her family and friends. Her mother set a bowl of moose stew before her. This she gave her full attention until her appetite had been appeased. Then she set the bowl down and looked from her father to the various members of the family circle. She had a real grievance, and she wanted to make sure that she had an audience before she began talking.

"Why you return to lodge of your father?" Tavenduwits asked. "You visit or you stay?"

"I stay. I not want to see Tupaku again!" she declared. Then she broke into uncontrolled weeping. Everyone looked at her questioningly, but no one made an effort to comfort her. She stopped crying abruptly and looked at Tavenduwits.

"Tell me, my father, chief of our people. Tell me, what's wrong? My face—" she brushed her fingers lightly from her forehead to her chin as if checking to see that all of her features were in place. "Me—" With a sweeping gesture, she indicated her well curved body. "What's wrong?"

Her father looked at her without change of expression, but the other members of the family circle shouted, "Nothing!"

"Tupaku never look at me any more than at Black Woman! He say, 'Bring my horse! . . . cut wood! . . . get food!' Daidŭtsi not like meat very good. She won't eat ants and crickets. She like currants, sunflower soup and wild strawberries. So I pick. She like camas bulbs. So I dig!

"Sometime I want to put water hemlock in her soup, but Black Woman watch me. When Tupaku away, I want to put black stone medicine man give me in her bed, but Black Woman not give me chance. I want to cut off Daidŭtsi's fine hair, but Black Woman not let me."

Tavenduwits, smoking his pipe quietly, listened to her tirade. Her accusations would hardly justify action in any way. After all, he had no complaint. Little Chief had paid well for his daughter. With her back in his tepee, he might have a chance to sell her for another horse or two.

Blue Beads told him that the only time Tupaku would share his blanket with her was when Daidŭtsi had to go to the menstrual lodge. Even then, she had to go to him, and he had little to say to her. When his favorite wife returned, he could see no one else.

"I'm his wife," she stated.

"Daidŭtsi's white," Tavenduwits said thoughtfully. "Maybe her people want her back."

"She'd be no good. She can swim, dance and ride horseback on her spotted pony. She do beadwork and make herself pretty, but she not know how to pitch tepee. She never lift an ax or tan a hide. She not know how to dig in the hard ground for roots. Black woman hover over her like mother hawk, ready to fly screaming."

After finishing her discourse, she asked a direct question. "You take her back to her people?"

Tavenduwits shook his head. Tupaku had fulfilled

his bargain with four horses, and he had given one more to Blue Beads. What did he have to show for the five horses she had cost him? But Tavenduwits was shrewd. He realized that there was a possibility that the white man might pay a ransom for a captive.

25

Little Chief would watch Washakie take out the gold nugget the ferryboat captain had given him following the episode at Green River. He seemed to like the way it sparkled in the sunlight. While he knew that the white man bought everything from corn liquor to women with his *puwi,* he carried it in his medicine bag, along with his other trophies. Whenever Tupaku found him looking at it, he could tell that the white man had done something to remind Washakie, for there was invariably a connection. Little Chief seated himself at his side and waited for him to speak.

"You think white men fight each other?" Washakie asked.

"You mean Gentile and Mormon?" Little Chief had learned the terms at Fort Supply.

Washakie nodded. Then he said, "White engineer Lander come while you hunt."

"What does he want?"

"Great White Father want new road so he not have to go through Salt Lake. He want road to go along base of Wind River Mountains to Salt River. Through Starved Valley to Fort Hall."

Tupaku was so angry he almost choked on his

words. "You mean Taivo want another road in our country?"

"*Ha.*" Washakie answered sadly.

"Captain John tell how sea gulls devour crickets. Gull is white like Taivo. We dark like cricket. What'll become of us?" Tupaku asked in alarm.

"*Kay shunbana.*" Washakie had to admit that he did not know.

"You say not fight? Our people hungry and will have no place to go."

"Did cricket fight sea gull? Did they drive 'em away? *Kay,* they wait. Finally gulls fly back to sea."

Tupaku, who was more familiar with the details of the story, replied, "*Ha'a,* when sea gulls fly away, crickets all gone. When white man take what he want, we be gone!" His patience was at an end. He could no longer stand by without a word and see the Shoshone nation crumble. He had made every effort to conform to Washakie's pattern even though it was contrary to his nature. Now his spirit was in revolt. "Tupaku rather die on battlefield than starve!" he exclaimed.

When news came that the government was sending an army to Utah, a cloud of uncertainty hung over the Indian camp. Everyone speculated as to what the chief might do. The missionary who brought the word had urged the Snakes to go hunting in the Big Horns and remain neutral. While the chief made no promise, he showed no inclination to enter the white man's fray.

At Little Chief's insistence, he called a council to discuss the matter. Washakie, who began with his usual eulogy of the white man, made no mention of the proposed road, of which his Indians were still unaware.

"Great White Father not make all his children do as he want any more than Washakie. He not like Chief Brigham's government, so he sends army to make him change. Washakie show he mean what he says, just like Great White Father. White man's trouble, no business of Shoshone. We fight own battles. Does he help fight Sioux?"

"*Kay*! *Kay*!" his councillors chorused.

Tupaku, taking exception to what Washakie said, arose and addressed the council. Tall and straight, he was as forceful as his chief when he said, "Tupaku think we should help soldier."

"Why?" one of the elders asked.

"We can't drive settlers out because they take root like grass. We help soldier drive 'em out. Great White Father's soldiers many and well armed. They have big gun on wheels. After they run the settlers away, they'll go back to their camp in far away country."

This was the first time Tupaku had openly defied the chief. The Indians, though surprised, looked at him in admiration.

"Tupaku speaks true. We should help soldier clear settler out of country," one of the elders agreed.

"Let Little Chief lead warriors!" another proposed.

Tupaku had not realized that his protest would arouse dissension. Now Washakie was forced to take a stand. "Your chief say he'll never hurt white man. When he make promise he keep it!" Then he made his first concession. "Tupaku, choose 50 warriors to go with you. Help white soldiers push settlers out."

Twelve hundred wanted to go, but Washakie insisted upon limiting the number. Again he surprised everyone by saying that the rest might go later if needed. "But first Tupaku must talk to military chief."

When Little Chief and his warriors found the Army for Utah, they were amazed by the size of the encampment. There were more tepees than they could count, stretched along the banks of Green River.

To Tupaku's delight, Blanket Chief Bridger, official guide for the army, was the first to come out to greet him. The mountain man showed his pleasure by hugging him.

"Blanket Chief gone long time," Little Chief commented.

"Yer right I been. Ef et hadn't abeen fer these here sodjers it'd abeen a damn sight longer. How's yer Pappy? He come, too?"

"*Kay.*"

"Jes sent his good medicine, eh? Well, 'fore I forget, tell 'im Rutta ain't Rutta no more. Her an' me got married with a parson. Her name's Miz Mary Washakie Bridger now. How you like thet?" He laughed hilariously and slapped the young Indian on the back.

"Et's sure nice a ya to come visit the sodjers. Why y'all dressed up? Who y'on the warpath against this here time, the Sioux?"

"*Kay,* on warpath with soldiers. Tupaku want to help drive settlers out so grass can grow and buffalo come back."

"Taint a bad idee." Bridger agreed. Then after he had had a chance to realize the full meaning of his words, the mountain man exclaimed, "Whatcha mean on warpath with sodjers? Washakie know 'bout this? Y'mean t'tell me he let y'come—"

"*Ha'a.*"

"Y'don't say! Don't tell me you've changed his mindt."

"Washakie send me," Tupaku replied.

Bridger, unable to comprehend, shook his head as he commented, "Reckon he couldn't take no more! I don't know how he ever come to let ya, but we're plumb tickled t'have ya with us. Wait 'til the sodjers hears about this!"

While Bridger held a conference with Colonel

Edmund B. Alexander, the officer in charge, more Indians streamed into camp. They mingled agreeably with the soldiers who purchased some of their curios with the tobacco they carried in their pockets.

A big council fire lighted the valley when darkness settled over the surrounding hills. The Yellow Noses, now painted and ready for battle, began their War Dance to the beat of the drum. The sound was portentous. Bridger took Tupaku with him when he went a second time to see the colonel, whom he found conferring with several officers. Alexander seemed to be awestruck by the primitive cries.

"Colonel, this here's Tupaku, son of Washakie, chief of the Shoshone. He's brung 50 fine warriors t'hep y' fight. There's more 'n a thousand standin' by."

Little Chief looked at the officer in a straightforward manner. When Alexander extended his hand, he clasped it firmly. For the first time, he felt that he and the white man had a common cause—to rid the Indian country of the settler. The Shoshones did not distinguish Mormon from Gentile. To them all settlers were Mormon.

The noise of the War Dance rent the air. With 50 making that much commotion, what would a thousand more be like? Alexander was appalled.

"What are they doing?" he asked.

"They're a gittin' ready t'go on the warpath with ya, Colonel. All y'need do is give the word."

The colonel's face was colorless when he turned toward his advisers. Little Chief could not understand his indecision.

"They're a splendid set of men. Better take them," one officer suggested.

"At least hire some as guides and hunters. We could use them," another affirmed, but Alexander was deaf to their advice. He also seemed dumbfounded by the primitive cries that had turned his orderly camp into a place of confusion.

All he would say was, "Arrange a council. Leave me for awhile! I'll give my decision in an hour."

As he turned to go, Little Chief was baffled. "When someone want to help Indian it make him glad. He says, '*Ha*!' But Taivo not know what to say."

The circle had been formed and all was in readiness for the council when the commanding officer appeared. The prolonged War Dance stopped abruptly. Alexander, a small, nervous man, was decorated with medals and insignias. He had more than once been cited for gallantry and meritorious conduct in his long military career. Soldiers and warriors clustered about to see and hear what was taking place.

When the pipe had made the rounds, Little Chief stood to offer his proposition to the white man. "Washakie friend of white man, who is always welcome at his fireside," he began. He spoke in Shoshone, and Blanket Chief served as his interpreter. "He go long way to Fort Laramie to meet Great White Father.

He even risk his life and life of his people to go in enemy country for medicine talk."

"He not fight white brother, but he know that unless settlers stop turning grass upside down there'll be no more buffalo. Washakie's people not Diggers. Buffalo hunters. We want settlers to leave. We come to help drive 'em out so buffalo'll come back."

The offer having been made, the colonel now had to accept or reject it. As he stood facing Little Chief, he tried to express his gratitude. "The Great White Father in Washington will be pleased by your offer. Colonel Johnston, who commands this expedition, has not arrived. I am temporarily in charge. It is not in my power to accept your offer, nor can I tell you when the colonel will be here. If you would like to come back after he arrives, you can make your wishes known to him. Thank you for coming such a long way to offer your assistance. It will help the morale of the troops."

Little Chief was puzzled. Did it mean that the officer would not accept his offer—that he would not let the Indians fight with him? He turned toward Bridger, who was vexed by what Alexander had said.

"Wall, I b'damned. Bet ef Johnston'd abeen here he'd a snapped up yer offer 'fore y'coulda said scat!"

"When'll he come?" Tupaku asked.

"I kain't say as t'that. He must not be expectin' 'im soon er he woulda said fer y'to stay 'til he gets here. Alexander don't know nothin' 'bout this here country. Bet he'll wisht he'd a took yer offer more times 'n one."

After a great deal of handshaking, the Snakes withdrew to their camp, where a feast was held in Bridger's honor. While Blanket Chief and the soldiers he brought with him were sitting around the campfire, the air was heavier than usual with smoke from grass fires started by the Mormons in their guerrilla warfare.

"Et's them Saints agin! We ain't saw hair nor hide a'em, but they're allus up t'somethin'. One night after we'd went t'bed an' was sleepin' sound, one a the guards yelled, 'sodjers turn out, we're attackedted! It was jest a scare 'cause all they done was t'try t'drive offen the mules. Ef the bell mule hadn't a caught his rope in the sagebrush, he'd aben runnin' yet. You shoulda heard 'im. He raised his head, lifted his tail, an' let outa bray y'coulda heard clean t'Wind River ef you'd a been listenin'. The other mules stopped an' jined in. I bet they skeered the Saints in Salt Lake. No harm done. Jest a little excitement, ceptin' fer one a the sodjers that died uv a heart attackt. It was jest too excitin' fer 'im.

"One a the emigrants tole us 'bout a song the Saints sung at their celebration in July. Et went like this:

Johnston's Army's on the way,
Doo-dah, doo-dah!
The Mormon people fer t'slay,
Doo-dah, doo-dah day.
An ef 'e comes, we'll have some fun,
Doo-dah, doo-dah!
T'see 'im an' his jennies run,
Doo-dah, doo-dah-day.

"They shore run thet night—jennies, jacks an' all, with the sodjers after 'em. The Saints ain't a bit afeareda the army 'cause it don't have no cavalry units t'force 'em t' a showdown. Ast me, they're a goin' t'have a pecka fun snipin' at us. Effen we had some a you Injuns what's mounted and knows the country, they'd be afeared t'try their capers. Effen I war heada this here army, I'd shore keep ya. I kain't understand the colonel!"

The fire, effectively forming a barrier between the military camp and the Indians, halted at the water's edge. Unable to progress farther, it fanned out each side, as if seeking a means of engulfing the Indians who had safely reached the opposite bank. The weary, soot-blackened soldiers were finally able to bring the flanking flames under control.

The Snakes had lost all desire to remain in the area. Little Chief ordered a return to Wind River, although night had fallen and their enemies' spirits might be on the prowl.

When Tupaku and his followers reached Warm Valley, they found Bear Claw preparing to go on the warpath. Logs had brought startling news of an encampment of Sioux on the Sweetwater, in easy striking distance of the Shoshones. Washakie had elected to go along, for he intended to take this opportunity to teach Nanagi the fine points of Indian warfare. So far he had shown no inclination to fight although he was an avid hunter.

Before the Snakes reached the Sweetwater, Nanagi rode up to his father's side and asked if he might go hunting.

"Hunting!" The chief was flabbergasted. "When Shoshone go on warpath they shoot Sioux, not rabbits," he snapped.

His son did not reply.

"Go!" Washakie shouted in disgust. The youth whirled his horse and left without a word.

A short distance down the trail, the Sioux rushed from ambush in surprising numbers. Bear Claw, overwhelmed by the enemy, ordered a retreat. Instead of following, the Sioux stayed to howl gleefully around their victims.

Nanagi, hearing the sound from a distance, returned to find his father in a bad mood. Stung by temporary defeat, he lashed out at the surprised youth. "Son of Washakie is coward and old woman!"

Recovering from the injustice of the insult, Nanagi whipped his horse and called back over his shoulder, "Nanagi will be brave like his father or die!" Then he raced toward the Sioux.

Washakie was galvanized with horror over the effect of his bitter words.

"Stop!" shouted Tupaku, but it was too late. Nanagi,

in range of enemy fire, was shot down. As he fell from his horse, the Sioux swarmed around him and hacked his body to pieces before the eyes of his father.

Rage swept over Tupaku as if the Sioux were responsible for every injustice in his life. Though he was not the war chief, he assumed command. Circling his horse, he shouted, "Avenge 'im! Drive 'em out!"

The warriors, incensed by what the Sioux had done, responded valiantly. . . . The fighting was so fierce that the enemy was repulsed. In the rear of the fleeing Indians, Tupaku spotted a young warrior wearing a crimson shirt, the distinguishing garb of Red Cloud, son of the Sioux chief by that name.

Emitting a thunderous war cry, Tupaku charged. The Sioux, realizing the plight of their young warrior, tried to come to his aid, but the Shoshones cut them off. In claiming the life of the chieftain's son, Little Chief avenged the death of his brother. The Shoshones pursued the enemy until they were completely routed.

Washakie was so grief-stricken over the loss of his beloved son that his hair turned white overnight. He bemoaned the tragedy that had come into his life, a tragedy for which he alone was responsible.

26

In the late fall, the Shoshones were returning from a successful hunt when they heard from a distance the moaning and wailing of the women they had left in camp. A runner met them with startling news.

"Daidŭtsi gone," he blurted. "Someone kill Black Woman!"

Gone! The impact of his words was like a physical blow. Tupaku sat, silent as a stone, too shocked to utter a sound. Though his subconscious mind reminded him that "nothing lasts for an Indian" he tried to tell himself that it could not be true. He had often anticipated disaster of some sort, but this particular time it had not occurred to him that it might happen while he was away.

Washakie was the first to respond. He was fond of Daidŭtsi, as fond as any father could be of his daughter, and he thought well of Black Woman. In his grief, he let out a cry that sounded like the bellow of a bull elk. It served to bring Little Chief to the realization that the runner's message was true.

Without a word to anyone, he pressed his heels in the flanks of his horse and sped back to camp. As he neared his tepee, he recalled his apprehension when Black Woman erected it at the edge of the village, where he had thought that they might be exposed to an attack. Why did be let her have her way? He should have been as firm as Washakie, who convinced Hanŭbi that he did not want his lodge moved in his absence. She had not defied him again. When Little Chief reached his tepee, he found willows piled high before the door to signify that the occupants had gone on a long journey. Tupaku, studying the few tracks that had not been obliterated by the excited Indians, decided that the abductors were three in number. There must have been two men and a boy or woman, judging by the size of their footprints. He thought for a moment that the smaller ones might have belonged to Daidŭtsi, but they could not have, because they were firm and purposeful. She would never have left of her own accord. As the tracks were fresh, he realized that he should lose no time following them.

But first, he must have a look at Black Woman, who, covered with a blanket, was lying under a tree. The women, keening loudly around her, stopped to stare when Little Chief lifted the blanket. They elbowed closer, for the knife with which she had been stabbed was still in her breast. As the Bannock removed it, he looked at it closely. The *Trois Tetons* were scratched on the blade. He would never forget that knife! It was the one he had wanted above all else among the Cheyenne peace offerings at Horse Creek.

Looking down at the woman whose motherly love had meant so much to Daidŭtsi, he made a pledge. "Tuwaipŭ," he said, "I avenge your death with this knife when I find Daidŭtsi." He spoke in broken English as if it might be easier for her to understand.

The women watching him shook their heads. They thought that he had lost his mind, he spoke so strangely. They were all the more sure of it when they saw that, instead of staying to take part in Black Woman's funeral, he jumped on his horse and went racing southward.

"Where'll he go?" one of the old women asked.

"To Ferries," another guessed. "Maybe get firewater. Make him forget!"

Shortly after the hunters returned to camp, Black Woman's funeral procession was slowly wending its way up the mountainside. Washakie, his face already drawn from sorrow, headed the procession with his *pohakantŭ,* singing a death song, immediately following. Bear Claw came next, then four Indians bearing a blanketed figure on a crude litter. Hundreds of mourners followed. A chief could not have been more honored than Liza, as she was carried to her final resting place.

Big Chief found a desirable spot where her remains could be dropped into a chasm too deep for the hungry wolves to reach. "Here!" he shouted as he turned to signal the litter bearers.

The howl was louder than ever when the body was hurled into space. The chief pushed a large rock over the edge. Then, filing by singly, each of the Indians paused to throw a parting gift down upon the remains, lying in a broken heap below. Among the objects were food, clothing, jewelry and other cherished items, including a pair of gauntlet gloves to keep Black Woman's hands warm on her journey into the afterlife. Even her oven was thrown down to her so that she might use it to prepare her meals. After the ceremony was over, the mourners plodded down the trail.

Little Chief's reason for going toward the Green River Ferries was one he could not analyze himself. While he had a feeling that he was on the right track, he was unable to see the picture clearly. He would have to think it out along the way.

His mind turned back to the time he first saw the knife, and he remembered his pang of disappointment when Tavenduwits selected it from among the Cheyenne gifts. Just how many hands it had passed through he had no way of knowing. He was aware that Tavenduwits was a shrewd trader. Had he not made Tupaku pay four horses for his disagreeable daughter, who had cost him another horse to get rid of her? If Tavenduwits had parted with his knife, he had done it for a price! There was no use going to his camp to find Daidŭtsi. He would be too smart to take her there. If he did and Washakie were to find out, he would destroy him as readily as if he were of an enemy tribe.

Several facts were clear. The knife had a direct connection with Tavenduwits. Walking Horse had joined him after being rejected, and Elk Tooth had ridden into camp on the horse he had given Blue Beads when he sent her back to her father. All three had to be implicated some way. Could the smaller tracks have belonged to Blue Beads who came along to help the abductors accomplish their evil deed?

The tracks near the camp were lost when the renegades rode into the stream, and although Tupaku had difficulty picking them up again, he felt confident that he was going in the right direction. He rode hard. When he finally found the tracks, he stopped to examine them and put his ear to the ground. Then he rode on.

He doubted very much that Tavenduwits was one of the abductors because it was unlikely that he would take such a risk. What would have been his motive? He would not have done it on Blue Bead's account since there was no love between father and daughter. Ransom could have been his only object. Someone who knew that Daidŭtsi was white was obviously trying to return her to her people. Tupaku had interpreted the omen of the hawks to mean that she would be taken from him. Now it had happened.

As he sped through the moonlight, he observed a glistening object on the trail. He wheeled around and alighted to see what it was. His attention had been caught by the beads on a moccasin Daidŭtsi had apparently lost or kicked off to mark the trail.

"We'll find her!" he promised Black Horse. "Go boy—go!"

The next time he dismounted to put his ear to the ground, he confided, "We gain on 'em!" Now that he had assured himself that he was overtaking the abductors, he would not need to listen at ground level again. He rode on, praying that his horse would not give out from the ordeal.

Finally, in the distance he made out several dark objects. Although the moonlight was bright, he could not tell their number. To his surprise, they jumped from their horses into a clump of willows as he neared them. So they planned to waylay him! If he were to ride into their trap, it would mean certain death.

Little Chief jerked his lathered horse to a quick stop. Jumping to the ground, he gave him a vigorous slap on the rump and sent him down the trail. The risk of losing him was one he had to take. He then rushed to higher ground, to an old buffalo trail used by the Shoshones in time of flood. Besides its being in the shadow of an overhanging ledge of rock, there were scattered evergreens to hide him from view. The abductors would have to expose themselves in the moonlight to resume the trail.

When the horse went galloping by without a rider, Blue Beads emerged from the willows and attempted to catch him, but he eluded her. Tupaku, leveling his rifle, fired. When she crumpled and fell, he had a feeling of satisfaction. Never again would she be able to harm Daidŭtsi.

Elk Tooth, jumping on his pony, gave chase. A second report from Little Chief's rifle brought forth a piercing scream as he tumbled to the ground.

When bullets started coming in his direction, Tupaku feigned injury by emitting an agonizing sound as if he had been hit. Following that, all was quiet. Tupaku then heard a voice he recognized as the Cheyenne's, ordering Daidŭtsi to get on her horse. Crouching to the ground, Little Chief scurried toward a boulder at the side of the road where the two paths merged. Walking Horse would have to pass by.

"Get on!" the Cheyenne ordered. "Get on!"

"You killed him!" Daidŭtsi screamed. "You killed Tupaku!" Releasing all of her pent-up emotion, she kicked furiously while he tried forcibly to put her on the horse.

"Stop!" he shouted. "I kill you, too." When she continued to fight, he gave her arm a cruel twist. "Get on!" he kept saying.

"*Kay*! I not go to white camp. What I care if you kill me?"

"I show you." He tied her wrists together. Then he threw her astride the horse in spite of her protests.

She began to cry hysterically.

"No one hear you," he scoffed. "Blue Beads, Elk Tooth, Tupaku all dead. You pull back on horse, you die, too."

The confused pony, with the girl drawing back on the reins and the warrior slapping him to go, began to rear. Walking Horse, at his side, attempted to force him to run. He was still trying to subdue the girl and the pony when they neared the boulder where Tupaku was crouching, ready to spring.

"Fool, he'll throw you!" the Cheyenne shouted at the girl.

With a savage war cry, Tupaku leapt from the shadow.

Daidŭtsi clung to her frightened horse, which was now completely out of control. She stayed on, strengthened by a sudden will to live. When she had quieted him, she urged him back to where the Cheyenne was struggling to gain possession of the knife. With his wrist held in a vise-like grip, Tupaku was unable to make use of it.

The sound of the panting Indians could be heard in the stillness as they rolled, first one on top and then the other. Daidŭtsi, her hands tied, watched helplessly. She could see that Little Chief was unable to break the Cheyenne's hold. Desperately as he tried, he could not lower the knife into position for a final plunge.

Daidŭtsi, fascinated by the writhing warriors clinched in their struggle to the death, had momentarily forgotten her abhorrence for warfare. With her life and Tupaku's at stake, she entered into the spirit of the occasion. She was no longer the gentle maiden who had argued against Tupaku's going on the warpath.

"Kill him!" she shrieked. "He show Liza no mercy! Kill him!" The forcefulness of her words served as a stimulant to Tupaku's lagging spirit. Exerting every ounce of his strength, he gradually forced the knife downward toward the region of the Cheyenne's heart. Then with the weight of his own body, he was able to drive it deep into his chest.

When Walking Horse fell away from him, he half crawled toward Daidŭtsi, who, with a joyous cry, slipped to the ground. She did not upbraid him for his savagery. On the contrary, she was elated. While he was removing the rope from her wrists, she told him what had happened.

"Pucho plan it," she explained. "She gave her horse to Elk Tooth, and Tavenduwits gave his knife to Walking Horse to help. Tavenduwits plan to meet us in a draw north of the Ferries, and he was going to tell Taivo he rescue me when he took me to the white camp for ransom."

Little Chief, too exhausted to hear more, wearily stretched out full-length on the ground. Seating herself beside him, Daidŭtsi gathered him in her arms and rocked back and forth, crooning like an Indian mother over her child. Contented, he leaned his head against her breast and closed his eyes.

Suddenly, there was a raucous sound overhead. Tupaku and Daidŭtsi recognized it before they saw the vision of the hawks. In awe, they again saw the second hawk take the twisting snake in midair, then the first regain its prize. This time they did not fly into a sunset, for the morning light was breaking. Although the path had been dark only moments before, it was now bright with the hope of a new day.

Epilogue

The settlements at the five Mormon mail stations connecting Salt Lake City with Fort Laramie were destroyed in 1857 by the Saints as they fled before the Army for Utah. The so-called Mormon War turned into a "push" since there was not a single confrontation between the two factions.

Washakie's decision to send warriors to the aid of the army did not disturb his conscience, nor did he abrogate his pledge of lasting friendship. He merely responded to the urge to help drive the settlers out of the country. To the exasperated chief, all were Saints, as he was unable to distinguish between Mormons and Gentiles.

After destroying an entire train of badly needed supplies, the Mormons forced the army to spend a miserable winter bogged down in deep snows at the ruins of Fort Bridger, which had served as one of the mail stations. In the spring, the war ended in negotiations. When Alfred Cumming, handpicked by the government, succeeded Brigham Young as Governor of Utah, the Deseret Empire was at an end.

Though vigorous, the Mormon missionary effort among the Shoshones had been short-lived. The first mission at Wind River, which was not established until 1883, was Episcopal under Reverend John Roberts, of Wales. The Shoshones are still predominantly Episcopalian.

The army rebuilt Fort Bridger, which it occupied until it was abandoned in 1890. There two important treaties were signed. The first, July 2, 1863, recognized the Shoshone Aboriginal Domain as extending from Salt Lake to the Platte, covering a total of 44,672,000 acres. In the second, July 3, 1868, Wind River Reservation was created for Washakie's Shoshones and Taghee's Bannocks, who were to remain only long enough to decide upon a reservation of their own. They soon left as they chose to live with the Northern Shoshones and Bannocks, or Northern Paiutes, on the Fort Hall Reservation in Idaho.

Although the Treaty of 1868 diminished the lands held by the Shoshones to 2,774,400 acres, the chief was pleased that he was allowed to name his reservation. His policy of peace with the white man had paid off. Had he resisted, he was convinced that he would have been relegated to Indian Territory. Speaking in council, he said:

> *"The Wind River Reservation is the one for me. We may not for one, two or three years be able to till the ground. The Sioux will trouble us. But when they are taken care of, we will do well. . . . I want for my home Warm Valley and the lands along Wind River and its tributaries as far as Popo Agie, and I want to be able to go over the mountains to hunt where I please."*

Eight years later, Camp Brown, where the agency was located, was renamed Fort Washakie in his honor. In appreciation of his loyalty and for his service to General George Crook as scout, a handsome saddle was presented to him. When the agent urged him to make a statement that might be carried back to the President in Washington, he made his most famous remark:

> *"Do a kindness to a white man, he feels it in his head, and the tongue speaks. Do a kindness to an Indian, he feels it in his heart. The heart has no tongue."*

In 1878, it became necessary to relocate 938 Northern Arapahoes who had been assigned to a Sioux reservation in South Dakota. They refused to live there or join their kinsmen on the Southern Cheyenne and Arapaho Reservation in Indian Territory. They had proposed several sites for a reservation, but they were too near to settlements, to trails or to the railroad.

According to the Indian Agent at the Wind River Reservation, Washakie had "too great a heart to say no" when asked if the homeless wanderers might be placed on his reservation until a suitable location could be found. They had previously come of their own volition to make peace and ask for sanctuary. By spring the restless warriors had departed, and the remainder of the tribe soon followed. So the chief, aside from accepting the white man's word, had every reason to believe that they would leave "when the grass comes again," as he specified they should.

The Arapahoes, under military protection, were settled on the eastern side of the reservation in the fertile Wind River Valley, while Washakie withdrew to his beloved mountains. Troops remained to make sure that the Shoshones did not run their uninvited guests off the reservation.

As time went on, the chief discovered that the Arapahoes as well as the troops were there to stay. Repeatedly, he asked when they would be removed, but his queries went unanswered. On January 31, 1891, he dictated a letter to the President of the United States in which he stated:

> *"We are willing to sell a part of the reservation to the Government for the Arapahoes, but until such arrangements are made we protest against any improvements that will in any way give the Arapahoes right to any of the land. At the time they came to this reservation, we did not tell them they could come here, and we have allowed them to live here since, thinking they would not hurt the land by living on it. We did not think that this would give them a right to the land."*

His suggestion of outright sale went unheeded, but he was not reconciled to sharing his reservation with his traditional enemies, the Arapahoes. Blind but still loyal, Washakie died February 23, 1900, at the probable age of 102; and he was buried with full military honors. Not only had he stubbornly maintained peace during his 60 years as chief, he had also outlived those who planned to deal with his successor for the removal of the two Wind River tribes to Indian Territory. The inscription on his tombstone in the military cemetery at Fort Washakie reads:

He Was Always Loyal To The Government
And To His White Brothers.

Thirty-eight years after his death, the Shoshones won their celebrated case against the government and were paid for the land the Arapahoes had occupied on a temporary basis for 60 years. It was a court order that finally brought justice. Ironically, when the offsets were itemized and deducted from the amount of the judgement, the Shoshones were charged for the famous saddle which had been given to their chief during Grant's Administration.

The Arapahoes gained title for the first time to the land in question, land that had been designated as theirs following the General Allotment Act of 1886. The Wind River Indian Reservation has belonged jointly to the two tribes since 1938 when the Shoshone case was resolved.

Linguistic Note

The Shoshone language is fluid and, with the help of the simplified key below, easily pronounced. Since it has not been standardized, the fundamental difference of opinion among the Shoshones themselves is one of spelling. Similar sounds result in spelling variance, yet the meanings remain the same. It is a spoken, not a written language.

A nontechnical approach is intended for the reader's pleasure, not to be construed as an attempt to formalize the language. The phonetic spelling of the selected words and the pronunciation key which follows show approximately the dialect as it is spoken at Wind River.

Accent is usually on the first syllable. Final vowels, if pronounced at all, are little more than breath sounds. Examples: in po'hakant(ŭ), or po'hagant(ŭ), the "ŭ" could be omitted. In the name Sacajawea (Sac'a-ja-we-a) the final "a" is a breath sound. Consonants are as in English. Vowels are as follows:

a	father
ai	aisle
e	bet
i	machine
o	wrote
u	as in food
ŭ	put

In the narrative, the popular "e" ending of the word Shoshone, preferred by the tribe to the more technical "i" ending, is used. The Shoshone people in Idaho are called "Sho-shones." At Wind River they are the "Shaw-shaw-nees."

Glossary

Bannock

aha	yes
Isha	Wolf
kai	no
Kamŭ Kaupa	Rabbit Leg
Pia Isha	Big Wolf
taibo'o	white man
Taghee; Targhee	meaning undetermined
tsŭa'a	little girl
Wŭda	Bear
yama	a form of greeting

Wind River Shoshone

A'a Kopŭp	Broken Horn
ahai'i	hello
Ahwaipŭtsi	trad. Young Crow Woman
Ashŭraba Kak	Spotted Crow
Daidŭtsi	Little One
Dam Apŭ	Our Father

Enga Kwitsaikite	Lightening
Enga Kwitsu	Red Buffalo
enga-tasŭa	smallpox, little red bug
ha; ha'a; haa	yes
Haimbi	Crowheart Butte
hanrih	beaver
Hanŭbi	Corn Woman
Huchuchi	Little Bird
Isŭf	Wolf
Izapŭ	Coyote
Kak Yorandegin	Flying Crow
Ka-tat-o	trad. Stays-at-Home
kay	no
kay shunbana	don't know
kesandŭ; kezant	bad; no good
Kitant Niet	Strong Wind
Kopŭp Mo	Broken Hand
Kuna	Firewood; Driftwood
Kwitawoyo Waipŭ	Magpie Woman
Kwina	hawk
kwitsu	buffalo
Mowumha	Tied-With-Rope
Mua Pavin	Moon-on-the-Water
Mŭatsi	Little Moon
mumbitsŭ	owl
Nanagi	Echo
Naroya	lit. to shuffle one's feet
Naroyan	Hides Away
Ninimbi	Little People
Ninimbu	Little Person

Nŭ-dŭtsowe!	Help me!
Oha Mo	Yellow Hand
Oha Mŭpi	Yellow Nose
ona	baby
Paishikantŭ;	
Pushikantŭ	a sore or a boil
panzukŭ	otter
Pariha (Paria) Tawa	Elk Tooth
Pariha (Paria) Ungu	Bull Elk
Pia Pungo	Big Horse
Pocatello	meaning undetermined
pohakantŭ; pohagantŭ	medicine man
Porivo	trad. Chief Woman
Pucho	Blue Beads
pungo	horse
Pungo Mia	Walking Horse
puwi	money
Satonzibi	some kind of flower
Shonip Gani	Grass House
Shoshone; Shoshoni	trad. Grass House People
Tagŭ Wŭnŭ	Sun Dance
taivo	white man
taivo nŭ	white men
Tavenduwits	White Man's Child
Tegwana Wanŭp	Blanket Chief
Tegwatsi	Little Chief
tivizant	very good
togoa	rattlesnake
Towiyagayde	Thunder
Tsanapui Pavish	Pretty Weasel

tsant	good
Tupaku	Black Arrow
Tupungo	Black Horse
Tuwaipŭ	Black Woman
Waipŭ Yagakantŭ	Crying Woman
Washakie; Washaki	trad. Rawhide Rattle
Weyavo	Night Hawk
Wobin	Log or Guard
wŭda	bear
Wŭda Mo	Bear Paw or Claw
Wŭda Pekanŭ	Kill Bear lit. He killed the bear.
yamba	wild carrots
Yŭ	Porcupine
yuavits	gopher
zant	good